HIDDEN CRIMES

Emma Holly

CONTENTS

❧ CHAPTER ONE

IF a cop was a werewolf, the half-fae city of Resurrection was a fine place to work. America's only supe-friendly metropolis offered plenty of excitement. Just as important, shifters didn't have to hide their dual nature. RPD detective Nate Rivera was glad of that. He liked being who he was.

He especially liked that his spacious loft apartment was a perfect expression of his personality.

The decor was sharp of course, every item selected for style and quality. He'd bought the converted warehouse space in his early twenties, with money his mother (a decorated cop herself) had left him at her death. A couple payments remained on the mortgage but—like the rest of his life—that was under control.

Nate never spent more than he could afford. None of his vintage modern furnishings indicated financial recklessness. Because detective salaries weren't princely, he saved up for his treasures on a strict schedule. His exposed brick walls displayed a gallery of miniature city scenes, which *weren't* purchased on first sight. Though he often fell in love with pieces in a moment, he took time to consider.

Did the paintings fit his collection? Would the amount he'd saved cover what the artist was asking? If it wouldn't, Nate denied himself. Okay, now and then he succumbed, but that was only because art gave him so much pleasure. Everybody needed a weakness. This one had the advantage of suiting his image of himself.

Just because he was a werewolf didn't mean he wasn't civilized.

What didn't suit his image of himself was the brown-paper twine-handle bag that perched on his authentic Arne Jacobsen egg chair.

With arms crossed over his gym-honed chest, he stared at it balefully. One alligator-booted foot tapped his polished cement floor.

1

Nate had bought a present for his pack alpha's wife. He'd gotten it on impulse, just spotted it in a shop window, turned on his heel, and went in. He hadn't asked what it cost. He'd simply handed over his ResEx card. Finding out what it did cost hadn't stopped him either. Instead, he'd clenched his jaw and told the owner he preferred tissue paper wrapping—plain white, if she had it.

Nate had no excuse for spending so much money on a woman he wasn't sleeping with. Ari's birthday wasn't until November, and her baby shower had been a while ago. For that matter, the baby wasn't new anymore. Kelsey was two months old, though this was the first time since her birth that the pack would eat all together at Adam's house.

"It's those damned women's faults," he muttered. "They should have let us come."

According to Rick's sister Maria, baby showers were for girls, and all girls deserved a break from testosterone now and then. To hear her talk, you'd think werewolves being real men was cause for regret. Ari was human and could be forgiven, but Maria was a werewolf herself. She should have known better.

Were-males had as much right to celebrate the birth of babies as anyone.

More wolflike grumbles were rising in Nate's throat when the deadbolt on his industrial style door turned. Instinct and training took over. He whipped his off-duty Smith & Wesson from its ankle holster. Half a second later, his sense of smell informed him who the intruder was.

"Don't shoot," said the half-laughing voice of Tony Lupone, fellow RPD detective and younger brother to their pack's second in command.

Like all Adam's wolves, he had a key to Nate's home.

"You could knock," Nate pointed out as Tony stuck his grinning head cautiously inside. His hair was a rich dark brown like his brother Rick's, slightly wavy and—per usual—in need of a good styling.

"Forgot," he said unashamedly. "Besides which, knocking would ruin my chances of catching you naked." Seeing he wasn't going to be shot, Tony stepped inside and gave Nate a onceover. He wagged his heavy Lupone eyebrows. "Nice boots, GQ."

"I told you not to joke like that. Just because you left the closet doesn't mean you can flirt with everyone. Hit on the wrong werewolf, and you'll find yourself taking a dirt nap."

"It's just you. I have to practice on someone."

Despite Tony's unconcerned attitude, Nate occasionally worried his teasing was more than *practice*. Rick's little brother had been out over a year now. While Resurrection didn't have a flourishing were-gay scene, he should have had sufficient time to hook up with someone. Back when Tony had played straight, he'd had no trouble snagging girls.

Tony was a good-looking kid, but Nate didn't swing that way. Nor was he a fan of awkward heart-to-hearts.

"What are you doing here?" he asked, pushing that idea aside. "Dinner is at Adam's place. You live in his same building."

Tony pulled an unexpectedly sheepish face. "I wanted to make sure I didn't walk in alone. I did something weird today."

The lowest ranking member of their pack was no clothes horse. Tony wore ripped jeans, beat-up running shoes and a clean but faded polo shirt. From behind his back he brought out a crumpled package. The pink and yellow duck-printed paper looked like it had been wrapped and unwrapped a couple times. The tape that was supposed to secure it no longer did.

"It's a stuffed bunny," Tony confessed, holding out the pitiful bundle. "I was picking up the beer, and there was this toy store across the street. I couldn't resist going in. I mean, I should have gotten a bear or something. A wolf at least. But I saw those stupid floppy ears, and I couldn't control myself. I kept thinking about the baby snuggling up with it for her naps."

"Kelsey is a girl," Nate said, trying to be fair.

"Maria's a girl. When she was little, she slept with a Transformer. She'd wake up with its shape dented in her cheek."

Maria was Rick and Tony's older sister, a married woman with a pup of her own. Nate cleared his throat uncomfortably. "I got something for the baby too."

Tony blinked at him, then flashed a delighted grin, causing Nate to regret sharing this with him. "You did? What did you get?" He spied the handle bag on his red-and-black cow print chair. "Ooh," he said, snatching it before Nate could stop him. His *ooh* changed to a gasp as he peeked inside.

"Oh my God," he breathed, lifting out the quilted white velvet blanket. He didn't usually sound gay, but that *oh my God* wasn't hetero. He shook out the baby quilt for a better look, making Nate want to grab it from him to refold. The intricate hand stitching formed the shape of a Tree of Life. "This must have cost a fortune."

"It's secondhand," Nate said defensively.

"It's *antique*. And it's fricking spelled." Tony looked at him wide-eyed, his werewolf senses having registered the enchantment.

"It's white. If it weren't spelled, stains wouldn't come out in the wash."

Giving in to his compulsion, Nate extricated the blanket from Tony's grip. The younger man watched him fold and restore it to its tissue paper nest. "You must have blown your spending budget for a whole month."

Three was more like it, not that Nate would admit that. Impatient to shut down the topic, he grabbed the keys he'd thrown in the vintage Cuban cigar box he kept for the purpose of storing them. "I'm sure it's just some primitive uncle instinct. In the wild, whole packs help take care of pups. We bought those presents because Ari married our alpha."

"I'll go along with that," Tony said. Seeing Nate was ready, he opened the door for him. Despite the classic subordinate behavior, his sudden smile was mischievous. "You could pretend you'd bought the rabbit too. Then only one of us would have to explain."

"Nobody would believe it," Nate was happy to say. "Not with that half-assed wrapping job you did."

"Sometimes," Tony said as they trotted down the warehouse stairs, "you're totally the gay one."

Nate knew some people believed this; he *was* particular. He didn't give a shit about their misconceptions, as long as Tony knew better.

The bright August sun turned the lush green shade of the pavement trees into an oasis. Nate liked to think of the neighborhood they lived in as upscale blue collar. Pretty century-old brownstones shared the oak-lined street with small bodegas and restaurants. Lots of folks who resided here had done so for generations. The area was maybe a quarter wolf, but other races had put roots down too. Even more than the street he'd grown up on, this one felt like home to him.

Tony waved to the corner grocer while Nate nodded. Mrs. Marinelli, the half-blind human music teacher, slowed her ancient Volkswagen to let them sprint across the street. Spells laid on the engine kept her from hitting people, as did the locals' knowledge of who she was. Fortunately, she rarely drove farther than ten blocks.

Tony twisted back to watch the sweet old lady try to gun the car, which was refusing to accelerate into the path of a squirrel. Leashed to his post and jealous, the grocer's friendly German shepherd barked wildly. "We really should take her license. She's ancient in human years."

"Adam submitted a request," Nate informed him. "The neighborhood association's been complaining."

"Well, good." Tony bounded up the next stoop. They'd reached Adam's well-kept brownstone, a mere two blocks from Nate's loft. "Not that I'd want to break the news. Mrs. M can swing that purse of hers pretty hard."

The street door wasn't locked, so Tony simply held it open, allowing Nate to precede him. "Too bad about the curse that witch put on her. Otherwise, we could take up a collection and have the elves fix her eyes."

Nate grunted in answer, his mind on other things as he climbed the stairs to Adam's apartment on the top floor. Rick and Tony owned the lower floors, and they all shared the big roof deck. Since the brothers were Adam's blood cousins, this had the effect of making the building smell like Adam's private turf. Nate was Adam's cousin as well, but only by marriage. For him, meetings with his alpha, who was also his lieutenant and therefore his boss, were always a bit tricky.

Nate, Adam, and Rick had attended the same class at the Academy. Of the three, Nate's scores in every form of testing had been the best. Rick and Adam had superior body mass, Adam being solidly six-one while Rick topped out at a muscle-bound six-four. In spite of Nate being a lean six-footer, in most styles of fighting he could take them. *He* won the sharpshooter medal. *His* times for the quarter mile on two legs broke a six-year record. Nate knew the RPD manual back and forth and swiftly grew famous (or infamous, depending on who you spoke to) for the precision of his reports. Despite these accomplishments, when the mysterious werewolf trait known as dominance entered the equation, Nate came up short on X factor.

The Resurrection Police Department was overwhelmingly made up of wolves. Squads were organized along pack lines, with leadership decided by ritual face-offs between members in animal form. Given his superior talents and intense drive, Nate had expected to be alpha. At worst, he'd braced himself to serve as beta. When both Adam's and Rick's wolves had been able to master his, it was a hard shock to him.

Adam was a good leader, and Rick was certainly affable, but sometimes that shock still stung. Nate didn't want either man to guess he resented coming third—in part for pride's sake, and in part because he liked them. Schooling his body language not to give him away was worth some concentration. By the time he strolled into the Santini entryway, no one would have thought he wasn't completely self-assured.

Directly across from the open door was Adam's cramped kitchen. Inside, Rick and his parents were putting the final touches on a giant pan of lasagna before it went into the oven. Nate threw them all a *hey*, then turned to the living room.

If he'd been a painter, he'd have tried to capture the scene he found. Adam's living space was the opposite of his own. Here comfort trumped style, hand-me-downs supplanted vintage, and no one got upset if the twenty-year-old curtains clashed with the threadbare rugs. Somehow, the place was beautiful anyway. Even empty of people, it radiated warmth. It soaked it up from Adam's goodhearted nature, from the bond he and Ari shared. The presence of pack on the old-fashioned furniture made the air glow gold. The wolf in him approved every inch of the Santini residence, even if the human chose differently.

When his gaze found Ari and the baby in the overstuffed rocking chair, a smile he couldn't have repressed tugged up his features.

The pair was adorable: Ari with her spiky and—at the moment—strawberry colored hair, the baby with her dark little tuft and her big round eyes. Built on the same slight lines as her human mother, the two-month-old's footie sleeper was printed with unicorns.

The previous year, Ari had earned Nate's respect by helping the squad take down a bad guy. Earning his admiration had required no more than being attractive and female. Her turning out to be a devoted wife and mother won over parts of him he didn't have names for.

"How are my favorite girls?" he asked, a shade of something extra in his trademark lady-killer croon.

He crossed the small cluttered room to Ari's shabby throne, his excellent peripheral vision marking everyone who was there. Ari's human friends Max and Sarah held hands on the love seat. Maria and her husband Johnny leaned forward on the couch, apparently ready to grab their five-year-old by the scruff if he forgot his P's and Q's. Ethan knelt on the window seat, craning to see the birds, but he glanced back at Nate's approach. Adam, alpha of them all, stood behind Ari's chair. One hand rested on its back while the other held a barely touched bottle of elf ale. He was casual but imposing, a smiling but alert paterfamilias.

Having reached his goal, Nate bent to stroke the baby's head and kiss Ari's cheek gently. Married lady or not, she was too pretty not to get his flirt on with.

"'Your' girls are fine," Ari said dryly, shifting Kelsey around to her shoulder to pat her little back. "We're waking up from our nap and feeling extremely grateful we're not cooking."

"Nate might be grateful too," Adam said with his own dryness. Ari had her talents, but cooking wasn't one.

Emotion swelled in Nate without warning, the feeling so intense he suspected it was his wolf's. Being with pack pulled his beast closer to the surface. The sensation wasn't unpleasant, just unnerving. Instincts drove his wolf's reactions, responses that weren't under Nate's direct control. He tried to simply go with the wave of warmth, but it was difficult. He needed these people. He loved these people. Sometimes, though, he knew he'd never be all he could as long as they were around.

"Boss," Nate said to his alpha, his tone touched by throatiness.

"Nate," Adam acknowledged.

Unaccountably tense, Nate's hand tightened on the bag he was carrying.

"Is that a puh-resent for Kelsey?" Nate's honorary nephew Ethan piped. The five-year-old was finally learning to say his *r*'s. The poorly hidden hope in his expression told Nate he should have brought a gift for him too.

"It is," he said, joining the boy on the window seat. "Since she's so little, do you suppose you could help her open it?"

Ethan considered this, then held out his arms to accept the bag. The tissue paper seemed to entertain him. The blanket he pronounced boring, though he did walk it over to Ari, where he plunked it grumpily on her knees.

"Ethan," his mother scolded. "Don't call other people's presents boring."

"You told me not to lie," Ethan returned reasonably.

Nate wasn't sure the boy understood why the adults laughed. Fortunately for Nate, their amusement smoothed over the awkwardness his expensive gift might have stirred. Subordinates weren't supposed to show their superiors up.

"Very thoughtful," Adam said, sending him a level look over his wife's spiky scarlet head. Nate was pretty certain he'd spotted the spellwork.

"It's beautiful." Ari's fingers stroked the white velvet. "If Kelsey won't take naps on it, I will."

"It's spelled," Nate felt compelled to explain. "Whatever gets on it will wash out."

"Well, that's convenient," Ari said, her brows beginning to rise.

"I have a present for Kelsey too," Tony interrupted, thrusting out his bedraggled package.

"Wow." Obviously not expecting such a fuss at a simple dinner, Ari took the gift. When she dug through the crumple to find the contents, her face split into a grin. "A bunny! Oh Tony, it's adorable!"

"It's not magic or anything," he said, his cheeks flushing at her pleasure, "but the saleslady promised it doesn't have any parts Kelsey can swallow."

"It's perfect," Ari assured him. "I don't know what I did to deserve you all being so nice to me."

She wasn't just saying this. As she turned between Nate and Tony, her cornflower eyes shone with tears. Nate couldn't decide if he was touched or uncomfortable. Ari was an Outsider, a human from the non-magic world that surrounded Resurrection's fae-created reality. Nate knew pieces of her story: that she'd been born telekinetic and her powers had freaked out her conservative parents, that she'd lived as a street kid in Manhattan before accidentally stumbling past their borders. Given her reaction to his and Tony's gifts, Nate concluded she hadn't been wallowing in love and care out there.

Seeing this, he understood why Adam strove so fiercely to make her feel cherished.

Ethan saved the moment from getting too sentimental by throwing his sturdy body theatrically on the floor. "Ugh," he declared. "Babies get all the presents!"

Nate scooped him off the carpet before his father could swat his butt. "Brat," he said, giving the boy a toss that made him giggle. "Why don't you and I play on the roof until dinner is ready?"

"Yes!" Ethan crowed. "No poopie girls allowed!"

"*Ethan,*" his parents scolded in unison.

"Let him be," Nate advised, aware they were embarrassed by their son's jealousy. He turned his attention to the boy. "Maybe Grant will play catch with us."

Grant was the gargoyle who nested on Adam's roof. Like most of his race, he was smarter than he let on. Despite being as big as a minibus, he was the safest, most protective friend Ethan could have had.

"I love Grant!" the boy declared, flinging his arms around Nate's neck.

Nate had to smile at that. Jealousy notwithstanding, Ethan's heart had plenty of love in it.

They'd almost reached the door when Adam's pager buzzed. Nate turned back and caught Ari giving Adam a look that blended resignation and wry humor, one that said whatever this was, he'd better be careful.

"Noo," Ethan moaned, knowing what the sound meant from his own cop father.

Adam lifted one finger to keep Nate waiting where he was. "It's the precinct. Don't go out until I see what's up."

~

The call from dispatch regarded a Russian wolf named Vasili Galina. Vasili had the questionable fortune of being the mobster Ivan Galina's younger brother. Vasili had worked as Ivan's right hand man until two months ago, when the siblings had fallen out. The cause was money and a woman, both of which Ivan claimed Vasili stole from him. Aware that Ivan was called "the Terrible" for a reason, Vasili had gone on the run.

Sadly for him, Resurrection was an island, surrounded not by water but normalcy. A few centuries earlier, the fae had created the Pocket city from the stuff of their dimension. Inside, werewolves were common. Outside, supes were at the mercy of much more numerous, monster-fearing mundanes. The Galina line hadn't set foot past Resurrection's borders since emigrating from Siberia. As a result, Vasili was intimidated by the idea of fleeing there.

If Adam's squad could catch the less ruthless brother before he grew desperate enough to try, they had a decent chance of getting him to rat on Ivan. Because Ivan knew this, they'd been in a race over who'd find Vasili first. This evening, he'd been spotted in the warehouse district, slipping into a tobacco shop owned by the disputed girlfriend's cousins. Surveillance had been watching the location for weeks now without a sighting. If Ivan's men were less patient than the RPD's, this could be a real opening.

Excited, but doing their best to keep a lid on it, Tony, Adam, and Nate hurried one floor down to Rick's apartment to strap on their vests and gear.

Rick's place was a messier version of Adam's. His front hall closet was fitted out as an arms cabinet. Barring a yen for a rocket launcher, whatever they wanted in the way of short-notice weapons he kept locked up there. Nate had a similar arrangement in his loft, though of course his locker was neater.

None of them needed an explanation as to why it was better to do this here than in front of family. Maria's husband Johnny they left behind with the lasagna. Johnny worked Special Tactics—operations you needed troops for, not just a gun or two. He wouldn't join a call like this unless matters turned extreme.

"We'll take Rick's car," Adam said, double-checking the clip for his gun before sliding it into his under arm holster. They were packing electrum bullets, the silver-gold alloy being effective against most supes. "His Buick has four doors and won't stand out like the response van. I don't want to spook Vasili or clue Ivan that we found him. Nate, you'll be at the wheel."

"Shit," Rick said even as he dug out the keys. He might not like giving up control of his car, but everybody knew Nate was the best driver.

"Should we call Carmine?" Tony asked. Carmine was the final member of their five-man squad, an older wolf with a wife and family.

"No time," Adam said. "He'll have to read about it in the reports."

Adam flashed his canines in a grin anyone would have called wolfish. Alpha energy boiled off him, his normally green eyes taking on a flame blue glow. As often as wolves went into law enforcement, that's how much they hated members of their own species choosing a criminal route. Nate's heart thumped faster despite his preference for keeping cool. His alpha's relish for this chase was infectious.

Because they might come up against anything, Adam shoved two depowering charms in his back pocket. Nate tucked the taser Tony handed him into his waistband.

"We ready, boss?" he asked, adrenaline tightening his fist around Rick's car keys.

"We're ready," Adam assured him.

~

Resurrection's warehouse district stretched along the banks of the North River. Once known for shipping and manufacture, today it combined actual warehouses with condo conversions. Aspirations to trendiness aside, the area's yuppie colonizers hadn't yet conquered its seediness. The address dispatch had given Adam was in the district's less savory reaches.

Nate spotted the sign for Quince Street painted on the brick of an old sardine plant, now a by-the-night boarding house for demons. If demons could behave themselves, the fae allowed them in Resurrection. They seemed unlikely to improve the locale's cachet. Wrinkling his nose, Nate turned Rick's dull gray Buick into the narrow thoroughfare. Quince ran uphill, its steepness creating the impression that the worn-down buildings were about to roll down on them. Nate had an urge to pull a U-turn right out of there.

"Do you feel that?" he murmured to Adam, who sat up front next to him.

His alpha nodded, hands braced on the dash—perhaps to resist an impulse to grab the wheel. "Someone has a go-away spell fired up nearby. Maybe not on this street but close."

The realization tensed all of them. Nate ordered his foot to stay on the pedal, sticking to a cautious but not unnatural rate of travel. Two workmen in spattered overalls passed on foot to their left, on the opposite pavement from where the repulsion spell was strongest. The pair walked briskly, like they couldn't get out of there fast enough.

"There's the sign for the tobacco shop," Tony said softly. The shop was also on their left, the exotic hookahs in the window suggesting it sold more than legal smokes.

"Repulsion spells are pricey," Rick put in, leaning toward the front seat as his brother had. "If Vasili didn't buy the enchantment, maybe he's been using its shadow to hide in."

This would require self-control but wasn't impossible, considering how intensely Vasili must want to steer clear of his brother.

"The shop door's opening." Nate turned the car to the side as if about to park. Not wanting to get too close, he slowed to an inching crawl.

The timing couldn't have been better. As they watched the glass of the door shimmer with movement, the gawky form of Ivan the Terrible's little brother emerged from the small smoke shop. He wore old clothes and a cap pulled low on his forehead. As disguises went, it didn't do much good. His was a face and figure they'd memorized.

"Gentle now," Adam cautioned, easing his door open.

Tony and Rick left the car just as silently.

It was Rick who caught Vasili's nervous eye. The strapping wolf was on the nearer side of the car and just too damn big to miss.

Vasili stiffened and appeared to curse as he noted their black bulletproof police vests. Warned, he took off at a dead run. His long legs were made for it. Nate wasn't certain *he* could have caught up with him.

They were pack then, even more than they were cops. Adam didn't have to bark instructions. They'd pursued prey together too many times before. Coordinating by instinct, Adam and Tony pelted up the street after Vasili, while Rick pulled himself monkey-style up the nearest warehouse's fire escape. From the vantage of the roof, he'd watch where their target went, then relay it to the others through their linked earpieces.

Alone in the car, Nate wanted to circle the block to his left but decided this was what Vasili was counting on. If he'd been hiding here a while, he'd have numbed himself to the repulsion spell. What Nate ought to do was drive as close to its source as the car would get.

Gritting his teeth, he did exactly that.

In spite of his good intentions, he was only able to do it at five creeping miles per hour. The closer he got to the skin-crawly thickness, the more his foot tried to ease up on the pedal. Swearing under his breath, he slung the Buick onto the sidewalk in front of a boarded up blanket factory. Sweating like *he'd* been buried in blankets, he ducked under the plywood that had been partially torn off the front door.

To his dismay, he heard footsteps running inside, presumably searching for Vasili. Tony and Adam must have reached the factory before him, which he—as the one person with a vehicle—was never going to hear the end of. His competitive streak wouldn't let him retreat, though his legs were shaking almost too much to walk. Going deeper into the dimness, he found a set of trash-strewn stairs and went up.

People had squatted here but not recently. The smells his wolf nose picked up were old. He forced himself to the second floor and pushed through a swinging door. The go-away spell was even stronger, like nightmares congealing the molecules of the air. He was in a long corridor, shut metal doors with glass porthole windows on either side of him. The floor was concrete, not polished like his loft but rough and broken up. There was nothing here. No sounds. No movement. He could leave if he wanted to.

Nate didn't like that he wanted to very much.

"Fuck this shit," he whispered.

He smelled something then, a whiff that was out of place. It reminded him of oil of cedar. Under that, he was certain he smelled blood.

The blood woke his wolf and, apparently, his wolf had some immunity to this particular magical compulsion. His spine straightened and his knees steadied. He strode to the third door down, from which the scent had come.

With his wolf's lack of consideration for consequences, he snapped the lock and went in.

For three long blinks, he had no idea what he was looking at.

The room he stood in didn't belong in a factory, at least not one that had woven blankets a hundred years ago. The space wasn't big, maybe twelve by twelve and about ten feet high, its walls sheathed in steel. Someone must have erected this metal box inside the factory's original loom bay. Its walls and ceiling were featureless, and it didn't contain furniture. A round drain, maybe a foot in diameter, marked the low spot on the floor. It was from this that the scent of blood and cedar came.

None of this should have frightened him. He was within the confines of the aversion spell, and it no longer affected him. He walked to the drain and knelt. The cover was steel, with generous holes piercing it. Nate used a thumb and two fingers to lift the thing away.

The pipe underneath was clean except for a small pale shape he couldn't quite make out. The object was lodged about three feet down where the pipe elbowed. Something more than squeamishness inspired him to dig out the latex gloves he kept in his bulletproof vest's pocket. His heart thudding in his throat, Nate stretched his arm inside.

He pulled it back holding a child's shoe.

It was a nice shoe: sturdy white leather in the high-necked lace-up style parents bought to steady wobbly ankles while their kids learned how to walk—the sort they preserved in bronze as keepsakes. Fluids had washed the leather; Nate saw that from the stains, but at the moment it was bone dry.

He nearly dropped it when Rick called his name from the hall.

"We got the bad guy, Nate," he said in a teasing way. "It's safe to come out now."

Nate stood, shoe cupped within his cradling palm. Werewolves weren't psychic, as a rule. Changing shape was the main magic they performed. All the same, he felt very strange, like his nerves were vibrating in ways they weren't meant to.

"In here," he called hoarsely.

Rick appeared in the steel room's door. His mouth fished open at what lay behind it.

Nate had never been so happy to see his beta's good-natured face. Rick was the epitome of normal, a slap-your-back high school jock who only occasionally wore wolf's clothing. Nate extended the hand with the baby shoe. "We need to get this to the lab. And probably ask the precinct Seer to take a scan."

"Shit," Rick said, a sentiment Nate understood perfectly.

~

The city's criminal forensics lab was backed up. Every pair of hands they had was sorting evidence from a secret burial chamber that had been discovered under a high rise on the East Side. Normally, residents wouldn't have minded living atop a tomb. Resurrectioners had strong nerves, and the units were rent-controlled. Problem was, the nearly departed weren't RIPing. Figuring out why they'd decided to cause a ruckus had become a nightmare.

To make matters worse, the precinct psychic was on vacation.

"Vacation?" Nate burst out. It was late. He sat at Adam's kitchen table with his boss and Ari. Earlier, Adam had promised to work on getting their case moved up in priority, and Nate had felt compelled to check on his progress. "Is that even allowed? Shouldn't she be working the East Side thing with the rest of them?"

Seeing how upset he was, Adam reached across the beat-up table to wrap his palm over Nate's forearm. "She *was* working it. There are hundreds of restless spirits at the site. Evidently, talking to them is exhausting the mediums."

Usually, the touch of any pack member soothed. To his wolf, the contact was instinctively comforting. It meant he wasn't alone, and that someone had his back. Tonight, he couldn't settle, not even when Ari also laid her hand behind his tense neck. Because he liked her, Nate struggled not to jerk away. She meant well. He simply wasn't in the mood to be calmed.

Maybe she sensed this. She let her hand fall away from him. "Why does an empty room have you tied in knots? You're usually laid-back, no matter what."

Nate wondered if Adam had told her about the baby shoe. Maybe not, considering her recent motherhood. "Something bad happened in that room," he said. "And that go-away spell was recently refreshed. Someone was planning on using it again."

"Vasili claimed he didn't know anything about it," Adam reminded him.

"Well, he would, wouldn't he? He's got enough on his plate without adding accessory to whatever the hell this is."

"All right," Adam said, though his temper seemed to be thinning. To his credit, Adam always tried to be an even-tempered boss. "I'll let Rick and Tony have at him tomorrow. Those two are good at interrogation, and they understand brother ties. If Vasili's hiding something, they'll crack it out of him."

"Are you hungry?" Ari pushed back her chair. "I could heat up some lasagna."

Nate looked at her, muss-haired and half swallowed by an old RPD T-shirt of Adam's. Her worried eyes made her look like an innocent, though Nate knew she wasn't that. He'd watched those same baby blues face down demons without flinching. At the moment, she looked sleepy. He'd woken her when he knocked on Adam's door, though thankfully not Kelsey.

"Sorry," he said, meaning it. "I shouldn't have bothered you with this. I'll go home now and catch a few hours sleep before tomorrow."

He rose and Adam rose with him, walking side by side with him to the door.

"We won't let this drop," Adam assured him. "We'll find out who was using that room and why."

Nate nodded, not quite meeting his alpha's eye. His throat was tight, his normally cast-iron stomach uneasy. Though he couldn't explain the feeling, he knew time was of the essence in solving this mystery.

❦ CHAPTER TWO

A man like Nate had passions. Three of his biggest were French press coffee, good red wine, and Outsider-style cherry pie. Something about those tart ruby fruits glistening in sweet sauce had the power to make his troubles seem like small things.

At present, his loft had coffee, a well-stocked wine closet, but not one bite of pie. Tony must have snuck in at some point and raided his supply.

That didn't seem fair to Nate. Tony's parents were the best cooks in the pack, and they spoiled their youngest child horribly—more so since he'd come out and made them worry for his future. His fridge wouldn't run out of anything.

What Nate had told Adam notwithstanding, sleep was the furthest thing from his mind. He grabbed the keys to his personal vehicle: a forest green Goblinati, fifty years old—the golden age of goblin automotive design. The sports car had two doors, was low slung, and could go six hundred miles on a single charge. Nate's mileage was more like four, but that was because he reveled in exceeding the speed limit. To his mind, cruising flat out down an empty road was a pleasure no car lover should miss out on.

He'd have his chance to indulge tonight. His favorite place to buy provisions was way the hell out in the cornstalks. The Poughkip Holy Foods was Resurrection's only all-organic, all-blessed grocer. The twenty-four-hour superstore was a notorious pick-up joint—which didn't make him think less of it. He'd enjoyed many a hot encounter following his forays there. His culinary skills weren't on the level of the Lupones, but women tended to like when he cooked for them. Getting them into bed on the first date and not the third seemed preferable to him.

All too often, he'd lost interest by then. Cutting straight to the chase was more efficient.

He and the car flew along Route 50, the hot August wind blowing back his hair. The rush of that *almost* blotted out the image of the sad little shoe he'd found.

~

Evina Mohajit was no stranger to compromise. As the fire department's youngest-ever station chief, not to mention a single mother of two healthy rambunctious cubs, she'd learned balancing work and home meant you couldn't do either perfectly.

Just in case she'd forgotten, her six-year-old daughter Abby issued a reminder the instant Evina shoved their sticky townhouse door open. Abby stood at the top of the inside stairs, her puppy-decorated cotton pajamas an acknowledgement of the fact that it was past her bedtime.

"Mo-omm," she wailed from her spying post. "You forgot Rafi's cakes for school!"

Evina glanced at the large canvas tote she'd slung over her left shoulder—in case two dozen chocolate and vanilla cupcakes wanted magically to appear. They didn't, and her daughter huffed like she was forty. "Mom, Rafi's going to be the only one without them *again*."

Evina knew why she'd forgotten. There'd been a three-alarm blaze at an apartment building, and her crew had been called to it. Though a weretiger like herself, her senior man had been injured in a flashover, a dangerous increase in heat that ignited the smoke blanketing the ceiling above his head. Evina had been watching the fire in her astral projected form. She'd warned him the flare was developing, but he'd pressed forward anyway. He'd heard two kids were trapped in a unit, and he'd wanted to get them out. Christophe had succeeded, but at the cost of wrenching off his fire retardant coat and wrapping them in it. He was in the hospital now, being treated for serious burns. According to his physician, the pain and shock he was in prevented him from changing.

None of which was appropriate to explain to a six-year-old.

"Maybe I could bake Rafi's cupcakes myself," she said, trying to sound hopeful.

"Mom," Abby scolded, her beautiful little moon face once again looking too mature for her years. "You *know* that's not a good idea."

Evina did know, and exhaled wearily. Her luck was no better than fifty-fifty when it came to following recipes. She pushed the front door with her hip to get it closed again. She lived in a tiger enclave on the edge of the downtown core. They had more land here than in the city, but of course feline neighbors had sharp ears. She'd just as soon hers didn't hear what a screw-up she was currently being. "Where's Gran?" she asked her daughter.

"In the den, watching *Downton Abbey* on the DVR."

Evina's mother was obsessed with the imported Outsider show, probably due to idolizing Maggie Smith's sharp-clawed dowager countess. Suspecting her own hide was about to be flayed for asking her mother to stay with the kids longer, Evina trudged up the stairs. Because Abby was still young enough to like it, she hugged and nuzzled her daughter.

"Off to bed with you," she ordered, swatting her small bottom. Thankfully, Abby giggled and ran.

The den was downstairs, along with their kitchen and living room, so Evina retraced her tracks. Weretigers didn't need the full moon to change. She found her son curled up on the sofa in his cub form, his furry head in her mother's lap, his striped tail slowly waving with pleasure. Though he was Abby's twin, Rafiq was much shyer. Turning tiger was his security blanket, something the rules at the mixed-race school he attended forbid him from doing there. Because he didn't focus as well as Abby, he was in a different class, a separation Evina knew made him self-conscious. Sensitive to this, her mother was gently stroking his ruff and ears, far more tender with her grandchildren than Evina remembered her being when she was a girl. Despite the resentment she might have felt, Evina treasured her for it.

The tigress in her agreed. Nothing could be more important than a mother you could count on to love your kids.

Her mother flicked off the TV and turned as Evina reached the den's doorway. Rita Mohajit was eighty—just entering her prime, as she liked to say. Evina couldn't deny she remained gorgeous, her figure trim, her striking face scarcely more lined than it had been in her twenties. Thick auburn hair formed a cloud of curls around her shoulders. Limber as ever, she'd tucked her feet under her. When she saw her daughter, her mouth pinched in sympathy. "Hard shift?"

Not expecting the kindness, Evina's throat tightened. She nodded. "I forgot to buy Rafi's cupcakes for school. Can you watch them a little longer while I run to the store?"

"You'll have to drive to the Holy Foods. Everything else is closed at this hour."

"I'll be fast," Evina promised.

"Be *careful*," her mother corrected. "And maybe pick up some wine for yourself. You've been working too hard."

Evina crossed to the sofa and kissed both her mom and son. Rafi greeted her with a baby's mewl, half asleep and somehow still smelling of little boy. She loved him so much she wished there were two of her, the only way she saw to guarantee she wouldn't let him down again. Her little boy *felt* everything so deeply, more than anyone in the family.

"It's okay, baby," Rita crooned, her hand falling to pet her daughter. "Rafi isn't as fragile as you think."

If Evina's eyes grew teary at hearing that, it was easy to hide in her son's

16

soft fur.

~

As long as Evina had driven all this way, she decided to grab a cart and shop. She was leaving the butcher's counter with her neatly wrapped packages of red meat when she recognized the man she thought of as the Holy Foods Romeo.

He was a character: sex on a shish kabob, as her sometimes bawdy mom liked to say. She'd watched him for weeks before he noticed her, seducing the single ladies and charming the cashiers. He knew how to tell one herb from another and would happily recommend a wine to complement whatever a pretty female had in her cart. He sauntered the aisles like the Emperor of Seduction, the bounce of confidence in his step better than any dance. Evina had observed he was good-natured when turned down, dazzling when accepted, and downright knee-weakening when he was on the prowl. Hearts fluttered at his approach . . . even hearts that knew better.

The first time he spoke to her she was flattered in spite of herself. He was smart and amusing, as quick with his tongue as he was to hop in bed. Maybe she was kidding herself, but he seemed to like that she could match wits with him. When he realized she was a tigress, his chagrin had struck her as genuine. He still talked to her after that, but they both knew he was just flirting for flirting's sake.

Historically speaking, cats and dogs didn't mix that way.

Though tigers and wolves couldn't have children, them hooking up wasn't a biological impossibility—more a cultural one. Tigers and wolves were rivals, no less so because both gravitated toward protecting citizens. If the RPD was a wolf domain, the **RFD** belonged to tigers. Wolves enforced the law. Tigers rescued people from disasters. Evina doubted any cop, werewolf or otherwise, liked the fact that firemen were more popular.

The two departments' annual soccer match was legendary for fur flying.

A tiger dating a wolf was almost unheard of. This, of course, didn't prevent Evina from occasionally daydreaming about a fling.

Oddly, her Romeo didn't appear in the mood for a fling tonight. His snazzy boots were rooted to the floor in the bakery section, and he was staring at a stacked display of boxes like they held the answer to life's meaning. His body was—as ever—truly admirable, turning snug black jeans and a dark silk shirt into a fashion ad. His brow was furrowed and his teeth gnawed his lower lip, something she couldn't recall seeing him do before. The sleek black ponytail that usually contained his hair was disheveled.

The mother in her couldn't help wondering what was wrong.

Oh what the hell, she thought, parking her cart by the tuna. She walked over to him, stopping arm to arm at his side so she could stare with him. Though he didn't look at her, she knew he knew who it was.

"I came for the cherry pie," he said casually, "but now that I'm here, suddenly I'm not excited."

Amused, Evina shot him a sidelong glance. "I could make a joke about that."

"Could you?" His lips were curving at the corners.

"Maybe you need some cherry pie Viagra."

He turned and smiled down at her. At 5'6" Evina was a good six inches shorter than he was. The wolf's smile was ordinary, no naughty sex-god-on-the-make in it. Evina thought the expression looked nice on him. Her grocery store Romeo had an interesting mouth, neither full nor thin but quirkily eye-catching. The peaks of his upper lip were so sharp she found it hard not to flush when she stared at them. His lower lip twisted to one side, a lack of symmetry that made him look as if he'd been born not taking anything seriously.

"Maybe," he said slowly, as if working out the mystery then and there, "I didn't come here for pie. Maybe I came here to talk to you."

"Watch out, Nate," she said, because they'd traded names and basic facts. "That sounded like it wasn't a line."

"How could a woman as rare and fine as you inspire anything but sincerity?"

Evina knew this was nonsense but enjoyed it all the same. In the process of trading quips, they'd turned to face each other. Other shoppers rolled their carts past them unseeing. Because it was the middle of the night, and even responsible single mothers sometimes felt reckless, she let herself stare into his eyes. They were dark and a little sad, which seemed extra dangerous to her. His lean cheekbones were dramatic, his clean-shaven jaw a symphony of straight lines. His high-bridged blade of a nose was slightly too long for beauty, but it added character.

Without that slight imperfection, he might have intimidated a forty-something tigress who'd had two kids.

"What are *you* here for?" he murmured.

Her brain took at least two seconds to supply the answer. "Oh," she said. "Cupcakes. Once a month, my son's class at school celebrates whichever kids have a birthday. They take turns bringing in the sweets, and Rafiq was up this time." She wrinkled her nose. "My daughter had to remind me that I forgot."

"Rough day at work?" he asked, like her mother had.

"Yes," she answered as simply as she could.

He touched her hand—or barely, his index finger brushing the side of it. Like all weres, his skin was warm. Tiny nerves trilled along her arm.

"Me too," he said huskily.

She wanted to kiss him, to cup his face and lay her lips over his. She wondered if he'd taste like his voice sounded, like hot black coffee or nice merlot.

"E-vi-na," he said, lingering on the syllables.

Neither of them moved, just stood there staring into each other's eyes. Nate finally broke the moment with a wag of his head. *Don't go there*, she could almost hear him thinking.

"Can I ask you something?" he said in a less seductive tone.

"Sure." She tried to sound more everyday herself.

"Most weretigers are psychic, right?"

"Some of us have gifts that fall underneath that term."

"But you run your own station. You're the alpha of your work pride. I read you won a competition when you were fifteen for how good your astral projections were."

Evina's brows shot up toward her hairline. "You Oogled me," she said, referring to a popular Elfnet search engine.

"I was curious." The faint darkening of Nate's cheeks suggested he was embarrassed at being caught. He seemed not to like this, because his interesting mouth pressed flat. "My question is, if you were in your out-of-body form, could you read a room's vibrations?"

"Possibly. It would depend on how strongly they were imprinted." She squinted at him. His expression was so worried he hardly seemed like the same person. "Don't the police have people on staff for that?"

"Usually, but the spirit infestation at the East End high rise has them tied up. I stumbled across a place today . . . I think it might have been a crime scene, and I—" He swallowed. "I think it might be important to know for sure quickly."

She could see he was struggling not to plead with his eyes. To her, this only increased his persuasiveness. "I can't promise I'd get an impression. Akashic reading isn't my specialty."

"But you'd try. I mean—" He seemed to recall himself. "Maybe I shouldn't ask you to look. What happened there might be bad."

"I've seen bad," she reminded softly, thinking of Christophe lying in his hospital bed, recovering from his burns so slowly he almost could have been human. "I pull people out of fires."

Nate's hands clasped her upper arms, his fingers squeezing them lightly. He made her sorry she'd worn a sweater for the store's AC. "I'll stay with you the whole time. You won't have to go inside physically."

She nearly smiled. Like a lot of men, he confused her relatively small human form with fragility. "Let me call my mother. Make sure she can stay with the kids. Just remember, I have to get home at some point. I won't be able to try for long."

"I won't ask you to," he promised. He squeezed her arms again. "Thank you, Evina. This means a lot to me."

She could see it did—and then she had to wonder if a werewolf's gratitude ought to please her so much.

~

The first time Nate laid eyes on Evina his nerves had sat up and woofed. She was female with a capital *F*. Exotic and curvy, everything about her said *soft*. He'd known a lot of women, but her face mesmerized: that creamy skin, those flying brows, the siren's mouth that—so far as he could tell—was naturally the color of a good cabernet. Her walk made him bite his lip, especially the rear view. Her long curly hair was as black as a raven's wing, the sort that made men fantasize about it brushing them. He'd only seen her wear it braided, and it hung to her rounded butt. Best of all (though it was a strange best for him) her eyes were huge and golden, surrounded by thick dark lashes like a doe out a cartoon.

Those eyes should have warned him she was a tigress; he'd sensed right off she was a were from her energy. When the truth had hit him, it was too late. He'd already caught a bad hankering for her.

He hadn't sealed the deal with a single female since his shopping cart first bumped hers.

This made what he was doing, waiting for her out in the parking lot, monumentally stupid. No matter what happened when she saw that room, Nate would end up worse off. If she weren't freaked out, he'd respect her more. If she were, she'd probably never want to see him again. The sudden sick dropping of his stomach warned him how much he'd miss that.

Even if it led to nothing, he looked forward to bantering with her.

Crap, he thought as she came back from making her cell phone call.

"Everything's fine," she said with the naturally sexy smile that never failed to tighten his trousers. "My mother has decided to be a saint tonight."

"Good." Gritting his teeth, he gently clasped her elbow to escort her through the rows of cars. She'd removed her light cotton sweater. Underneath, she wore a sleeveless fitted blouse the color of tangerines. She'd paired it with plain white capris. Bare now, the skin of her arm was satin, its muscles warm beneath his fingers. They'd put her groceries in the trunk of her car, which was spelled to keep things cool. For now, they were leaving her vehicle here. All she carried was the giant tote no mother seemed able to leave home without.

She clutched it and laughed when she caught sight of his transport.

"Really?" she chuckled, little snorts coming from her nose. "You drive a vintage Goblinati? Nate, you know that's a total skirt-chaser's car."

"I know it's fast," he said, secretly amused by her hilarity. "And I think I ought to get points for not buying it in red."

He held the passenger door for her, noting how neatly she swung her trim calves inside. Because noticing made this feel too much like a date, he worked a frown onto his face and circled to the driver's side.

By the time he slid behind the wheel, she'd buckled up and turned her body toward his. Her legs were pulled up beneath her, her cheek at rest on the soft leather. The pose was catlike, her gorgeous curves relaxed and molded into the car's contours. Nate thought about how flexible she must be, how small compared to him. His cock hardened without warning, stretching his black jockstrap. Just looking at her and having her look back was more powerful than most kisses.

Unsettled by that knowledge, he inserted the key and spoke. "Where we're going isn't far, at least not the way I drive."

She smiled at him sleepily, a tired woman at the end of her day. He realized she was comfortable with him. He liked that better than he could say.

"Feel free to catnap," he teased drolly.

She smiled again and, to his surprise, took him up on the offer.

She slept until he stopped the car at the old blanket factory. Adam had made some inroads with his string pulling. Though the plywood still listed crookedly on the front entrance, a cat's cradle of police tape warned people to keep out. Better still, the RPD had installed a discreet watch spell. If their mystery perpetrator came back this way, his image would be recorded.

Nate looked around but didn't sense anyone nearby. Apart from a distant clanking down by the river, the neighborhood appeared abandoned.

"This is the place?" Evina asked, shutting her door quietly. Stiff from her nap, she laced her fingers above her head and stretched. Despite the circumstances, Nate couldn't tear his gaze away. The way her breasts lifted with her movements was gasp-worthy.

She caught him staring and laughed softly. "You are excellent for my ego, Detective Rivera."

Her use of his title, pleasurable though it was, reminded him of their mission. "We should go inside. I know it's important for you to be undisturbed when you're projecting."

Though her eyes stayed warm, her smile slipped away. She nodded for him to go ahead of her. Once they'd both ducked beneath the tape, Nate led the way with the powerful police issue flashlight he kept stowed in his glove box. The dirty stairs didn't look any better under its beam. Evina sucked in a breath when a rat the size of a rabbit scampered across their path.

She wasn't afraid. Rats were prey to tigresses, even if they did make for disgusting meals—definitely not interchangeable with chicken.

"Wait here," Nate said when they reached the swinging doors to the second floor corridor. "I want to check the way ahead."

Evina gave him an eye roll, reminding him she faced danger everyday.

"I'm the one with the gun," he said, pointing to his ankle.

That comment widened her eyes. He supposed it hadn't occurred to her that he'd go armed to the grocery store. Satisfied she'd stay, he checked the length of the hall. As he'd expected, no one was there but them.

He returned to her, belatedly sorry he'd left her by herself in a pitch-black stairwell. His estimation of her nerves went up another notch when he saw how calm she was.

They continued together to the strange room he'd found. It too was webbed in crime scene tape. Nate reached through the plastic strips and pushed the door open. The repulsion spell had dissipated, but Evina felt something. A shudder big enough to see shook her slim shoulders. She set her jaw more determinedly.

"I need to sit down for this," she said.

Abruptly regretting that he hadn't grabbed his leather jacket from the back of the car, Nate used his boot to scuff a circle clear of clutter on the cracked concrete floor.

Evina grimaced and lowered herself to it, her face oriented to the doorway. "It'll help if you stand behind me. Touching another person anchors me."

Nate moved behind her so that his knees touched her back. Cross-legged, she wrapped her arms around his calves. He was anxious enough that the contact didn't give him the sexual charge it otherwise would have.

Evina closed her eyes and started to breathe slowly.

He saw why she'd won a medal for this skill. In seconds, he felt her energy slip into a trance state. Light flickered through her aura, which was expanding rapidly. The air around them grew cooler as she drew on the ambient magic their half-fae city was famous for. The swiftness with which she threw herself into the act made him want to protect her. Nate dropped one hand to her head, which didn't seem to disturb her.

His wolf let out a whine, audible only in his mind. It wasn't a sound of submission, despite Evina being alpha when he was not. To him, his beast sounded as if it were concerned. If it was, it didn't have much time to be. Light flared brilliantly in Evina's heart center. Not wanting to be blinded. Nate narrowed his eyelids.

The light coalesced into the form of a tiger and padded out of her.

Nate's breath—and probably his wolf's as well—caught like cotton candy inside his chest. Evina's tigress was the most beautiful feline he'd ever seen.

Though only a projection of astral energy, her were form appeared solid. Night black stripes marked the richest possible orange fur. She was much bigger as a tiger than a human—bigger than his wolf, if it came to that. Her back came to Nate's waist, muscles rippling under that gorgeous pelt. When she glanced back at him, light flashed behind the pupils of her gold eyes. A growl rumbled from deep within her chest, her lips pulling back in a obvious threat. The hairs on Nate's arms stood up, but the sound inspired a thrill more than it did an urge to flinch.

He got the impression her beast was testing him.

"Snarl all you want," he said equably. "You're here because I trust you."

She huffed, the resonant sound like a train would make. Her lips relaxed back over her long canines. She swung her great head away as if dismissing him.

Solid-looking or not, she prowled straight through the crime scene tape.

~

Evina had practice concealing fear. As the boss of people who risked death on a regular basis, she needed to set an example. Level heads pulled firemen through tight spots. Losing focus because of dread never helped anyone.

She ignored how much her tiger didn't want to enter that room.

Having Nate behind her helped, knowing he had the gumption not to back down at her tigress's threat display. She allowed her awareness of her human body to slip away in favor of more fully inhabiting her projection.

The metal beneath her paw pads was cool and smooth, the sensation more elusive than it would have been if she were solid.

She sniffed, pulling back her lips and opening her mouth to taste the scents that were there. Beneath the tang of steel, she picked up blood and perfumed smoke—perhaps from a wood-based incense. The skin along her muscular shoulders crawled, just as it had when Nate first opened the door. She quartered the room, a big cat pacing a small cage. Three strides took her long body across it.

Her more primitive mind opened, along with the senses Nate called psychic. A cry teased her ear from someone who wasn't there. The sound was cut short. Evina's tail flicked at the distress this caused.

Barely aware she was doing it, she lay down in her cat form and closed her eyes.

Images flooded her, as sharp as if the events were happening in front of her. The vividness surprised her. She hadn't known she'd get such a clear reading. Three men stood in the room, garbed in hospital green and masked like doctors. They were huddled around a table with raised steel edges that formed a tray. A child perhaps a year old lay in its center. The child was on its back, sleepy but awake, dressed in clean blue pants and a striped short-sleeved top with a cartoon fox on it. "I'm Tricky!" the shirt declared. The barely scuffed condition of the child's leather shoes said it was only just walking.

The child seemed unalarmed by its strange surroundings. Its big brown eyes gazed around, its chubby legs and arms wriggling. The movements had caused its T-shirt to ruck up over its navel.

One of the doctors pulled the shirt down and patted the child's belly. "He needs to die without violence, and with as little fear as possible."

His voice was low and soothing, nothing to alarm the child. The other two doctors nodded behind their masks. The one who'd spoken brought out a small pillow, the kind stewardesses hand out on planes.

Evina's astral tether gave a sharp tug, trying to snap her back into her physical body. The part of her that was a mother didn't want to see what came next. The part of her that faced whatever her job required countermanded it ruthlessly.

"Hold his hands," the first doctor said.

The other two complied, gently rubbing the dimpled fingers with their milky white latex gloves. The first doctor pressed the pillow over the child's face.

The little boy laughed at first, thinking it was a game. When he finally began to struggle, realizing he couldn't breathe, his back arched like a bow off the steel table. His short arms and legs flung out, his entire body straining to get air.

No, Evina thought, correcting her misimpression. The baby wasn't straining to get air. He was straining to change forms. Young though he was, instinctively he was hoping to defend himself or escape.

This child was a shapeshifter.

The shock catapulted her into her human form, which was bent over and moaning. Nate had dropped to his knees, though she hadn't been aware of him moving. His arms wrapped her from behind, not tightly but close enough that his wolf warmth sank into her. She needed it. She was shivering violently.

"I'm okay," she said through clenched teeth. She didn't sound okay, even to herself. "Jesus." Taking three slow breaths, she pushed herself around to face him. His dark eyes were wide, his supportive hold on her arms cautious.

"Let me tell you what I saw right away," she said. "I don't want to forget details."

~

Nate let her go through the story once while her memory was fresh, then took her out to the car. His digital memo pad was there, and he wanted an audio record. He kept his arm around her all the way down the stairs, her weight leaning on him more heavily than he suspected she realized. Once she was settled in the passenger seat, he dug out the micro-recorder and had her repeat what she'd seen.

She was steadier now, her telling more organized, though it didn't change appreciably.

As she described what had happened in the room, Nate ignored how cold the back of his neck had gotten. No matter what he'd felt when he found the shoe, her story was sufficient to chill his blood. "You sure you didn't see the doctors' faces? Maybe their hair or eye color?"

She shook her head, her lips pursing in frustration. "I know I should have tried. I *thought* I was paying attention. The truth is, as soon as I saw the little boy, all my focus went to him."

"That's natural," he soothed, rubbing her pants' now-black knee. The floor of the blanket factory had been filthy. She must have transferred the dirt with her hands. A pang ran through him for getting that stain on her. "You noticed more than a lot of pros would have."

"Two of them looked Caucasian," she said. "The doctor who talked and the taller of the listening pair. The third was shorter and a couple shades browner than you are, but I couldn't say precisely where his genes hailed from."

"Did you get the impression they were shifters?"

"I'd be guessing if I said *yes*. Their bodies were human, not elfin or fae—at least not pureblood. I'd have noticed pointy ears or that sparkly skin unmixed faeries have."

"That narrows it down some."

"Not enough." Evina shoved her hands through her hair, forgetting it was braided. She stopped when her fingers snagged. "What gets me is how matter of fact the head doctor was. He wasn't—" Her face twisted. "He wasn't getting off on what they did. He was businesslike. 'He needs to die without violence,' was what he said, and it didn't seem like it was out of compassion."

"A ritual maybe?" Nate suggested, though this seemed like a long shot.

"The way they were dressed?" Evina shook her head. "If a bunch of humans get into that black mass stuff, they tend to wear silly costumes."

Nate rubbed his lower lip, looking out the Goblinati's windshield into the night, trying to will useful thoughts to form. The nearest streetlight was broken, the next seeming far away. The clock on his dash clicked to 2:30. "You couldn't be mistaken about their victim being a shapeshifter? One year old seems young to try to change, even as a fight or flight response."

"Weretigers first change around the time they're weaned. My son Rafiq learned to run on four feet long before he walked on two. Other shifter races turn early too. Foxes for one—not that I'm assuming the child was a werefox just because of his shirt."

Nate brought his gaze back to hers, the dark car and the situation cocooning them. "That was a good detail. We can run your description of the boy's clothes and age through the Missing Persons database. See if we get a hit."

Evina shivered. Nate remembered the tailored leather jacket in the back seat. The weather didn't call for it, but sometimes he needed to look sharp on short notice.

"It's warm out," she said when he shook it out for her.

"Put it on anyway," he advised. "If you were one of your crew, you'd be ordering yourself to be checked out for shock."

"Low blow." Smiling wryly, she swung the coat around her shoulders.

Nate liked the look of his garment cloaking her. To smell his scent mingling with hers satisfied him on a deep level. Knowing this wasn't wise, he clicked off the recorder and slid his key into the ignition.

"I'll drive you back to your car," he said, privately deciding he'd follow her home as well. "I'll call you tomorrow, if that's okay with you. My boss will probably want to talk to you in person."

She nodded with her head turned away, lost in her own musings. She had a surprisingly cute profile, her nose turned up a bit at the end—like a kitten's, he thought. Sensing she didn't want to talk anymore, Nate let her sit in silence for the return trip to the grocery store.

~

Evina's head was full of things she wished weren't in it. She wanted to be home that instant, her arms wrapped around her kids. She wanted to drive to the hospital to hold Christophe's poor bandaged hand. If she could have swaddled everyone she loved in industrial strength bubble wrap, she'd have done it then.

The Holy Foods parking lot was emptier than when they'd left. Nate was able to pull up beside her car.

"Thanks for the ride," she said.

He laughed on a sardonic burst of air. The response made her look at him. The store lights angled through the windshield onto his face. He was incredibly handsome, his looks illogically improved by the line of worry between his brows.

"Evina," he said, "you shouldn't be thanking me."

Maybe she shouldn't have done it, but she laid her palm on his hollowed cheek. The touch made him freeze, then thrummed like etheric fire through his energy. She couldn't recall a man's aura reacting to her like this. His eyes went darker and his breathing quickened, the sound turning her soft and molten between the legs.

The hint of stubble beneath her hand didn't discourage the steamy surge. Smooth-talker though he was, Nate Rivera was all man.

"Evina," he repeated in a much different tone.

He leaned to her across the seats, his fingers brushing an escaped curl back behind her ear. She shivered—and not from cold. She knew her eyes had widened, and that her breasts rose and fell too quickly to pretend she wasn't aroused. She couldn't have said why he had this effect on her. She might be out of practice, but she was no shy miss when it came to dancing this tango.

Nate slid his hand around to cradle the back of her head. "You have no idea how much I want to do this."

He pressed his lips over hers. Their surface was warm and soft, molding to hers so gently it seemed silly to object. She didn't want to object. She nuzzled closer to him and moaned, her hands finding natural spots to rest on his chest. He was hard there, as if he didn't have an ounce of fat on him.

He turned his head just so and slipped his tongue inside.

He tasted good, better than anything she could have invented in her most torrid fantasy. His tongue stroked hers, his cheeks pulling inward to suck sleekly. When she let her mouth answer the way she wanted, he moaned for her. His head turned again, opening her more. He kissed her harder and more aggressively. Evina's nails dug into his shirt like claws. He gasped and started breathing like he'd been running flat out in wolf form.

That idea was so perversely exciting she had to push him away.

"Sorry," he said, retreating immediately. "I shouldn't have done that."

"I wasn't telling you not to," she pointed out, rather breathless herself.

Nate eased back into his seat. "You were overwrought. I—" He smoothed his hair around his head, his ponytail ragged now. "I never should have dragged you into this."

If there was one thing Evina hated, it was being treated like she was weaker because she was female.

"You didn't drag me into anything," she bit out. "Even if I weren't a mother, I'm alpha just like you. It's my nature to want to protect children."

He stared at her in shock. Her sense of insult climbing, she unlatched her door and got out. "Call me at work today. My shift starts at eleven. We'll arrange a time for me to meet your boss. Since you Oogled me, I assume you know what station I work for."

He shut his mouth. "I do," he said. "I'll call you after eleven."

She slammed the door, satisfied he'd gotten the message that her spine had starch. Her anger steadied her, allowing her to start her crotchety old converted Camry on the first try. As empty as the lot was, she couldn't fail to notice his Goblinati trailing out of it behind her.

When he still rode her bumper after two lights, she knew he intended to make sure she got home safely.

"Idiot," she muttered to her rear view mirror. Even as she did, a strange warm ache blossomed in her chest.

She couldn't remember the last time a man had tried to look out for her.

♦ CHAPTER THREE

NATE drove to work by himself in his Goblinati. Most days the squad rode together in the response van, but this morning they weren't enough in synch. Nate had fallen into bed and slept after he got home, though he couldn't remember it. To him, it felt like he'd opened his eyes a minute after he shut them.

This might have been for the best, because who knew what he'd dreamed about? The square steel room and the creepy doctors? Evina's delicious kiss? The fact that she was under the impression he was alpha?

Nate had told her he had a boss. He'd assumed she understood. How awkward would it be to explain he wasn't in charge of anyone?

Conscious that he was running late, even by the squad's loose standards, he made a coffee stop on the way.

When you weren't the alpha, a caffeine offering never hurt.

The detective squad room was located in the bowels of the precinct house. Nate left a mocha grande on the grateful watch sergeant's desk, then trotted down the stairs with the rest of his purchases. More than the usual bodies were in the half beat-up, half high-tech room. The extras were uniforms, being organized by Rick for the continuing pursuit of Ivan Galina.

"I'll take that off your hands," Tony volunteered, neatly grabbing his cardboard tray of Star's Brew and scones. When it came to food, he and his brother Rick were known for their hollow legs.

"Where's Adam?" Nate asked, bemused by the hive of activity.

"Office," Tony said around the scone he'd already dug out and stuck in his mouth. He chewed and smiled brilliantly. "He's requesting a search warrant. Vasili gave up the location where he and Ivan dumped their last accountant."

"You and Rick got a burial site out of him?"

"We squeezed him good," Tony crowed.

28

Despite his surprise—and maybe a tinge of envy—Nate gave the side of Tony's shoulder a congratulatory punch. "I need to talk to Adam. I'll catch up with you on this later."

Their lieutenant rarely used his small office, not wanting to establish a separation between him and his men. Battered file cabinets took up most of the space. Room remained for a desk and Adam's landline phone, which he was talking on. Despite the hum of noise outside, Adam hadn't shut the door. He set the receiver back in its cradle as Nate came in.

"You got a minute, Lieu?" he asked.

"Just." Adam leaned back in his chair and stretched. "This Galina thing is popping."

Nate shut the door behind him, then set his digital memo pad on the desk. Adam wasn't one to waste breath on pointless questions. His brows went up, but he tipped his chair back to level and pressed the play button.

Nate had listened to Evina's account of her astral survey one last time on the drive over. Now he pulled an uncomfortable guest chair closer and watched Adam's reaction. It wasn't what he was hoping for. Though his superior listened attentively, he didn't seem bowled over.

"You took a civilian to a crime scene?" Adam asked when the recording finished.

"Evina isn't any civilian. She's the station fire chief for Company Number 5."

"*Evina,*" Adam repeated.

Nate felt heat rise into his cheeks. "She's an acquaintance. We met at the grocery store."

"And presumably she's as young and pretty as she sounds on this tape."

"It wasn't like that. We aren't dating. She's a tigress." Nate could see from his boss's amused expression that he was making this worse. "The department psychics were tied up, and I thought this was too important to sit on. You have to admit her debriefing is impressive. The pros we use aren't always this detailed."

"Or this imaginative." Adam's elbows were on his desk, his broad hands folded together before his mouth. "There's a reason cats aren't suited to police work. They chase shadows when nothing's there."

"And dogs chase cars," Nate spat back angrily.

"Fortunately for us cops, chasing cars is a useful skill."

"You can't be suggesting we ignore this."

"We can't be sure what this woman saw."

"She saw something awful! She's a mother. You should have seen how shaken up she was. Plus, I didn't tell her about the shoe I found. How could she have known this involved a child if she was 'chasing shadows' like you say?"

Nate had jumped to his feet in front of Adam's desk. He was a hair's breadth from encroaching into his boss's space.

"Look," Adam began in a conciliatory tone. Nate was so infuriated he wanted to sock him. Sensing this, Adam patted the air. "Put the description she gave you into Missing Persons. If we get a hit, we'll proceed from there."

Nate had already done this from his home unit, and was waiting on the results. That didn't seem diplomatic to admit right then. "I want to pursue this," he said instead.

Adam let out a sighing breath.

"Give me Carmine," Nate insisted, knowing the older man was the only detective Adam might be willing to pull off the Galina case. Carmine was a good solid cop, but not what you'd call brilliant. Nate didn't care about that. Carmine's belly laugh and easy manner had a way of disarming witnesses. "Carmine can coordinate a door-to-door around the blanket factory. See if any vagrants or shopkeepers saw our trio of doctors. It wouldn't hurt to canvas the area anyway—in case the dumpsite doesn't pan out the way you want. Vasili *was* holed up there for a while."

"Fine," Adam said. "You can have Carmine and two uniforms. Make sure you don't waste them. I might need to pull them back again."

"Thank you," Nate said, possibly conveying more exasperation than gratitude. He didn't ask if Adam wanted to speak to Evina personally. He already knew the answer to that.

~

The fact that Nate's boss thought Evina couldn't be trusted didn't seem like news he ought to share by phone. Because it was past eleven, when she'd mentioned her shift started, he made the ten-minute drive out to Company Number 5.

He parked across the street half a block from their garage bay. This was where their lime-green tiger-striped fire trucks would pull out. Evina's station owned two apparatuses. The first was a pumper. As Nate understood it, pumpers increased the pressure of hydrant water, to ensure it would blast from hoses onto a blaze. The second truck was a lengthy ladder and platform deal, designed for attacking fires or entering buildings from high floors.

The pup in Nate was excited to be close to these life-size toys. The man in him preferred the prospect of sniffing around Evina. From the moment he'd seen her behind her cart at the Holy Foods, his sexual antenna had been hyper-tuned to her. His pulse quickened as he left his car, his outlook brightening in spite of the awkwardness of his errand.

A second later, he realized seeing her wasn't going to be simple.

A tiger were the size of a refrigerator was working in the bay. He was folding a soft-sided hose so that it accordioned neatly into a compartment on the truck. The taut set of his giant shoulders told Nate the tiger knew a stranger was approaching.

"You can't park there," the firefighter said without bothering to turn his head.

The implication that Nate posed no threat was a classic wereanimal insult.

"There's no sign," Nate said, taking in the man's height and build. He was bigger than Nate's packmate Rick—6'7" if he was an inch and equally muscle-bound. He could bench press Nate without effort but wouldn't be as fast. This knowledge was in his voice as he continued. "I made sure your trucks would be able to get by if they went out in that direction."

The man tucked up the last of the hose and turned. His hair was strawberry gold and wavy, his skin a rosy cream color. Many weretigers were of Indian descent but not all. This fellow looked like a Celt to him. When he spoke, a growl rolled under his voice.

"You misunderstand me, dog. *You* can't park anywhere near here."

A grin broke across Nate's face. He wasn't any more afraid than if this had been his pack's beta. Nate knew how good he was at hand-to-hand. Civilized or not, some big lunk spoiling for a tussle put him in his happy place.

"I *can* park there," he said, "and I have. If you want a piece of me for that, by all means give taking one a shot." Enjoying this, he spread his hands and grinned more broadly, his fingers beckoning the other on.

The fireman lunk measured Nate scornfully with his gaze, tiger gold bleeding into Irish blue. He rolled onto the balls of his feet and tucked in his shoulders, clearly preparing to pounce into an attack. Laughing silently to himself, Nate thought: *here, kitty!* Then the tiger did the last thing he expected. Rather than spring, he blinked twice and backed off. Nate's game-for-anything attitude had averted fights before, but guys this big didn't generally give up so fast.

"Huh," the fireman said, the sound of dismissal at least half cat. He narrowed his eyes at Nate, as if suspecting the wolf had played a trick on him. "Don't be planning to park there long."

"I won't," Nate promised, his meekness almost sincere. "Is your boss around?"

The tiger's eyes slitted more. "Evina is in her office."

Though Evina was this pride's alpha, as a female she'd be considered a pride possession—one they'd instinctively do anything to defend. Nate walked through the garage bay with the awareness that hostile eyes followed him. It didn't seem wise to challenge his watchers by staring directly, but he couldn't help noticing every cat he passed was as massive as the first guy.

Evidently, when it came to the RFD, runts of the litter need not apply. Females weren't barred from serving if they could pass the physical, but except for her, Evina's crew was male.

He was a bit surprised when he completed their gauntlet without trouble.

Well, he thought, passing into an empty sitting area. *That was interesting.*

Inhabited as it was by felines, the building's smell caused Nate's wolfish nose to twitch. The aroma wasn't unpleasant—musky, he guessed—and not what he was used to. The lounge-type furniture wasn't bad. Secondhand and worn out by large bodies, heaps of colorful pillows brightened it. Nate's inner neat freak approved of how clean the place was underneath its slight messiness. Rick and Tony were way bigger slobs than this.

A station house run by cats did have its upside.

He ascended a set of wooden stairs within the big open space. The steps led to an enclosed office, or maybe *perch* was a better word. Like Nate's boss Adam, Evina worked with her door open. Metal support columns were the only barrier between the lounge space and the garage. From her big square window, she could view everything.

She didn't seem to have watched him run her men's gauntlet. She was on the phone leaning on one elbow, her graceful hand shielding her pretty eyes. Knowing she must have heard him by then, Nate waited politely outside the door.

She ended the call soon after and looked at him. Although she seemed curious about his presence, she gestured him to a guest chair whose seat had been repaired with bright blue duct tape. Patch job notwithstanding, it was more comfortable than Adam's.

"That was the hospital," she said. "One of my men suffered third degree burns yesterday. The doctors are trying to adjust his pain meds so that he's not too drugged to change. He's expected to make a good recovery, once he can manage that."

"I'm sorry," Nate said, wincing at the thought of not being able to heal such serious injuries. "Is there anything I can do?"

The question came out automatically. Nate saw it surprised Evina. She widened her lustrous eyes at him. "Not unless you can compel another shifter to change form. I'm afraid that's not among my gifts."

"My alpha can do it sometimes," Nate said, "but as far as I know, his influence only works on wolves."

"Your alpha . . ."

Nate smiled, glad redressing her earlier misconception had been easy. "Yes. As it happens, I have a beta too."

"I thought . . ." She trailed off.

"I know. I realized last night. Believe me, I'm flattered."

She shifted in her swiveling chair, her eyes considering him in a similar fashion to her hulking Irish guard cat. "I'm surprised. You give off quite the aura of confidence."

"I'm confident about a lot of things," Nate said, not quite straight-faced.

She blushed, delighting the most masculine part of him. "Yes," she said dryly. "I noticed that."

She pulled one foot up onto her chair, hugging her shin with both arms.

Her foot was bare, her shin clad in worn blue jeans. Something about the pose, or maybe the curry orange polish on her toenails, gave Nate an instant erection.

"Why are you here?" Evina asked, seeming unaware of this. "I expected you to call."

"Ah." With one finger, Nate scratched his cheek in embarrassment. "It appears my alpha doesn't find your vision of what happened in that secret operating room as compelling as I do."

"He can't be planning to ignore it."

Nate shrugged uncomfortably. "He doesn't think what you saw is evidence of a crime."

"Well, fuck," Evina said, the word too hard for her lush soft mouth. "*You're* not going to ignore it, surely."

"No. I convinced him to give me a detective and a couple uniforms. They'll canvas the area around the factory. Hopefully, someone will have seen something."

"And the child's description?"

"I'm afraid I came up empty-handed at Missing Persons. No one's reported a shifter child that age disappearing in the last eighteen months. They'll check farther back, but I'm not holding my breath."

"Those psychic impressions I read were fresh," Evina said firmly. "Not more than a few months old."

She jumped up and began to prowl the width of her office behind her desk. She reminded him of her tigress, the sight of which had enchanted him last night. She was more than wild; she was shifter sex on two legs. Muscles moved in her body that had him imagining her in bed. His hard-on shifted from uncomfortable to raging. He ordered himself not to tug his trousers and draw her eyes to it.

When she stopped and faced him dead on, excitement slapped through his blood. She'd come around the desk and was only feet from him.

"We'll go to the media," she said. "My mother's dating a news producer at WQSN. Non-wolves don't always report trouble to the cops. A direct appeal for information could generate some leads."

Nate considered. WQSN was Resurrection's third largest TV network. Their all-shifter soap operas were very popular.

"A sketch of the boy you saw would help," he said, shoving aside his awareness of how ticked his alpha was going to be if they did this behind his back. "I know an artist who could work with you on one."

"Good." Evina smiled ferally at him.

She stood in front of him, her bare feet planted, her fists pushing at her waist. The teeth her smile bared seemed especially white and sharp. To him, she was a miniature Valkyrie.

A tiger queen, he corrected. One any male would be privileged to surrender to.

"I want to fuck you so bad I hurt," he blurted.

She jerked, startled by his bluntness—as he was himself. Nate usually played his seduction cards more smoothly. A second later, her lovely bosom went up and down. Nate realized the tips of her breasts were sharp. That spurred a surge of heat he didn't know how to squelch. Luckily, he didn't have to.

Evina reached down, grabbing him by the skinny tie he wore with his black silk shirt. "Come with me," she said huskily.

His hormones went haywire. Skin humming with arousal, he fought not to stumble as she tugged him onto his feet. Stronger than her size would suggest, she pulled him to her desk and around it. In his current panting state, he was *almost* willing to cast caution to the winds and let her take him on top of it, in clear view of her oversized pride members. His pretty hide was grateful when a panel in her rear wall swung open. The hidden door revealed a small private compartment.

"Welcome to my kitty hidey hole," she purred.

He caught a glimpse of tufted saffron-colored leather, which padded both walls and floor. The floor was no more than three foot square, not big enough to lie down unless you were as small as she was and curled up. To want a private space like this must have been a cat thing. At the moment, the lack of size didn't matter. Evina shoved the door closed behind them. A light came on, an exotic bazaar-style lantern dangling from a chain above.

"Rrr," she said—part funny, part serious—as she slammed him unresisting against the wall. The little growl skipped along the nerves of his penis, making it thrum and throb. By this point, his cock was hard enough to pound railroad spikes. He reached for her bottom to pull her softness closer. She groaned as he hitched her up.

Nate wondered if a person could die of thankfulness.

"No one can blame me for this," she said. "Wolf or not, you are too damned yummy."

When her lips seized his and her hard-tipped breasts flattened against his chest, Nate decided no one could blame him either.

~

Evina's memory hadn't exaggerated his skill at kissing, or how hard his lean body was. He pulled her up him effortlessly, big hands arranging her thighs around his trim waist.

That done, he kneaded her bottom enticingly.

Her pussy tightened at the press of the bulge that stretched his trouser front. God, he was big—and exactly what she needed. The ache inside her had been building ever since he arrived. Now her head fell back, and Nate

34

kissed a licking, stinging path down her neck. He was almost biting her, almost sucking hard enough to leave marks.

This should have dismayed her, but every nerve she had sang with excitement. Her hands tightened on his shoulders, so wide, so spare of any cushioning but muscle. She rolled her pubis over his large hard-on, hungry to stimulate both herself and it. Nate grunted and shoved his crotch at her harder.

"My God," she breathed, loving how strong he was. "This is going to be good."

"We're doing this?" he panted. "This is on?"

"This is *so* on."

He let out that grunt again and turned her, shoving her spine into the wall. They kissed openmouthed and urgent, growing increasingly aggressive now that they'd given in to their attraction. Nate's clever seducer's fingers opened her jeans and slid in. His hand was underneath her panties, the smooth hard tips of his fingers moving into her wet folds. He understood she wasn't breakable. When he found the pulse and swell of her clitoris, he gave it a good strong squeeze.

Her private break room was soundproofed, but her throaty moan still struck her as too noisy.

Not too noisy for him. Nate kissed her harder and continued to rub her clit, his thumb and fingers rolling it between them. He was skilled at this, seeming to know exactly where the little rod was most sensitive. She supposed he might be reading her energy, not an uncommon gift among weres. Whatever his secret, he took advantage. He rubbed her sweet spots over and over, alternating the pressure just enough not to numb them out. Sensation coiled inside her groin, tingling, spreading, rising so swiftly it startled her.

"Don't," she gasped into his mouth.

"Do," he urged, breathing raggedly.

He wanted her to come without him, and that wasn't how she intended this to go. She fumbled for the front of his nice trousers—some designer brand, she could tell. "I want you inside me. I want you *with* me."

His fastenings were more complicated than hers. Getting nowhere with opening them, she gripped his erection through the cloth. He growled at her. He sounded a little angry, but she'd gotten her message through.

"Crap," he said when she refused to let go. Capitulating for now, he released her pussy and butt, allowing her legs to slide down his. He dropped then, managing to reach his knees in the confined space. Anger forgotten, he nuzzled her belly through the traditional tunic shirt she wore. He inhaled, long and slow, and she knew he was drawing in her essence. The room was too cramped for him to bend lower.

Considering his hum of pleasure, she had no doubt he would have otherwise.

She looked down just as he turned his face up to her, his cheek against her stomach. His dark eyes glowed gold within his lashes, almost like a tiger's would. He smiled so sweetly and yet so wryly that her heart felt momentarily uncomfortable. He knew how impractical their attraction was. Her hand had fallen to his hair and was stroking it. It was hard not to notice his was silkier than hers.

"This is liable to be fast," he warned humorously.

"Then I guess we'll have to do it more than once."

"Good. I don't want to hear any nonsense about us getting this out of our systems."

That startled her. She had been thinking along those lines. He distracted her by grinning, after which he yanked her worn denim jeans and panties all the way down her legs. Since he wasn't able to kiss them, his hands claimed the honor of admiring her naked calves. He smoothed his touch from their shifting muscles to the back of her knees, where the warmth and sensitivity of his palms did amazing things to places he wasn't close to touching.

Evina wondered if he had a roadmap to every woman's erogenous zones. He certainly seemed to be taking a tour of hers. The energy with which the nerves in her clit were jumping completely unnerved her.

"Are my legs all you're interested in?" she asked tartly.

He snorted out a laugh. "I'd remind you patience is a virtue, but as it happens, I'm not feeling virtuous myself."

He proved it by rising so awkwardly his elbow thumped the wall.

"The room is padded," she pointed out when he cursed softly.

"It's *small*," he countered.

"So am I," she teased.

His eyes locked onto hers like lasers. In spite of his clear good humor, the predatory lowering of his brows caused her to shudder erotically. Cream trickled from her, filling the space with scent. Nate's nostrils flared, one hand moving between them.

To her surprise, he wasn't aiming for her sex. Quicker with his trousers than she'd been, he lowered his zipper with a spine-tingling rasp. Evina's pride couldn't prevent her from starting to pant like him.

"Touch me," he ordered.

No one ordered her. Not at work and not in bed. Her head spun from his male scent, different from what she was used to but apparently effective at calling to her sexually. In truth, the differences made him call to her harder. Evina couldn't remember being this desperate to do the deed before.

"You want me to touch your cock?" she asked, the question soft and breathy.

He took her wrist and placed her hand over him. Though he wasn't rough about it, she wasn't certain she could have resisted. She wanted to touch him too badly and—oh—his cock was silky. His skin burned beneath the curve of her fingers, the pulsing of his flesh too exciting not to savor.

"Touch it all over," he instructed. "Dig me out of my jockstrap."

Feeling odd for being so biddable, she freed him from the stretchy cotton. With her second hand, she eased out his testicles. They were tight and full, their skin roughened by light hair. Her fingers had their own cleverness. She played with his sac enough to have him biting back swear words.

Then she dragged both her hands up his long hard shaft.

He watched her do it, his head hanging helplessly. The tip of him was wet, luring her thumbs to massage the moisture around his crest. Under the rim seemed worth getting slick, and that killing spot on the throat. Nate seemed to like when she worked pressure into that.

She treated him as if he weren't breakable either.

"God," he gasped as she returned to his tip for more lubrication. She pushed across his hole until he shuddered. "God, Evina."

"Take me now," she said, judging he'd give in.

He looked at her. Lust had burned away his sadness and his humor, narrowing his focus to her alone. Tension caught in her throat as he lifted her by the rear again. Her legs bare, she gripped his waist with her thighs, needing no urging to squeeze them around him. He shifted his hips, and his crown nudged her labia. His eyes went dark a second before they flared.

She knew why his irises had lit up. She was even wetter than she'd been when he was fingering her.

He pushed inward without a word, and she took him the same way. His cock was smooth and hot and thicker than she'd expected, stretching her soft wet walls. When he needed a different angle to penetrate completely, she cocked her pelvis to it for him. He closed his eyes to slide in that last fraction, his hips wriggling against hers in a lovely rooting motion she couldn't doubt he enjoyed. Her pussy clenched around it, the ache his deep pressure stirred marvelous.

His lashes rose and he smiled at her.

"What do you like?" he asked. "Fast? Slow?"

She blinked. It bothered her that he could ask this, that his control remained unshaken. Shouldn't even a Romeo lose his cool for her? Rather than spoil the moment, she shoved her pique aside.

"I like it fast," she answered. "And hard."

He pressed his lips to hers once, gently. "As my lady commands," he said.

~

Nate liked all sorts of women and all sorts of lovemaking. That said, there was nothing quite like letting loose with a fellow were. He could hardly imagine a better match than for his preferences than Evina.

She fit him in ways he hadn't known a woman could.

Her slighter size made him want to protect her while her curves urged him to maraud. The groan of enjoyment that welcomed his first hard thrust told him he could get away with that. Even better, her assertiveness challenged the side of him that just knew it could take charge. He wanted to devastate her with every trick his years of lovemaking had taught him.

Unfortunately, he was too busy rocketing to Crazy Land for that.

No matter how fast and deep he drove his cock into her, his nerves urged him to grab more. She was helping, her ankles hooked tight in the small of his back, her heels digging in each time she thrust with him. Their bodies slapped each other more noisily than they did the padded wall.

Evina was so wet it would have been a crime not to make the most of her welcome. Nate braced one foot on the wall behind him to add to his thrusting power.

He grunted at the immediate enhancement of sensation. Each time he slung in her was like visiting heaven. Knowing her tigers were outside, he tried to be quieter. He might have saved himself the trouble. Evina was making more of a racket than he was.

"Shit," she said, her fingernails pricking holes right through his nice silk shirt.

The idea that she was excited enough to lose control of her shape sent his arousal into the stratosphere. His own fingertips were hot, his claws trying to lengthen too. He reined them in with all his will, preferring not to bloody her cute bottom.

"God, you're hot," he swore, pumping still harder into her.

Evina bit her lip and tensed. Her head lashed from side to side on the tufted leather, the motion a silent *no, no, no.* Nate concluded she didn't want to let go before he did.

"Me too," he whispered, jerking his mouth closer to her ear. "My balls feel like they're about to explode with come."

It seemed she liked dirty talk. She whimpered and went for him, the strong contractions of her pussy incredible on his cock: soft wet ripples dragging him to the brink. Nate gasped, the fullness in his testicles increasing by what felt like a power of ten. He couldn't have held on for anything. Sheer primal need overtook experience.

This was the moment when he and his beast were one.

Losing it, he cried out and shoved in as the heat of ejaculation rushed intensely from him. Her heels pulled in on his tailbone at exactly the perfect time, locking him as deep as he could go inside her while her sex clamped like a vise around him.

The pleasure of all those pressures made him groan. Pain, of course, wasn't what pulled the sound from him.

"God," he breathed as the ecstasy petered out.

She'd flung her arms around him at the climactic moment, instead of simply gripping his shoulders. Nate doubted she'd planned to do this but liked the full-on hug. He nuzzled her sweaty temple, relishing the feel of her hard breathing.

Because her pussy was quivering slightly—still coming, was his guess—he took a firmer grip on her hips and stroked gently out and in. His erection was mostly hard and this felt really nice to him. To her as well, he noted. Though she was very wet from their mutual orgasm, he couldn't miss the increase in her interior temperature.

"Jeez," she said in a worried tone.

Her concern inspired a chuckle. "We can do it again, you know. That didn't take all that long, and weres are hard to exhaust."

She lifted her head from his chest. Her eyes were suspicious but still glassy with pleasure. "Don't take seducing me for granted."

"Did I seduce you?" He laughed, more ebullient at that moment than he could recall being in a while. "I thought it was the other way around."

"Shut up." She shoved at his shoulder, to which he responded by kissing the fist she'd made. "Stop it," she said in exasperation. "I need to get back to work."

That irritated him a bit, since he couldn't see why she'd be angry. Hadn't they both enjoyed themselves? Years of stepping carefully around women's sometimes mysterious reactions told him not to push the issue.

He released his grip on her and helped her to stand. Her knees were shaking, and that seemed to irk her too.

"You're standing on my jeans," she said, doing a poorer job than he was of concealing her annoyance.

Nate stooped as well as he was able and handed them to her. She tugged them on in the narrow space, her movements forcing Nate to flatten against the wall.

"Please zip yourself," she said.

Nate did, then stopped her from opening the door by stretching his arm across it. He wanted to ask if she was okay, but was pretty sure he'd dislike the answer.

"Your hair," he said. "Turn around, and I'll neaten it for you."

She grimaced, but did as he suggested. He handed her a handkerchief so she could blot the sweat from her face.

"You're just Johnny on the Spot," she said acidly.

Done reassembling her braid, he dropped his hands to her tense shoulders. Something in him hurt that she wasn't happy. Unsure how to acknowledge that, or even if he wanted to, he spoke to her gently. "You knew I'd done this kind of thing before."

Evina exhaled gustily. "I did. Forgive me for being grumpy. I'm . . . out of practice being a good sport about these things."

Now that he had her apology, Nate wasn't sure he wanted it. "You're not the same-old, same-old," he assured her. "I really hope we can do this again."

She twisted around and patted his chest lightly. "You're very sweet."

Well, that wasn't a real compliment, no matter how she meant it to sound. Stiff now himself, Nate pushed the hidey-hole door open. He had just enough room to let her exit ahead of him.

She froze in her tracks about a foot outside. "Mom. What are you doing here?"

"Seeing if you're free for lunch," said a sultry voice, "though it looks as though you've already had a bite."

Nate couldn't help but grin. This sounded more entertaining than fighting with Evina. He tucked his shirt into his now-zipped trousers, smoothed his hair, and stepped into her office. Evina's mother didn't look much like her, but he'd heard feline genetics were unpredictable. Unlike her daughter, the elder Ms. Mohajit was tall and willowy. She too had curly hair, though hers was a bright auburn that hung loose around her shoulders. She was made up expertly.

To his dismay, she seemed familiar. Women weren't so mysterious that he didn't know *ever* having hooked up with Evina's mother would be extremely bad.

His heart lurched when she cocked her head to the side. "Do I know you?"

"I don't believe so," he said as Evina quietly sighed *oh God.*

"I do," the woman insisted. "You bought a baby blanket in my shop just the other day. Elf-spelled in white velvet."

"Oh," he said, the strength of his relief shocking him. "Yes. Rita's Treasures on Tenth Street."

Evina's mother offered him her elegant long hand. "I'm Rita, of course."

"Nate Rivera," he returned automatically.

She kept her hold on his hand, not flirting so much as not letting him get away. "I trust the present was a success."

"Very much so. My alpha's wife loved it."

"Your alpha's wife." Rita's slight smile deepened. "So . . . you have no children yourself?"

Nate fought a smile of his own. He rather her liked her playing the mother card, checking him out for her daughter. "No children, no wife."

"Ah," she said, "and you such a handsome man."

"He's a handsome *wolf*," Evina broke in sharply. "I think even your plate is a little full for that adventure."

Rita's expression was startled for a second, after which it turned delighted. "Oh darling, that's sweet of you, but I wasn't vetting him for me."

Evina's cheeks turned the red of Nate's favorite pie filling. Seeing mortification had struck her speechless, her mother took pity. She dropped his hand to give her daughter a quick hug. Then she undid whatever good she'd accomplished by whispering that she was glad Evina was finally letting herself have fun.

"It wasn't fun!" Evina said. "I mean—" Flustered again, she shot Nate an apologetic look. "You were wonderful of course, but, Mom, I'm helping him on a case."

"A case?" Concerned, Rita turned her gaze to him. "Are you the reason my daughter came in late last night?"

"I'm afraid I am, though she wasn't in any danger. In truth, both of us were hoping *you* might be of assistance . . ."

❧ CHAPTER FOUR

UNABLE to resist the one-two punch of Nate's charm and Evina's determination, Rita Mohajit agreed to set up a meeting with her producer friend later that evening. She made Nate promise he wasn't endangering her baby girl. Nate gave his word solemnly, endeared by Rita's behavior. Evina was less enthralled.

"Mom," she finally said. "You do remember what I do for a living."

"Of course," her mother soothed, bending slightly to kiss her cheek. "But this is different. This could involve criminals."

Her walk as she departed was a different kettle of sexy from her daughter's. Nate would have bet good money Rita had been practicing being slinky all her life. Her sway in her high-heeled sandals was too deliberate. Being who he was, Nate admired the performance. Evina's crew appeared to as well. More than one male nose twitched at the trail of tigress and patchouli Rita left behind her.

"You can pull your tongue back into your mouth," Evina said sourly.

Nate grinned, happier with her than he could explain. "When you get snippy, it makes me want to kiss you."

"Snippy!" The way she pursed her lips suggested she was remembering kissing him. That was fair, he thought, since he was doing the same thing.

The next order of business was bringing Evina to meet Nate's favorite street artist. They argued over taking one car or two, but Nate's Goblinati was more reliable. Converted Outsider cars like her Camry never ran on ambient energy as well as those that were built for it.

"Stop smirking," she demanded from the passenger seat, where he'd been appreciating how nice she looked with her legs curled up. "It's not a sign of weakness to do something sensible."

"Should I offer to let you drive?"

"I'm not as good as you," she grumped. "I'd be terrified of scratching your paint job."

Nate showed respect for her honesty by letting a short silence pass. Then, because the rebel wolf inside him couldn't leave well enough alone, he asked the question that was needling him. "Tell me, Evina, are you always this bad-tempered after a nice quickie?"

"Yes," she retorted. "My crew is constantly warning me I'd better not get laid."

This was so silly both of them had to laugh.

Nate reached out to rub her thigh. For just a second, she put her hand over his. Brief though the contact was, it finished calming them.

It occurred to Nate that they were reacting to each other like they were pack.

That idea shut him up until they reached the not quite legal street market under historic Irving Bridge. The cast iron bridge marked the boundary of a thriving artist's district. Some tables sold junk, others genuine finds. The vendors were a mix too, from barely scraping by to commanding thousands at galleries. Dave Redfield was at the upper end. He set his booth up here every Monday so as not to lose touch with the community who'd inspired him to begin with.

Ironically, considering his name, Redfield was a blue elf, his skin an indigo so dark it was nearly black. The best way to tell it wasn't was to compare the color with his ebony waist-length dreads. His ice blue eyes added to his striking appearance, as did his high cheekbones. Built on more solid lines than most elves, who could be ethereal, the pointy ears he sported declared the purity of his blood.

Nate liked him even better for not being snooty about his lineage.

"Nate," he said, rising from a cheap beach chair to swing out a hand to him.

Nate gripped the dark blue mitt and then bumped knuckles, their personal manly greeting. "Dave. I'm hoping I can introduce you to a new friend of mine."

"Always happy to meet a beautiful female."

"Oh boy," Evina said, though she was smiling. "I see why you two get along."

Dave looked from her to Nate. "Both of you are wearing serious auras. Something tells me you aren't here to admire paintings."

His latest creations hung on makeshift pegboard walls that angled in a squared *U* behind him. One had already caught Nate's eye—a picture of this very bridge at night with a pair of moonlit gargoyles poised on its railing, their wings lifted for the moment of taking flight. The simplicity of Dave's style made the image charming and spooky at the same time, as if Chagall and Grandma Moses were smoking faerie dust together.

"Not today," he admitted regretfully. "I'm hoping you can do me an under-the-table semiofficial police favor."

Dave burst into a laugh. "Under the table *and* semiofficial. That sounds like you to me."

Nate put his hand on Evina's shoulder. "My friend saw something psychically, a child we think might have disappeared. We can't confirm that until we have a picture to go with what she saw."

"I can do that," Dave said, his handsome features falling back into graver lines. "Why don't we step into my office?"

His "office" was the space between his rear pegboard wall and a pier of the old iron bridge. He'd stretched lengths of fabric across clotheslines to give him privacy from the bargain hunters and sightseers. Weeds grew from the uneven ground, but the broken glass and clutter were cleared away. With a flourish that reminded Nate elves were related to royalty, Dave opened another folding beach chair for Evina. He set it at a small paint-caked table.

The elf looked down at her as she sat gracefully, the dappled light underneath the bridge making quite a picture of her. Evina was feminine yet fierce, sexy but natural, her catlike curiosity overruling her slight shyness. She seemed simultaneously vulnerable and imposing. Nate didn't think he'd ever met a woman whose contradictions fascinated him so much. To his irritation, he wasn't sure Dave had either.

Obviously dazzled, the blue elf pulled out a sketchpad and sat across from her. "You can come back and pose anytime."

Evina's hand flew up to her curly hair. Unbeknownst to her, Nate had used his shifter speed and dexterity to arrange it in a flattering French braid. She looked even prettier than she suspected. "Oh," she said. "That's . . . very nice of you."

Redfield's chuckle was low and male. "What's nice is watching my old friend glare daggers over you."

~

Was the good looking elf serious? Was Nate *glaring daggers*, as he put it? She didn't look, as this might indicate more interest than she wished to betray. Nate certainly knew fascinating people. Shifters didn't always make friends beyond their own kind. She knew the thought that Nate was jealous shouldn't have gratified her. The last thing she was looking for was that sort of relationship. Possessiveness was not a tiger ideal.

Unsettled, Evina pushed her tunic's sheer sleeves to her elbows. She jumped when Redfield put his ink-blue hand on her bare forearm.

"Relax," he said. "I'm going to read you lightly while you tell me what you saw. It's a check and balance between what I picture at your words and what you actually perceived. It'll help me bring the sketch alive."

Evina had never had her mind read before. Elfin magic was a step down in power from that of the fae, but elves had lots of mojo compared to weres. This made sense when you thought about it. Faeries and elves were cousins.

"Um," she said, "are there confidentiality ethics elves follow?"

"There are," he said, "and you can count on me to only read what's relevant."

She looked up at Nate, who nodded. She didn't know Nate that well, but she supposed she trusted his judgment. They wouldn't have been here if he hadn't trusted hers.

"Okay," she said. "Have at it."

Whatever Dave did, she didn't feel a thing. She went through the story as she had for Nate, her memory of the happy little boy being smothered bringing a chill to the warm bright day. When she'd finished, Dave turned the sketchpad around for her to see.

She gasped, her hand flattened to her chest. He'd caught the child exactly, right down to his "I'm Tricky!" striped T-shirt. "That's it. That's exactly what I saw."

The elf's pale eyes were sad enough to give her goose bumps. "I didn't put in the room," he said, turning his face to Nate. "I thought that might be a detail you wanted to hold back."

"It is." Nate touched the picture's edge. He shivered like she had. "This helps. Thank you." He shook the elf's hand as he had before, though this time their knuckle bump was slower.

"If you can," Dave said, "tell me how this turns out."

~

Their moods were thoughtful as they returned to the car. Nate's tie was still loose from her yanking it for their quickie, and he'd rolled his cuffs halfway up his arms. With his hands thrust into his pockets, he made the dishabille look impossibly fashionable. Evina got a shock from noting the tiny holes her claws had left in his dark silk shirt.

Somehow, Nate made even that stylish.

She got into his sports car in silence, wishing she could think of a reason to extend her time with him. That was childish; she needed to get back to work in case a call came in. All the same, she couldn't deny his company was pleasant. Riding in his Goblinati was pleasant too: the sunshine, the warm breeze, his expert hands on the wheel. There was something fundamentally girly about letting a man drive her.

"We could get coffee," he suggested at the first red light. He sounded as tentative as she felt.

Reluctantly, Evina shook her head. "I shouldn't leave Liam to fill in for me too long."

"Liam is the big Irish guy?"

"That's one way to describe him. He didn't harass you about seeing me, did he?"

Nate smiled, private amusement glinting in his eyes. "Only enough to prove he valued you."

"Christophe is my usual backup. He astral projects as well as I do."

"Christophe is the one in the hospital."

"Yes." She watched Nate's right hand spin the wheel as he made a turn. His fingers were a lovely toasted color and very elegant. She struggled not to recall the feel of them gripping her bottom. "You're good at remembering details, aren't you?"

Nate flashed his killer grin. "Part of my job, sweetheart."

Evina was willing to bet it was more than that. Nate had a good brain between his ears.

He exited the neighborhood side streets for River Drive—not exactly a short cut but more scenic. Evina watched a pleasure boat cut a wake through the green water. The extra glitter around its passengers told her faeries were aboard. Faeries were the city's biggest celebrities, like royalty and rock stars rolled into one. Though she was no gossip junkie, Evina couldn't help wondering what this group was up to.

"Can I ask you something?" Nate said. "Why do you think your mother is more attractive than you are?"

This brought her gaze back to him. "You've seen her, right? She's a sex goddess on a diet. Men's eyes follow her everywhere she goes."

"Men's eyes follow you."

Evina released a snort. "Not like they do Rita."

"Trust me, who's a sex goddess and who isn't is very much in the eye of the beholder. And you hardly have to worry about your weight."

"Well, you would say that, wouldn't you?"

"Is that how it's going to be?" he joked. "You think I'm a pick-up artist, so you won't believe anything I say?"

"If you told me the sky was blue, I'd probably believe that."

Nate shot a strangely fond look at her. "Your mother isn't alpha, which I suspect secretly bugs her. That could be why she feels a need to compete with you."

Evina could only gape at him. He was more than smooth, he was scary insightful.

"Hey," he said, "I'm more than a pretty face."

"No kidding," Evina muttered to herself.

~

Rita's friend the news producer was a bit too excited about scooping his rival networks on a possible big story. Nate was glad they'd met in a small Greek restaurant instead of the studio. The fewer eyes on this meeting, the better. He didn't want Derrick Black's ambitions putting Evina in jeopardy.

"You can't use Miss Mohajit's name or image," Nate said, leaning across the table toward the silver-haired werepanther. "We don't know what happened yet, but we have to treat her as a witness whose identity needs to be be shielded."

"'Have you seen this child?' doesn't make for much of a story," Derrick Black complained.

"It isn't a story. It's a favor WQSN is doing for a member of the RPD."

This was splitting hairs but honest. Sensing something off but not what, Black crossed his arms. He was a lean older shifter, handsome enough to be on-air talent, were it not for the Wall Street sharpness around his eyes. The four of them sat in an isolated booth at the back of the family restaurant, untouched cups of coffee in front of them. "This isn't how the station usually gets requests from the police."

"This situation is delicate, and maybe time sensitive. I give you my word I'll remember I owe you one."

"Sweetie," Rita interrupted, her manicured hand stroking Black's expensive suit jacket. "They're trying to help a kid. Surely you don't have to profit from everything."

The producer struck Nate as the sort who did, but evidently Rita's pull on him was strong. "Fine," he said. "We'll air the picture at eleven, six and noon. You need more than that, you'll find you owe me two."

"Understood." Sensing it was time to withdraw, he rose and shook Black's hand. Evina stood with him, all of them understanding Rita would be staying. This seemed all right with her. As far as Nate could tell, Black's rough edges didn't rub her the wrong way.

"Phew," Evina said once they'd stepped out into the fresher air of the street. "Good thing my mother doesn't mind swimming with the sharks."

~

Maybe he shouldn't have, given his ranking in the pack, but Nate subscribed to the adage that it was easier to beg forgiveness than to ask permission. That said, he knew he'd arrived at the point where his knees had better shine the floor. He hoped he hadn't gone too far for his alpha to accept groveling.

A quick cell call to Carmine yielded the information that Adam was at the precinct.

"Where you been, bruddah?" the stocky werecop asked, putting on one of his many fake accents. If pressed, Carmine could pass for almost any nationality on the phone. "You missed some excitement."

Wincing, Nate allowed his pedal foot to grow slightly more leaden. He was ten minutes out from the station house, eight if he finessed stoplights. "What happened?"

"Well, nothing regarding your door-to-door. Me and the unis came up with nada. Nobody's seen nobody, doctor or otherwise. Rick and Tony's crew, however, unearthed a corpse."

"The Galinas' not-so-naturally-deceased CPA?"

"Looks like. Nice and stinky too. The bad news is a sorcerer worked some mojo on the body and the site. The techs are saying there's no trace to test. Without hard evidence to link Ivan to the murder, there's nothing to prove Vasili didn't do the number cruncher all by himself."

"Aiy," Nate said, imagining this wouldn't please Adam. Their lieutenant controlled his temper better than most, but he wanted the werewolf mobsters bad. He cursed as another driver made him miss the light for his turn on Mott. Damn taxis shouldn't cut people off.

"*Aiy* is right," Carmine agreed. "Story goes, suspicion for Vasili's alleged embezzling fell on the accountant first, which led to him being given his premature sendoff. If the accountant could have proven Vasili stole the money, younger bro would have had motive."

"Except why give up the dump location if Vasili didn't think it would implicate Ivan?"

"To stall us maybe. He looks like he's cooperating, so we keep him around. Ivan's going to tear Vasili limb from limb, probably in slow motion, the minute we let him go."

"Maybe." Nate got his chance to turn at last, glad his shifter reflexes allowed him to multitask. "I feel like we're missing something with this Galina thing. I just can't put my finger on what it is."

"You want your finger to be useful, get your head back into the game. Rick and Tony are good, but your brain is more devious than theirs. Adam could use you on this."

Nate wished he could drop the snake tail he and Evina had got their claws into. He couldn't though, no matter if the snake twisted around and bit him. He believed a child's fate hung in the balance, possibly more than one. Noticing where he was, he shifted more of his attention onto the street. Older buildings surrounded their station house, tiny businesses tucked into their ground floors. Nate shot a wistful glance at his favorite espresso bar, regretting it wasn't strategic to stop right then.

"I'm coming up on the garage," he informed Carmine. "I'll see you in a few."

"Put up your umbrella," Carmine advised. "Boss-man looks like a thundercloud."

By the time Nate parked and joined his squad, Adam and the others were wolfing down Chinese take-out in the break room. Seated closest to the door, Tony handed him a full box of beef lo mein. Nate would have appreciated the gesture more if he hadn't seen the pity in Tony's expression.

He was about to catch it good.

Adam was tipped back in a chair, his feet stacked on the break room table, his chopsticks stabbing into another box. Carmine's mention of thunderclouds was accurate. Their alpha looked as frustrated as Nate had ever seen.

"Well," he said sarcastically at Nate's arrival, "look what the cat dragged in."

Nate was certain the feline reference was deliberate. Evina's race might not be appropriate for dating, but it was hardly cause for shame. Not about to apologize for it, he pulled his spine straight and faced his boss head on. "You got a minute to talk?"

Adam's face darkened. Apparently, his mood dictated that he say *no* to anything he was asked. "Whatever very important business you've been up to, I'm sure you can share it with the team."

"Fine," Nate said, his own temper stretched. "I commissioned a sketch of Evina's vision. I've released it to WQSN. They'll be airing it on the eleven, six and noon broadcasts. I gave them one of our open tip lines. The calls will go to recording, but I could use Dana's help screening them."

Dana was their dispatcher. She liked Nate and wouldn't mind, but that didn't cut him slack with Adam. The others knew this. They'd fallen silent, holding their breath for the explosion that now seemed inevitable.

Face like a mask, Adam dropped the front legs of his plastic chair to the floor. His voice came out as a half-wolf growl. "Any other way we can serve you?"

"No," Nate said, something in him suddenly, crazily unable to bend at all. "That'll do me for now."

Adam launched his body out of the chair, his spring carrying him over the table to crash into Nate's chest. Nate fell backward beneath his weight, too startled to defend himself.

"Lieu!" Tony and Carmine called in protest.

They'd hopped out of their chairs, but only Rick, Adam's second, dared to lay his palm against Adam's back. Adam snarled at the touch that was meant to calm him.

"I'm not hurting him," he said, which was true enough. His grip had caught Nate's shoulders and his eyes were practically shooting flames, but all he was doing was holding him submissive under him.

His alpha energy pushed at Nate like it would keep him down forever.

"Is it too late to apologize?" Nate ventured humorously.

Adam wasn't ready to laugh. "What is it with you lately? You catch a whiff of this pussy's pussy, and suddenly you're unhappy with your place here?"

Nate's jaw fell at his crudeness. Adam wasn't species-ist, that he knew. "I love this pack," he said once he'd recovered. "You guys are my family."

"You love this pack," Adam said darkly, "but you don't love your place in it."

Nate couldn't deny this, no more than Adam's alpha instincts could tolerate insubordination. Nate's gut clenched uneasily. They'd come to a confrontation that had been building for a while.

"I love the pack," he repeated, his voice shaking. "I respect every one of you."

"Ease up, Lieu," Carmine said, the most experienced shifter among them. "Let your wolf relax. Nate's backed down enough for now."

The fire in Adam's eyes guttered to a glimmer. He pulled in his claws, which Nate only just noticed were extended. They hadn't broken skin, but they made a soft ripping noise as they left his nice black shirt. Between Adam and Evina, the expensive Ermenegildo Zegna was history.

If his pulse hadn't been drumming like a rabbit's within his throat, Nate might have laughed. As it was, when Adam shifted his heavy weight off him, what he mostly felt was relief.

Grudgingly, Adam offered him a hand up.

"I am sorry I made you angry," Nate said as he took it. "I don't know how to let this case go."

Both statements were honest, as Adam seemed to recognize. He rolled the last of his alpha tension out of his big shoulders. "You've got to show me results, Nate. Not just weird rooms and visions and behind-my-back meetings with reporters."

"We will," Nate assured him. "I know there's something here."

He realized only later that his reference to *we* didn't mean him and Carmine.

❧ CHAPTER FIVE

EVINA had finally gotten the twins tucked in bed when Rita used her key to saunter through the front door. Dressed to the nines in a sleeveless red cocktail dress, she joined her daughter in the kitchen. Evina was washing up dishes there. How three people dirtied so many she'd never figure out.

"You're back from your date early," Evina commented.

Rita poked a fork at a piece of leftover brownie, then set the utensil down. Though shapeshifters had fast metabolisms, she didn't believe in tempting Fate. "Derrick had to go to the studio."

"I've got the kids tonight. You didn't have to come over."

"This thing you saw . . ." Rita twisted her mouth. "It makes me want to stick close to my grandcubs." She gave Evina's arm a rub. "You should go out."

"Me?"

"I know. That delicious man you've been flirting with is the Big Bad Wolf. That makes it better, if you ask me. No expectations on either side."

Not so sure about that, Evina dried her hands on a clean dishtowel.

"You can't mourn Paul forever," Rita pointed out.

"I'm hardly mourning him. He's not dead."

"No, he just got married—which if you're honest, you'll admit is worse."

"Mom!" Despite not wanting to encourage her mother's outrageousness, Evina had to laugh. "He's the father of my children. He loves them, and he was never unfair to me. I couldn't wish him dead."

Temporarily neutered, maybe, but not dead.

"That wife of his is barely thirty," her mother said as if the insult of Paul finding a lifemate had been to her. "And she's not even a full tiger."

Paul's wife Liane was a quarter fae and very beautiful—more beautiful than Rita, which could explain why her mother had taken such a dislike to

51

her.

"That wolf is way sexier than Paul," her mother said silkily. "You know what they say about the best revenge."

"That it isn't a mother's business to get it for her daughter?"

"Very funny." Her mother pulled a single wine glass down from the cabinet. "You know you're itching to have at that wolf again. And, who knows, maybe you'll help him solve the case. Cats are cleverer than dogs."

Her mother was cleverer than a fox, as she proved with her next words. "What'll it be, sweetie? Sit home drinking cabernet with your mother or work out your frustrations with a very handsome and willing man?"

"Fine." Evina stopped Rita from pulling a second glass out of the cabinet. "I'll go. And I'll be back before breakfast."

"Bring milk," her mother said. "Rafi drank the last of it yesterday."

~

By the time, Evina parked in front of Nate's address, she was sweaty-palmed anxious. She was also uncomfortably aroused. Too many fantasies of what she wanted to do to the sexy wolf had accompanied her drive over. She couldn't remember the last time she'd simply showed up on a man's doorstep. She would have called ahead, but that had seemed too much like playing supplicant.

Tigresses shouldn't have to ask if they were welcome.

She stepped out of the car with her nerves trying to jump in too many directions. The area where Nate lived was nicer than hers: more trees, more expensive better-kept buildings. The four-story warehouse he called home was wider than three of her neighborhood's townhouses.

Tasteful brushed aluminum letters announced the building's name as "Alchemist's Lofts." Evina wondered if RPD detectives earned more than station chiefs, or if not having two kids to feed and clothe made the difference. Paul contributed now and then, but regular child support wasn't expected of male tigers. The ones who were alpha enough to breed tended to have too many offspring for that to be practical.

Maybe Nate's a good saver, she told herself.

Stalling, she ran her gaze up the building's front. When he'd given her his address and private phone number, saying she could get in touch with him anytime, he'd mentioned his unit took up fourth floor. Though the hour was past ten, his lights were on. When she strained her ears, she thought she heard faint music.

That seemed promising . . . unless the sultry R&B meant he already had female company.

"Rrr," she growled underneath her breath, disgusted with her dithering. If he had company, so be it. If she wasn't welcome, she'd live. The only truly lowering decision would be *not* pressing his buzzer.

She marched herself to the glass front security door. *N. Rivera* was the uppermost of the seven buttons. At her mother's insistence, she'd dressed up a bit. To her dismay, the moment she pushed the buzzer, wet heat ran out of her pussy to dampen the fancy panties she'd pulled on.

"Yes?" said Nate's smoky voice, the answer coming too soon for her to compose herself.

The building's intercom was set high into the wall. She lifted her chin to speak to it. "It's Evina."

A startled pause greeted that. "I'll buzz you right up," he said.

~

Following Nate's instructions, Evina took the old-style freight elevator to his floor. He must have guessed she'd enjoy working the contraption. Like any shifter, she had no trouble climbing stairs—even if that involved jogging up them in three-inch sandal heels.

He opened his door as she shut the accordion gate behind her. Naturally, he was his usual smooth self. His gaze slid over her leather miniskirt and snug wrap top. The blouse was printed to look like a field of flowers. Her cleavage in the V of the crisscrossed neckline was not subtle. When it came to admiring that, Nate was no different from most men.

A wolfish smile spread across his face. "Dare I hope this is a booty call?"

Evina lowered her brows and glared.

"You mean it is?" He laughed with quick delight. "Oh let me shut my mouth and give thanks for my good fortune!"

Resenting his charm and miffed at being seen through so easily, she sauntered past him into his apartment. Her first glimpse at that had her forgetting to guard her pride.

His place was huge—airy, modern, the ceilings so high a tribe of monkeys would have felt at home swinging on the exposed struts.

"Wow," she said, taking in what looked like museum-quality retro furniture. "Your pay grade must be a few levels above mine."

When she turned back to him, he'd colored up slightly. "I save," he said. "Most of my things are refurbished eBay finds. And my mother left me some money after she died."

"She was a cop?" Evina asked, suddenly intensely curious.

He nodded. "It was a line of duty death. My father cut out when I was four, so the two of us were close."

The back of Evina's eyes burned. Life bonds were uncommon among tigers but not wolves. His father leaving couldn't have been easy.

"I'm sorry."

He smiled, either not upset about it anymore or good at pretending. "Let me get you a glass of wine."

Evina trailed Nate into the spotless kitchen, noting with some amazement that he had two dishwashers. They were Brownie Hygienics, a brand she could only dream about affording. "I can't stay long."

"So this is one of *those* booty calls," he teased. "Planning to ride me hard, then toss my ass back in the stable."

"I wasn't *planning*. Exactly."

He pulled two beautiful balloon glasses from the open shelving that was arranged like an art project on his long side wall. "I'll just serve you a couple ounces. I can see you're nervous, and I *do* want you to relax, but I understand you might need to drive later."

With a deftness that was wonderful to see, he uncorked a bottle with an Argentine label. He poured a small amount in each glass, turning the bottle like a wine steward. Then he passed hers over.

"*À votre santé*," he said, chinging the delicate crystal rims.

"You should give lessons," Evina said dazedly.

Something in her tone caused him to lower the glass before it touched his lips. "I *am* glad you're here, Evina. Genuinely. I don't mean to seem insincere. I'm just . . ."

"Really good at this?" she suggested.

Nate set his wine on the black marble countertop. "I didn't light candles," he offered hopefully. "And I did have time before you came up."

She laughed, set her own glass down, and stepped toe to toe with him. Time to give him her own honesty. "I'm glad I'm here, even if your . . . extreme suaveness knocks me off balance."

Nate slid his arms behind her waist. "Everything about you knocks me off balance. You are so effing gorgeous you make me hurt."

His dark eyes had taken on a luster as he pulled her cautiously closer. Though their hips rested only lightly together, Evina noticed certain developments had already taken place for him. The ridge of his erection lay hot between them, its size and hardness making her pussy squirm. "I thought about you all the way over here in the car."

Nate's breath came faster. "What did you think about me?"

"That I wanted to see you naked. That I wanted your hands all over me in bed." She cruised her palms up his chest, over the simple black pocket T he wore.

"Would you like to start working on that now?" he asked.

She covered his ears with her hands and pulled his mouth to hers.

The kiss was good—deep, hungry, angling this way and that as he took control of it. It seemed natural to let him, to give way when he turned to press her lower body into the shiny Italian cabinets.

"E-vi-na," he moaned, his hips and cock digging in. "You are the best thing that's happened to me all year."

All year struck her as a surprising claim. He appeared to mean it. His hands ironed down her back, around the curve of her leather mini where it clung to her butt.

"Mmm," he hummed, pulling her lower parts closer still.

"I could use some help with this," she said, struggling to drag up his black T-shirt. "You're taller than I am."

He backed off far enough to grip the hem with both hands. He took a second to smolder at her, then whipped it over his head.

"Wow," she said, enjoying her eyeful of his anatomy manual chest. Helpless not to, her caresses followed her eyes, trailing up his ribs and circling his sharp nipples. She gave each of these a quick love bite, not hard enough to break skin but just to make him inhale sharply with excitement.

Smolder didn't describe what his eyes did then.

"That outfit is nice," he rasped. "I think you'd better take it off before I rip it."

He lifted his hands, displaying the wolf claws that were starting to extend. The sight of those small erections made her shiver.

"Move back," she said, her voice as rough as his.

He retreated to the nearest of his two dishwashers. She made a little presentation of stripping off her stretchy shirt, letting him absorb the visual of her pushed up breasts in the blue satin and black lace bra. He'd pressed his palm to his heart by the time she reached behind herself to unzip the miniskirt. A single push and wriggle sent the garment dropping around her high-heeled sandals.

Thanks to Rita's bullying, her bra matched her underwear. Thanks to Evina's genuine interest in impressing Nate, the coordinated panties were a thong.

Nate's eyes traveled very slowly back to her face. "Women like you in underwear like that make life worth living."

She laughed. How could she not when he was this generous with his praise? "Take down your ponytail," she said, wanting to see his hair spread around those broad brown shoulders.

"Undo your braid," he returned.

Evina's hair was longer, and he finished before she did. Despite being available to help, he didn't offer. He seemed to enjoy watching her unbind herself. His clawed hands curled tellingly at his sides, the bulge of his erection sinfully enticing. Its shape was outlined so clearly behind his zipper she had no doubt it pointed upward in his jeans.

The slant of it couldn't have been more rakish.

"There," she said, shaking the last of her dark curls free. The lowest tendrils were tickling her hips.

Somewhat to her surprise, the sight poleaxed Nate. "I want you on top of me," he declared, soft and guttural. "I want your hair hanging all around us while you ride me."

His intensity was catching, clutching at the soft flesh between her legs. "Where's your bed?"

"Opposite corner of the loft."

"Get me to it fast, and I'll give you a reward."

Her tone was teasing, his snarl of answer all business. He grabbed her off her feet as only a shifter could, zipping her across his home so quickly their surroundings blurred. They landed on his wide platform bed with a mutual gasp for air.

His sheets were impractical white silk—forgivable, considering how fine Nate's lean body looked lying back on them. Not wanting to ruin the fabric, Evina kicked off her shoes.

That done, she didn't waste an instant attacking his zipper.

"God," he said as she freed the button. She wrenched the tab down next, careful not to clip him but quick enough. His penis was hot and thick as she extricated it from his jock. Lust flushed its skin darkly.

Evina knew exactly what she wanted to do to it.

"Fuck," he gasped when she slid her lips over the hot satin of the head.

He bucked into her, like he couldn't control himself, his half-clawed fingers forking through her hair. She took him to the verge of her throat, her alpha's command of her reflexes able to handle pressure there. He groaned and heaved, his narrow ass thumping on the mattress as he went up and down. Evina pressed her forearms down on his hips. She needed strength to prevent his writhing from jerking him out of her.

"Ahh," he cried as she tightened her lips still more and sucked upward.

Her tongue dragged a lightning circle around his cockhead's rim. Half dozen times she repeated this suck and tease, knowing his most sensitive nerves would love the slick friction. His claws tightened in her hair, his whole body straining for more pleasure. Evina sank down once more and swallowed against his glans.

Fluid spurted into her throat. She wanted it, wanted to suck him up until he was empty. Nate let out a growl that sounded more wolf than man, every muscle in his body clenching as he willed his ejaculation to cut short.

Evina was impressed. Only alpha tigers could control themselves like that.

A second later, she found herself flipped over and on her back beneath him. That pushed her buttons like she wouldn't have believed. Nate's muscular thigh slid between her legs, her thong absolutely useless for hiding how sopping wet she'd grown. The noise he made when he realized this was surprisingly like a purr. Strangely panicked, Evina pushed at his chest. She liked what was happening too much, and the feel of him weakened her. The force of his heartbeat shook his bones and muscles.

"I thought you wanted me to ride you," she panted.

Eyes glowing like gold flames, he lowered his head and kissed her.

No word existed to describe what she did but *melt*.

She opened to him—mouth, arms, even her energy seeming to part and give his access. He moaned at her and she moaned in answer, wrapping her legs around him to hold him close. Long delicious minutes passed while they tasted and stroked and rubbed against each other. To her delight, wolves seemed to like this as much as tigers. Nate managed to get her fancy bra off without tearing it. He brought both hands up to squeeze her breasts, using careful claws and strong fingers to tease the nerves within her nipples. Her vaginal muscles began to flutter, though it was difficult to say whether this was due to the stimulation or his obvious relish for touching her.

Because he'd curtailed the climax she'd tried to drive him to, he was twice as wound-up now. All the while as they writhed together, his cock trickled pre-ejaculate on her skin. The pulse inside its hardness was wild and uneven.

Finally, he pulled his head back and looked at her. Feeling like she'd been faerie-struck, she touched his quirky asymmetrical lower lip, reddened now from them feasting on each other. The R&B he had on swelled toward a crescendo, as if they were in a romantic movie. Probably the music was skewing her emotions. She wanted to tell him he kissed like an angel, but found herself speechless. His tongue snuck between slightly lengthened canines to lick her finger. He nipped it playfully.

"Don't move," he ordered. "I'm taking my pants off now."

She lay there on the silky sheets, passive but disinclined to change that while he rolled nimbly off her and stood. His modern platform bed was low to the ground, its simple wooden headboard no more than foot tall. Evina reached back to grip it and stretch her spine. Nate seemed to tower above her as he shoved his jeans down and got naked. Though she'd seen his cock thrusting out already, he had more to appreciate. The muscles of his legs were gorgeous, lightly furred and very long. His balls were full but drawn up.

Seeing them, aroused by them, Evina cupped her hand around the front of her thong and tried to squeeze her ache away.

"God," he said, his gaze locked to her fingers. "Pull them off."

Figuring he meant the panties, she wriggled out of them. She put her hand back where it had been before. Nate dropped to his knees over her. His palms were planted to either side of her shoulders, his neck craned down to watch her stroke her clit. His now loose and shining hair hung down, shielding his expression—though she couldn't doubt he found her show inspiring. A warm drop of pre-cum splashed from his cockhead to her belly.

"Nate," she said, dragging his attention reluctantly to her face. "I think you ought to take me now."

"Unh," was his flatteringly incoherent answer.

Evina released her crotch to rub one side of his ribs. Nate shook himself and blinked.

"Condom," he said.

Evina shook her head. "You don't need one with me. Wolves can't get tigers pregnant, and neither of us could be diseased."

His eyes flared again. "I haven't ridden bareback in forever."

This amused her. "No, not since yesterday in my hidey-hole."

"Oh my God, I—" He stopped and peered sharply down at her. "I guess there were a few things I wasn't paying enough attention to."

"Nothing wrong with getting lost in the moment." She dragged her index finger down the centerline of his wedge-shaped chest, loving the sweat she found on her path to the root of him.

"Mmm," he hummed, his lean face softening as she gripped his shaft and pulled upward.

"Come inside me, Nate," she purred. "Pay attention to me now."

He didn't lower himself, he raised her, lifting her by the hips with her thighs splayed around him as he kneeled up. Her head remained on his pillows, her arms flung out for balance.

An important logistical problem soon became apparent. His erection stuck up at too high an angle to enter her.

"Tip my cock down," he said. "Put the head in you."

She placed that part of him where they both wanted it. She licked her lips at the wonderful pressure against her gate, realizing as she did that her canines had sharpened. They both breathed quick and shallow, one ball of heat joining them. Nate gripped her thighs more firmly and pulled her down his length.

When he rocked his hips to squeeze in the last millimeter, she could have sworn he filled her up to her throat.

With a groan that should have been recorded, he started to lean forward.

"Don't," she said, which opened his bliss-shut eyes. "Don't shift over me. I like my view of you right there. I want to watch you take me until you come."

Sweat glistened on his pectorals, his ragged breathing moving his tight six pack. "Evina . . ."

She walked her fingers up his yummy front as far as she could reach. "Please. You're so pretty."

In case that wasn't convincing, she dug her bare heels harder into the muscles of his butt cheeks. He liked that, shadows of pleasure flickering though his face. She thought of games they might play later, but later wasn't now.

"You're killing me," he said to her.

Evina bit her lower lip and smiled. "Can you blame me for wanting to see you unravel?"

The question drew an odd expression into his eyes. "All right," he said with unexpected determination. "I'm going to show you the real deal. I'm going to fuck you exactly the way I want and let you watch it all."

"Bring it on," she dared.

He took her at her word. His first thrust was hard and deep. His second didn't begin until he'd finished enjoying it. He set a rhythm that suited him—though Evina would have had to be dead for it not to pleasure her. He was steady and focused and each succeeding upward jump in his arousal was on display for her. He closed his eyes first, grimacing with pleasure as her sheath tightened on his shaft. Next came a huffing noise she couldn't have liked better if he'd been trying to excite her. Around the time the veins in his biceps started popping out from his skin, his pumping sped up dramatically.

She couldn't help crying out for that; the repeated thumping of her pussy felt too incredible. Her mewls got him grunting, his thumbs stretching inward to work the upper folds of her labia against her engorged clit.

Even then he was thinking, rubbing the slick swollen flesh together just enough to keep her with him but not so much that she couldn't avoid coming. She wanted to come, of course, her claws punching holes through his nice silk sheets. Her body arched with her efforts to hold back her climax.

"Shit," he said, his eyes opening briefly to watch her. He pumped faster and panted. "I want to move over you. I want to fuck you under me."

His instincts drove him to desire that, the old male urge to dominate a female very strong among weres. Blotches of pre-orgasmic color were appearing on his chest. Tendons joined the veins in standing out on his neck.

"Come . . . like this," she pleaded, so close she could barely get it out. "Empty yourself in me and . . . next time, you can take me doggy style."

He snarled, driving his cock into her so hard she thought her words must have shoved him over the edge. Then he drove in the same way again, the concussion inside her pussy impossible to resist. Her head tried to arch back as she climaxed, her eyes wanting to screw shut at the sweet whole-body-tightening contraction. She kept them open and got her chance to watch Nate utterly let go.

His lips pulled back as he shouted, his upper and lower canines driven all the way out by lust. Heat shot into her with his final thrust, more and more, and then at last his body relaxed.

He pulled from her, his cock wet and rosy and not quite softened. Evina's bottom rested on his hairy thighs. Her legs didn't immediately want to uncramp; they'd been squeezed around him so urgently. He kneaded them, working his magic fingers down into the muscles. He looked at her sex, which was very exposed to him. She sensed he could have watched it longer, shining and plumped from what he'd done to it. Instead, his gaze lifted to her face.

She'd never seen a man as gorgeous as he was then. His eyes gleamed like stars within his dark lashes.

"Can you get up?" he asked, slightly hoarse from his climactic bellow. "Are you steady enough to turn around for me?"

Evina's eyes widened. He smiled at the reaction, the expression transforming his features. If angels could be devilish, that's how he looked to her.

"Can't tigers have sex more than once in quick succession?" he asked.

"Sure but—"

"So can wolves," he said simply.

He helped her up onto her knees and turned her, arranging her in the ever-popular presenting position. Evina's inner tigress let out an approving purr, evidently convinced her appropriate master was taking charge of her. Unnerved but tightening once again with arousal, Evina wrapped both hands around Nate's headboard.

Her arms were straight to brace her, her hips tilted upward to let him in. Nate folded himself around her and slid back into her heat with a happy sigh. He didn't wait to begin thrusting. His hands gripped the headboard outside of hers, his now very hard erection swiftly picking up speed in her. It seemed ridiculous, but his shaft felt even thicker than before.

"Oh yeah," he praised, his face nuzzling her hair aside from her neck. "That flips my switches good."

He remembered what she'd said about wanting his hands on her. He took one from the headboard to run caresses along her body's front. Her breasts were fondled, her nipples pinched, her belly stroked by his warm broad palm. His low moans assured her he reveled in touching her. Truth be told, his hands weren't tools enough for him. Bringing his mouth into play, he kissed her shoulders and licked her nape. When his lengthened teeth dragged over that vulnerable skin, a sexual quiver ran down to her tailbone.

"Can I bite you?" he whispered against her vertebrae.

Tigers didn't experience bite-bonding like she'd heard wolves did. They weren't tied to the moon that way. Still, this was an intimate request. Sexual biting tapped into deep instincts. Any male who did it was hoping to stake a claim. Any female who let him was saying she surrendered.

Evina hadn't done that since she and Paul parted ways.

She reached back to bury her fingers in Nate's dark waterfall of hair. She meant to tell him maybe another time, to soften her refusal with the caress.

She didn't get a chance to explain. Nate interpreted the touch as her urging him onward. With a groan that seemed to come from his marrow, he widened his jaw and bit.

Heat flashed through Evina's body as the points of his teeth took hold, hormones she had no control over surging into her bloodstream. The effect was a hell of a lot stronger than she remembered it being with Paul. She would have panicked, except the sensations felt amazing. The pain of her skin being pierced was nothing. This was about being trapped by a male and being taken care of at the same time. She was safe, cherished. She began coming and couldn't stop, hot crashing waves of pleasure that started deep in her groin and rolled out strongly in every direction.

Nate made a sound like something had hurt him. She hoped she wasn't accidentally being rough. As if to prove she wasn't, he drew back and rammed into her again, even deeper than before. He ground his pelvis into her ass, holding there like he never intended to pull out. The pressure in her pussy increased impossibly. He made the sound again and shot into her.

This time, he really flooded her.

She didn't know how long his climax lasted, his being difficult to separate from hers. When her knees gave way, he followed her to the mattress, his hand cupped around her pubis to keep himself tight in her.

She didn't mind, despite not knowing him all that well. His weight couldn't bother her, and the continued snuggling was surprisingly pleasant.

He let go of the skin he'd gripped at her nape, licking it gently to encourage it to heal. Evina doubted it had bled much. He'd been careful even in extremis.

"Mm," she said, reaching back to pet his hair weakly.

"Mm," he answered, shifting his chest slightly to one side. "That was amazing."

Evina laughed quietly, amused by his phrasing but sensing he meant it. "That's what all the skirt-chasers say."

"Nuh," he said, too drowsy to get the whole *nuh-uh* out. "You rocked my world, *chica*."

Strangely touched, Evina smiled to herself and slept.

✤ CHAPTER SIX

NATE woke when his lengthy R&B playlist ran out of tunes. He was sprawled atop Evina, who seemed unbothered by his weight. She neither stirred nor grumbled when he pushed up, the easy rise and fall of her breathing proving he hadn't smothered her.

Nate watched that for a moment, oddly lulled by the slow rhythm. Her incredible waist-length curls lay across her face, which was turned to the side. That didn't bother her either, but perhaps—as was the case for housecats—she liked sleeping under layers. Nate drew the sheaf of curls gently behind her, baring the softness of her profile. Did she really have two children? She looked like a child herself. Her cheeks were rosy, her nose too kittenish not to smile at. He smoothed one hand lightly down her back, her skin like velvet under his fingertips. God, her bare ass was gorgeous, round and lush and tempting enough to bite.

He stopped himself in the middle of leaning down.

What the hell was going on with him?

Nate didn't let women sleep over. He fed them, he fucked them, and then he ushered them as charmingly as possible out the door. If a repeat encounter so much as hinted at leaving her toothbrush here, she was history. He didn't think of women as possessions. To him, they were entertaining loans.

Evina looked so right snuggled in his bed he wanted to keep her there forever.

Alarmed, he dragged one hand through his tangled hair. He needed a shower and a stiff whiskey. Okay, maybe not the whiskey. Under the surface sheen of anxiety, his body was seriously relaxed.

That second time, when he'd taken her from behind, his bulbus gland had activated. Located low down on the underside of werewolf penises, the organ was a vestige of their canine halves, meant to improve the chances of conception. When werewolves hooked up with a likely genetic mate, it swelled at orgasm, tightening their fit within their partners. Because the bulbus was nerve-rich, it could produce killer orgasms. Nate's scalp had just about peeled off when he'd exploded in Evina.

The reaction didn't make sense to him. Evina was a tiger: by definition inappropriate to mate. Of all Resurrection's races, only faeries could interbreed with anyone they chose. Nate had only had his bulbus swell twice before, and each time for wolf partners. On those occasions, he'd found the phenomenon mildly uncomfortable. With Evina, the ecstasy had been breathtaking.

To his dismay, he saw that as he sat there pondering, he'd laid his hand on her hip and was rubbing it with his thumb. That too was making him feel good.

Shower, he ordered, drawing back the caress.

He needed time alone to sort this out.

~

Evina roused to the murmur of a television with its sound on low. The flicker of the screen led her across the open loft, whose lights were otherwise turned off.

Unsure whether she was welcome to wander around naked, she'd wrapped the slightly ripped silk sheet around her, toga-style. Nate sat in the living room, watching a large flat screen from a very sculptural low white couch. Thanks to her inner cat night's vision, Evina had no trouble seeing him. Nate's hair was damp, and he'd pulled on a pair of navy silk boxer shorts. They'd have been laughably Casanova-ish on anyone but him. As it was, she noted once again how tight and sexy his body was.

He glanced up as she padded over. "The WQSN spot was on. I'll play it again for you."

She sat, and he used the remote to rewind for her. The spot was simple enough. The sketch of the child was shown, along with a tip line number. The newscaster asked if anyone had information about the boy, explaining that the police believed he might have gone missing between May and August of that year. The timeframe seemed right to her. She turned to Nate and found him biting his thumbnail.

In a man as self-assured as he was, the nervous gesture was a big deal.

"Nate," she said, "did you get into trouble over this with your boss?"

He grimaced, then caught himself and shrugged. "It'll blow over."

"Well, forgive me for noticing, but that Grand Canyon-size furrow between your eyebrows is contradicting you."

He hopped up from the sofa before she could touch his arm. "I can handle it."

She looked at him. His body language was as troubled as her daughter Abby's when she couldn't find a way to protect her twin from a slight.

"It's not a problem," Nate insisted.

His tone didn't convince her. Would his alpha throw him out for going behind his back? Some lead shifters were too rigid to tolerate defiance.

"Do you have family besides your pack?" she asked. Her voice was too sympathetic. She knew that from the way he drew his pride closer to himself.

"I've been a lone wolf before," he said dryly.

Evina knew she ought to shut up. She rubbed her knees through the sheet, trying to get herself to do just that. Then she caught sight of the time on Nate's Elfnet cable box.

"Crap!" She jumped up in horror. "It's nearly 5 a.m. You recorded last night's news. Oh my God, I have to get home." She smacked her head in annoyance. "Milk. Rafi drank it all yesterday. I was supposed to buy some before breakfast."

"I have milk," Nate said soothingly. "Nearly a whole gallon. Why don't you shower and get dressed?"

She needed to wash up. Both her children had sharp little cat noses, and Nate's scent clung too strongly to her to pass muster. She wasn't ready to answer questions about him—not even her own, if it came down to it.

"Go," he said, shooing her.

"I'll pay you for the milk," she promised. "I'm afraid my son is a bottomless pit for it."

His eyes went soft, his own troubles forgotten in solving hers. "It's a gift, Evina. A small one. You don't even need to thank me."

~

He might not need her thanks, but Evina couldn't forget Nate's kindness. She'd seen him bristle at her attempt to poke into his problems, and still he'd been sweet to her. Twice, she caught herself stroking his plastic milk container instead of pouring it. That was completely stupid. He'd given her some milk, not volunteered to help feed her litter from now until adulthood.

Sometimes having a primitive half was a pain in the ass.

"Mommy?" Rafi said from his seat at the kitchen table, where he and his sister were shoveling in their favorite Faerie-O's cereal.

To her relief, he'd been sleeping in his boy form when she came in to wake him up. She hated chivvying him to change first thing in the morning. For one thing, it took forever. For another, the fact that she had to so often worried her. How was her little boy going to grow up happy and socialized if he felt more kinship with his tiger than the world of mostly one-formed people?

"Yes, sweetie?" she asked, hoping none of that sounded in her voice.

64

"If you had faerie blood in you, would Daddy have married you?"

Unprepared for this, Evina barely stopped her coffee from spurting out her nose. She stood in front of the sink with her back to it. This, she'd learned, was the best position from which to goose her sometimes wandery children through breakfast. When she recovered her breath, she spoke.

"Why do you ask that?"

Rafiq's face was thinner than his sister's, his eyes the same big round pools of blue. Though both had her dark curly hair, those azure eyes came from Paul. Right then, Rafi's were round and curious. "Grandma said Liane cast a spell on him. That's what faeries do, isn't it?"

"Sometimes," Evina said carefully, "but we don't know Liane did. I expect your father just fell in love with her."

"Grandma called her the *B*-word," Abby added helpfully.

"Grandma has her opinions. I hope you know you shouldn't repeat them."

"Ever?" Abby asked, which Evina suspected was a trick question.

"Not if you think someone's feelings will be hurt. Even Grandma wouldn't call Liane the *B*-word to her face."

Abby looked like she wasn't convinced of this, possibly proving what a sharp tack she was. "When I grow up. I'm going to get some faerie blood in me. Then I can marry if I want to. Or change mean people into toads."

Abby's practical turn of mind was hard to argue with. Evina wondered where to begin explaining that she'd have to be *born* part fae—and that this wasn't always a blessing. Liane was beautiful, it was true, but because of her heritage, her and Paul's mixed-race child was facing challenges.

A knock on the kitchen side door saved her from searching for the words.

"Daddy!" Abby and Rafiq chorused. Evina supposed his arrival explained the twins' choice of breakfast topics. Little felines especially had access to information that sometimes seemed psychic. To them, the coincidence was nothing to be startled by. They ran to hug their father as he stepped in.

Paul gave them the growls and tickles they both adored, his playful side part of what had made her fall for him.

"I didn't know you were coming by," she said when the chaos had subsided.

Evina's ex was a big tiger. His smile and his bright blue eyes were his best features, though he wasn't unhandsome. He had Rafi tucked under one wrestler's arm, while Abby rode his big shoulders. He was so tall Abby's mop of black curls brushed the ceiling.

"I thought I'd take them to school," he said. "Plus it seemed like I ought to talk to you."

His choice of words joined a whiff of belligerence to put her on full alert. "It seemed you *ought* to," she repeated.

Paul set his jaw, trying as usual to be more alpha than he was. "Liam called me."

Liam must have given him and earful about the wolf who'd come sniffing around the station house.

"He had no business calling you. No more than you have lecturing me."

"I used to run that station."

"*Used to*, Paul. And never without me to back you up."

"Mommy!" Abby complained as a brickish color washed up her mother's ex-boyfriend's face.

"You're in the wrong," Evina said quietly.

She didn't use her dominance on him. Though her will packed more watts than his, it didn't seem right to do that in front of their children. The resentment in Paul's expression said he knew she could force him to back down.

"They're my cubs too," he blustered. "You shouldn't be doing . . . unnatural things around them."

Rafi squirmed out of his father's hold so he could look at her wide-eyed. "What unnatural things, Mommy?"

Hell, Evina thought, unable to lie to him. "Mommy made a friend who's a wolf. He's a police detective and very responsible, but some people don't think cats and dogs should be friends."

"I like puppies," Rafi offered, which made her laugh. She ruffled his mop of curls, cut to match his sister's, then reached up to pat Abby's cheek.

"I like puppies too," she warned her ex darkly.

~

Nate, Carmine, and Dana their dispatcher had nearly a hundred tip line calls to sort through when they arrived at work. Carmine's experience came in handy for deciding who was or wasn't worth calling back. Since every recording had to be listened to regardless, screening the crazies from the maybes ate up the whole morning.

After that, Carmine insisted lunch was a must. Though Nate was itchy to get going, he had to admit filling his stomach helped him get through the afternoon.

They were on their tenth follow-up visit when it looked as if their luck—which had sucked so far—might be changing. They'd come to an older and poorer section of the city, to an address in a goblin warren. Buildings in Goblinville, as the projects were colloquially known, appeared bombed out but were perfectly sound inside. The goblins who clustered together in them simply altered the original human apartments to suit their own aesthetic.

Dank and crumbly was the prevailing theme.

The rate of crime in the area made Nate thankful they'd signed out a department vehicle. Goblins didn't have as much spellcraft as elves or fae, but the average do-not-steal charm wouldn't deter them. Nate's Goblinati would have been especially enticing, having been assembled in a goblin-run factory. The goblin lower classes, whose neighborhood this was, sometimes resented the owners of the goods their miniscule upper strata profited from selling to.

"Jeesh," Carmine said, shaking his head as he stepped heavily from the car. His huge work boots crunched a soda can that lay in the sidewalk's weedy strip of grass. "Why do people live like this?"

"They feel at home here. Everyone has their comfort zone."

Nate's attitude wasn't universal. Every so often, some supposed do-gooder group started a campaign to have goblins deported back to Faerie. The efforts invariably died on the vine. Goblins were too useful as cheap labor in too many businesses. Despite their occasional propensity for theft, they never went on strike, and they weren't usually violent. If they wanted to live in squalor, lots of folks decided that was the immigrants' business.

"There's Building B." Carmine pointed out a marginally less gloomy building among the depressing huddle of dark brick.

They picked their way to it through more trash and knee-high weeds. Just in case, they kept their hands on their weapons and all senses on alert. Glittering eyes watched them silently from windows, causing their hackles to crawl a bit. They ducked through a vestibule that had been purposefully lowered. Few goblins were more than four feet tall. High ceilings, so they claimed, made them feel oppressed. Low ones certainly made policing them uncomfortable for the cops.

Forced to crouch but resigned, they took the creaky lobby elevator to Unit 1204. The graffiti that embellished it was in a language neither of them spoke.

They announced themselves and, when requested, pressed their gold shields to the low peephole.

The door was opened by a female goblin whose skin was a surprisingly beautiful shade of red. Lower class goblins were mostly gray.

"You're Hephaesta Erg?" Nate asked, wanting to be sure. "You called in a tip about a child last night?"

The goblin inclined her hairless and pointy head. "I am and I did. Please come in if you wish to speak."

Nate and Carmine entered, relieved to discover the goblin's ceilings reverted to normal height. The interior wasn't dirty, though it did give off an impression of shadowy disarray. All the hand-built wooden furniture was child-sized. Necessarily not invited to sit, they stood.

For a moment, the goblin simply stared at them, wringing her long red hands in front of her bony chest. She wore clothes, which her kind didn't always do. In her crocheted cardigan and white-collared dress, she reminded Nate of a very small lunch lady.

"Tell me," she said, her large amber eyes pleading. "Did you find a body?"

It was at this point that Nate's interest pricked. Maybe this stop wasn't another waste of time. "Did you recognize the child in the picture on WQSN?"

"Yes," she said without hesitation. "His name is Joel Martin. I used to be his nanny."

"You used to be," Carmine said without making it a challenge.

She nodded emphatically. "The Martins didn't have a lot of money, and they both worked. They had to hire goblin childcare or none at all. Look." She pointed to a wall of pictures in mismatched frames. Silver duct tape affixed them at odd angles to the chipped paint. "There I am rocking Joel's cradle. He was a sweet baby. No trouble to anyone." She covered her mouth to hold back a little sob. "Joel was always laughing. The silliest things could make him giggle."

Nate didn't miss her use of the past tense. Wanting to see her face when he asked his next question, he went down on one knee in front of her. "Mrs. Erg," he said, taking her shoulder as if she were made of glass. "Why do you think Joel is dead?"

"They didn't appreciate him!" she blurted, tears spilling from her snake-pupil eyes. "They were always taking him to specialists, trying to get him fixed."

"The Martins, you mean."

"Yes. I'd hear them arguing about where they'd get the money to try again. Once, Mr. Martin said he didn't know how much longer he could bear the shame. Joel was a good boy! They were lucky to have him!"

She wiped her tear-streaked face, mumbling a *thank you* when Carmine handed her a Kleenex. To the squad's frequent amusement, his wife stuck a packet of them in his pocket each morning.

Nate waited for Mrs. Erg to dry up enough to speak. "What were the Martins ashamed of?"

"Joel couldn't change," she said, waving the hand that held the tissue. "As if any sensible parent wants a child who turns into an animal. No offense," she added, belatedly remembering to whom she was speaking.

Carmine let out a quiet snort, but Nate was too intent to take offense. "Mrs. Erg, what sort of shifters were the Martins?"

"Foxes," she said as if it ought to be obvious. "Werefox children change very young."

Nate rose and rubbed one finger across his mouth. Mrs. Erg's windows were blocked by parchment shades, but he stared at them anyway. Everything she said jibed with Evina's vision. It wasn't proof, but it was getting there.

"When did you leave the Martins' employ?" Carmine asked, holding the picture she'd pointed out earlier.

"Two months ago." She drew her slender shoulders back stiffly. "Mrs. Martin called me one morning. No explanation. She just said they didn't need me anymore. I went back secretly to check on Joel. I was worried about him.

Mrs. Martin wasn't so good with him."

"And?" Carmine prompted, because she'd flattened her lips and stopped.

"And he wasn't there! The neighbor's goblin maid told me they'd said Joel had gone to stay with cousins. Who sends a one-year-old away from his family?"

Carmine patted the picture of her and Joel. "If you thought something bad had happened, why didn't you go to the police?"

"Me?" The goblin's open mouth exposed her square white teeth and long tongue. "And give them the chance to accuse me of harming Joel myself? I don't think so!" She shut her jaw again with a snap, reminding Nate why goblins were at risk of such suspicions. Once upon a time, they'd been known to make meals of children around Joel's age.

"I know what you're thinking," Mrs. Erg accused, wagging two of her six red fingers. "Those were the bad days, when we lived in the Old Country." She tossed her head angrily. "I'd like to see you werewolves account for every bite your ancestors gulped."

Nate admired her spirit, but that didn't mean he'd take her word on faith. "Sometimes people backslide," he said softly.

"It was *ritual*," she huffed. "*My* favorite food is spaghetti with meatballs."

Her arms were crossed, her gaze nearly shooting sparks. Nate was still going to check her background, but right then he relented.

"Thank you," he said. "We'll get back to you if we have more questions."

The anger fell away from her manner. From the movement of her fingers, Nate was guessing she wanted to clutch his arm. "What about Joel? You never said what happened to him."

"We're not sure. We think . . . If we're able to confirm Joel was the child in the picture, chances are it wouldn't be inappropriate for you to say a prayer for his soul's passing."

"Oh," said Mrs. Erg in a little voice, her citrine eyes welling up again. Her hand pressed her thin-lipped mouth. "Thank you for telling me."

~

Nate and Carmine left the claustrophobic building without speaking. Once free of its confines, both rolled cricks from their necks and shoulders. The gloomy atmosphere of the courtyard seemed like Palm Beach right then.

Because the bland department car didn't require Nate's expertise, Carmine was driving. "What do you think?" he asked after sliding behind the wheel. "Do you buy her story?"

Nate closed his door with a solid *thunk*. "We'll check it out. First, though, I think we'd better make the acquaintance of Joel's parents."

~

69

Little Jersey was, by Nate's guesstimate, a ten-minute bus ride from Goblinville, easy enough for a nanny to take every day. The borderline suburban area reminded him of Evina's neighborhood. Ugly modern construction alternated with tired old, little of Resurrection's downtown charm having extended out this far. There were more trees and grass here, but Nate didn't see the point.

Then again, he was a city boy.

The Martins lived in a square brick apartment complex. Since they'd crossed into the dinner hour, cooking smells suffused the hallways, none especially appealing.

Carmine looked at Nate when they reached the Martins' door. His bushy brows went up in question.

"You take lead," Nate said, realizing what Carmine was asking. "Unless they give you reason not to, do your nice guy thing. I want to watch their reactions."

Nate stood aside with his weapon drawn while Carmine gave the plain brown door a thumping triple knock. "RPD. We need to speak to the Martins."

A male opened the door, presumably Mr. Martin. He was medium height and narrow, with ginger hair and a thin mustache. Nate thought his watery blue eyes weren't as pretty as the goblin's, strange though those had been. He seemed nervous to have cops on his threshold.

Nate tucked his gun away. Martin's vibe was weasely but not aggressive.

"What's this about?" Joel's father asked, his gaze darting between them.

Carmine showed his ID. "Police business, Mr. Martin. We need to speak to you and your wife."

His pale eyes grew shiftier. "We're about to sit down to dinner."

"This won't take long." Carmine pulled one of his trademark moves, giving the ball of Roger Martin's shoulder a friendly squeeze even as he stepped past him. Martin gaped at his presumption, but wasn't bold enough to protest. Amused, Nate followed Carmine into the living room.

A cheap hotel painting of a blurry forest hung above a dull brown couch. The seating wasn't in any way improved by a row of beige pillows. The lamps on the small end tables came from a low-end department store, as did the knockoff Oriental rug. A wedding picture of the Martins hung opposite the couch. Ironically, their decorations were less homey than Mrs. Erg's. Nate saw no photos of Joel, nor any sign he'd once lived here.

That was telling. Whatever had happened to their son, they weren't making a show of remembering him.

Mrs. Martin came into the room. She looked more like a mouse than a fox, her clothes too old for her slim thirty-something body. Her unstyled hair was a lackluster brown. "What's going on?" she asked her husband.

"It's the police," he said, his manner striving for natural and failing utterly.

"They want to ask us a few questions."

"We were wondering what happened to Joel," Carmine said gently.

Mrs. Martin's hands tightened on the napkin she was carrying. "Joel is staying with his cousins. We thought it would be good if he had relatives his own age to play with."

"Could you give us an address?" Carmine asked even more softly, pegging her as the weaker link. "We'd really like to check that he's fine."

"I . . . I think I might have mislaid it." Mrs. Martins' eyes were white-rimmed with panic. Carmine lifted his hands like a priest about to give a blessing.

"You know that's not true," he said in a tone so compassionate, so comforting it would have calmed a rabbit in the thick of a chase. "Joel isn't with his cousins at all."

"I think you need to leave," Mr. Martin summoned the spine to say. He was too late. Two fat tears were already rolling down his wife's gaunt cheeks.

"I'm sorry," she cried, completely unraveling. "I knew I shouldn't have agreed. I just was at my wit's end!"

The truth as the Martins understood it came out between defensive pleas for understanding and tears of self-pity. Carmine exhausted his supply of Kleenex before they had the whole story.

Overcome with shame at having sired a flawed offspring, and unable to afford more dead-end cures, the Martins turned to a lawyer they'd heard could arrange "special" adoptions. In return for a then welcome sum of cash, they were promised their son would be placed not with a family in Resurrection, but in a loving home beyond its borders. To mundanes, their non-shifting son would seem normal. Raised Outside, he'd think he was normal too. He'd forget the place he'd been born existed and, as a result, would never be able to track down his birthparents.

"They showed us the adopters' file," Mrs. Martin claimed passionately. She leaned forward on the couch, one of the pillows clutched to her belly. Her husband sat beside her and nodded at all she said. "We read their letters. They really wanted a child. We know the way we gave him up was illegal, but surely Joel will be happier with them."

Nate didn't know how to respond to that. Carmine didn't either. He looked at Nate helplessly.

"Mrs. Martin," Nate said, his throat tight enough that his words came out rough around the edges. "We'll need the name of the lawyer and anyone else you met at the adoption agency."

"I'll get it." Mrs. Martin hopped up, eager to redress her wrongdoing now that it had been exposed. "I wrote everything in my datebook."

When it came to wrongdoing, Mr. Martin was more resistant to remorse than his spouse. He waited until his wife left the room, then spoke in a low worried voice. "They don't want to return the boy, do they?"

Nate's answer was more heartfelt than he expected. "Mr. Martin," he said, "you should be so lucky."

~

The subsequent takedown was pulse pounding in its execution and oddly anticlimactic afterward. More or less hiding his surprise that Nate and Carmine had obtained warrant-worthy affidavits, Adam convinced a judge to issue one that night. Then he called Special Tactics to assist them with the arrests.

The Martins were taken into protective custody, mostly so they wouldn't have a chance to give the lawyer a head's up—had they been so inclined. With them under wraps, a force that included Adam's squad, plus Johnny Lupone's Special Tactics unit quietly surrounded the adoption agency at 9:30 the next morning. The Wings of Love Placement Agency did business from an unremarkable storefront in a strip mall. Considering the amount of man- and weapon-power they'd brought, the only real suspense was how many fish they'd catch.

As it happened, Adam chose his timing well. They netted the lawyer the Martins had used, his partner, two paralegals, and one office manager. Tony had the presence of mind to paw through their file room before it was boxed up as evidence. This led them to the trio of masked doctors Evina had seen in her vision. They turned out to be dentists who worked in the same strip mall two stores down. They'd gone out for breakfast and had missed the RPD's mostly stealth entry.

When they spotted the half dozen police vehicles circled around their associates' door, naturally they tried to run. This gave Nate, Carmine, and Johnny the satisfaction of chasing and subduing them personally.

Carmine looked slow, but he could haul ass when he wanted to.

Nate's sole complaint was that none of their catches were talking.

Now Adam and he stood shoulder to shoulder behind the two-way glass that overlooked the largest of the precinct's interrogation rooms. They'd separated everyone they arrested, to prevent them from strategizing tales. The leftovers were down in Holding, enjoying the station's cells. The Wings of Love head lawyer sat alone at the table in the room they observed. He was a smarmy lion shifter who came off as too stupid to be a mastermind. That he hadn't demanded representation Nate understood; he probably thought he could represent himself. That none of his co-conspirators had asked for counsel was bothering him.

"They'll crack," Adam assured him, bumping Nate's arm with his elbow. "And if they don't, the evidence in those files Tony found is damning. These guys are aren't going to walk."

The files went back a disturbing eighteen months, during which no less than two dozen shifter children had been "placed" in new homes. The Special Crimes department was at work notifying the birthparents, none of whom seemed to realize the offspring they'd given up weren't perfectly safe and sound. They'd all gone to the agency voluntarily, having heard about it through an amorphous grapevine they couldn't yet pin down. The only definite link between the parents, aside from being non-wolf shifters, was that their children all suffered from a defect that prevented them from changing.

Their eagerness to let them go reminded Nate of stories of Outsiders who abandoned unwanted infants because they weren't boys. The shifter children had been healthy apart from their one flaw. They simply weren't the progeny their parents had dreamed of.

Their behavior sickened Nate.

He watched the lion lawyer check his Blancpain watch and click his tongue in irritation, as if he were a simple white collar shit being made late for an appointment. Did he even care that these kids he was preying on were cousins to his own kind?

"$80,000 per child," Nate said, the amount the agency's books had recorded as their facilitation fee.

Adam grunted beside him. "Could have been ten times that much once they reached the end buyers."

"You know those babies were being cut up for parts."

Other entries in the files had made that horribly clear.

"I know," Adam said.

"We have to find the distributors."

"We will. Even if we don't squeeze it out of these bastards, there are only so many people with the balls to sell supplies for flesh rituals. Convictions for that carry mandatory death sentences."

"They should send them to hell dimensions," Nate growled. "Preferably ones where they can be killed repeatedly."

"We'll get them. It might take some old-fashioned detective work, but between us and Special Crimes, we'll get them all."

Nate turned toward him, suddenly grateful his shoulders weren't the only ones carrying this. "Thank you for letting me run with this. And for backing up me and Carmine when we needed it."

Adam dragged his hand uncomfortably down his mouth. "I'm not sure that's necessary. It's thanks to you and your instincts that we cut the head off this snake."

Unease spread through Nate at his alpha's words. Did Adam really think they'd caught this scheme's leader? Didn't he find it strange these mooks weren't tripping over themselves to inform on one another and cut a deal? At the least, the paralegals and the office manager should have been squealing their fool heads off. Maybe that happening was a matter of time.

And maybe fear of the real snake was keeping them silent.

He drew breath to speak but thought better of it. It was good to have Adam back on his side, to not be wondering how uncomfortable life would be if he pushed his boss past the breaking point. Nate would wait and see what happened with their suspects. Then, if he had to, he'd go to the mat again.

"It's not over," he burst out in spite of that very sound reasoning.

Adam's black eyebrows shot up above his soft green eyes. "That's what your gut is telling you?"

"Yes," Nate felt he had to admit.

He braced for an explosion, but Adam's only response was a weary sigh.

❧ CHAPTER SEVEN

THE squad's traditional victory barbecue for a big arrest was held on Adam and Ari's roof. Everyone but Nate was in a festive mood. Carmine and his wife were demonstrating a salsa for Ari and Adam, who weren't having much luck imitating the steps. Tony rocked baby Kelsey, fast asleep in his arms. Ethan, the former baby of the pack, tore through the partygoers with a pair of barbecue tongs he'd stolen from his father.

"I'm the king of the grill!" he proclaimed in a mock-adult growl.

Rick probably saved the next batch of ribs from burning by snatching the boy off his feet mid-run.

Nate slanted his bottle of faerie stout to his lips, wondering if he'd ever feel like himself again.

Maybe his keel would have been even if Evina had been there. He'd considered inviting her. He'd called her station, wanting to let her know they'd made arrests. Whoever answered coolly told him that she was at a fire. He hadn't left a message, but worry for her safety had nagged at him ever since. Grimacing, he took another swallow of strong beer. Maybe he ought to worry for himself. Thinking about Evina as if she was or could be part of his life was unlikely to lead anywhere useful.

"You're quiet," said a rumbling voice behind his left shoulder.

Grant the gargoyle had flapped down to his reinforced roost on the edge of Adam's roof a quarter hour ago. If gargoyles ate, Nate had never seen one do it. Though indifferent to ribs and beer, Grant seemed to enjoy watching the others enjoy themselves. Most gargoyles pretended they only spoke Pidgin English, but Grant was a rebel among his kind. The size of a minibus, he had a goblin's head, a lion's body, and the wings of a bat. He was fur and flesh, but when he fell motionless he could pass for a statue carved out of stone.

Nate glanced at him. The only exceptions to his grayness were his great goblin eyes, which Nate noted were a brighter yellow than Mrs. Erg's. That the mind behind them was highly perceptive, he had reason to know.

"I'm just tired," he said, looking away again.

"Hm." Grant resettled his batwings with a warm stir of air. "You must have worked harder than Carmine. He seems quite energetic now."

Nate knew Grant was poking fun at him. Rather than laugh, the words *I'm afraid I'm in love* popped into his head. He shook himself. That had to be the stout talking.

"You know a lot about magic, right?" he asked.

"Most gargoyles do," Grant said.

"What sort of spell would a person do with the body . . . or parts of the body of a shifter child who couldn't change?"

Like most gargoyles, who considered themselves the protectors of Resurrection, Grant was fascinated by the police. Despite his familiarity with the things they faced, Nate's question widened his eyes. "You mean children who can't change because of a genetic flaw?"

"Yes."

Grant mulled this over. "Shifters who can't change are rare. The gene for were-ism is usually dominant. Even mixed bloods express it. Traditional wisdom holds that those who can't change still possess the magic. It's simply locked within their cells."

"Why is that important?"

"It's important because if it's *un*locked, their flesh contains more magic than ordinary weres. Gargoyles use communal mind power to enact big spells, but others employ objects. Practitioners who tap the power of . . . material such as that could gain the ability to change form themselves. The bones of non-shifting wereanimals are known—though not widely, for obvious reasons—to heal otherwise incurable diseases. A human sorcerer might want to add wattage to a spell, without paying for it with his or her personal life force. If a magic worker didn't care about morals, those kind of ingredients would be priceless."

"How priceless?"

"This is hearsay, you understand. No one familiar with gargoyles would let us catch direct wind of this. They know we'd inform on them at the drop of a hat."

"But?"

Grant's claws clicked on his concrete platform, as if he had fingers to drum. "I've heard of non-shifting were flesh going for as high as half a million dollars for a few ounces."

Nate barely had breath to whistle. "That's a freaking lot of cash."

"Yes, it is. Is that what the case you just closed involved?"

Closed was stretching it, in Nate's opinion. He tried to multiply half a million by two dozen and who knew how many cut-up bits. Where was all that money going? Maybe more importantly, what was whoever was collecting it hoping to do with it? For some people, money was an end in itself. For others, it was a lever that could move worlds.

Grant nudged Nate's leg with his gray lion's paw. Too big to pat Nate's back without knocking him over, he was doing the next best thing. "You should be proud. These crimes are terrible, but at least you and your pack put a stop to them."

Nate never could decide how young or old Grant was. He often seemed wise, but he had an earnestness about him that made it hard to judge. The longing in his voice when he said *your pack* caused Nate to feel an unexpected kinship. By not hiding his intelligence from Adam and the others, he'd set himself apart from his own people. Nate wondered if finding a slightly awkward place among a bunch of cops was worth giving up all that.

He put his hand on Grant's surprisingly warm foreleg, the buzz of the gargoyle's magic palpable through his fur. "You're a good friend," he said. "The pack is lucky you chose to live near us."

"Hear-hear," Ari said, salsaing to them for the tail end of this. Nate noticed her footwork was better without Adam to partner her. "I came to see if you two needed anything."

"We're well," Grant said. "Or I am. Perhaps Nate would like to dance with you."

Ari winked at Nate. "I don't think so. Nate knows how to ask a woman to dance himself."

She hopped up to sit on Grant's platform, parking her little butt between his giant paws. Settled, she blew a two-finger whistle to Tony. "Bring Kelsey over," she said, because he was dancing around with her dozing on his shoulder. "Grant hasn't met her yet."

Ari and Grant had always struck Nate as having a real friendship, maybe more than Grant did with anyone in the pack. Sometimes Nate suspected Ari knew things about the gargoyle the others didn't. If she did, her offer startled him all the same.

"Maybe you shouldn't do that," he said, shifting uncomfortably over her. "Your daughter is very small."

"I'll hold her, silly." Ari accepted the blinking bundle from Tony. "There you are," she cooed to her slowly waking daughter. "Time to meet your Uncle Grant."

Kelsey blew a spit bubble while Grant looked stunned. Nate guessed the gargoyle hadn't realized Ari thought of him in those terms. With a caution that was amusing, *Uncle* Grant craned over Ari's head to look down at the wriggling girl. Kelsey was too young to know how fortunate she was. Not only would she never be given up, she'd never lack for protectors who'd lay down their lives for her—including Grant, he was sure. Smiling at the gargoyle's air of wonder, Nate put his hand on Ari's shoulder.

"I'm taking off," he said when she looked up. "Thanks for the great party."

"You're sure? It's early."

"I'm sure," he said. "I've got beauty sleep to catch up on."

He only had two blocks to cover between Adam's house and his. The night was misty but pleasant in temperature. As the grocer chained and locked his shop's accordion-style gate, his German shepherd woofed. The sound of someone's TV trailed out an open window, canned laughter mixing with the real deal from Adam's roof. Nate shoved his hands deeper in his pockets. His fingers bumped his car keys.

Damn, he thought as a longing to see Evina seized his muscles.

The curse didn't stop him from striding to his building's underground garage.

~

The EMT who was bandaging the bullet hole in Evina's bicep was a weretiger, a friend, and a single mother like herself. Familiar with—and understanding of—Evina's aversion to emergency rooms, Freda had agreed to patch her up in her loft office at the fire station. With luck, she'd be healed by morning. The twins wouldn't have to know their mommy had been hurt.

"You owe me drinks," Freda said, snapping her first aid bag shut. "We'll pool babysitters and make it a girls night out."

"Don't call it that," Evina pleaded, gingerly probing her gauze-wrapped arm. "My mother will want to come."

"I *love* drinking with your mother," Freda declared. "She's so handy when it comes to snagging the man-candy."

The sound of a low male growl down in the garage bay drew Freda to the office's big window. "Talk about man-candy," the EMT murmured.

Heat pricked the back of Evina's neck, a flush she couldn't fight climbing up her face. Freda was a fun friend and a free spirit. She knew all Evina's tigers, quite a few of them intimately. From her tone, Evina surmised the man-candy was someone new to her.

Evina didn't need three guesses. Her body was already telling her who it was.

Sure enough, when she went to look, Nate was at the back entrance. Nights were getting cooler. Over slim black jeans, Nate wore a snazzy fitted leather jacket with lapels, the same he'd loaned to her outside the factory. Mist surrounded him like a halo, but he was no angel. From his shiny ponytail to his Varvatos boots, he was an advertisement for how devilish bad boys could be. Tonight, Liam wasn't his challenger. Her third man Jonah—his temper short from being stuck here holding the fort while his alpha and pridemates had battled danger—was barring Nate's path into the fire house.

It probably didn't help his control that his alpha was currently injured.

All Nate did in response to Jonah's growl was lift his groomed eyebrows.

"I have business with your boss," he said.

Jonah's growl lowered and drew out, the animal sound seeming to issue from his chest. Real tigers made that noise before they attacked.

"Wait," Freda said when Evina moved forward to intervene.

"I'm Evina's friend," Nate said, cool as a cat himself. "You need to step aside for me."

Jonah wasn't in the mood for that. His fireman's arm, which was half again the size of Nate's, crooked, bunched, and delivered an uppercut straight to Nate's breadbasket.

At least, his fist would have landed there if Nate hadn't grabbed his wrist before it connected. Nate's entire body spun, the motion tight and controlled. He used Jonah's weight against him, one designer boot sweeping his feet out from under while the momentum of his upper body twisted Jonah's arm to an awkward angle behind his back. When the smooth-as-a-dance move finished—in milliseconds, it seemed to her—Jonah had been forced to his knees, his face dripping sweat from the pain of his captured arm. Because the firefighter was too proud to cry out, Evina had no trouble hearing what Nate leaned down to say.

"Evina is your *alpha*, tiger. It's not your place to question who she wants to see."

"Wow," Freda said with a little purr. "When you're done tapping that, can I have a go at him?"

Though it was a joke, or at any rate friendly, Evina had to fight back her own growl. Good Lord. Was she really thinking of Nate as if he belonged to her?

Preferring not to answer that, Evina shoved through her office door.

Nate must have sensed she was around already. From what she understood, werewolf noses were sharper than tigers'. Even so, her appearance seemed to take him by surprise. He looked up and his head jerked back, his hold on Jonah slipping.

"Oh my God," he said, "you've been shot!"

Jonah was halfway to taking advantage of his lapse in attention when the genuine concern in Nate's voice sank in. Stopping so close to attacking forced him to catch his balance on his freed arm.

"I'm okay," Evina said, coming quickly down the stairs. "It was a through-and-through."

"A through-and-through!" He had her by the forearms, his fingers rubbing gently as he clasped her above the wrists. "Didn't you change? Why are you still bleeding?"

"Of course I did. The bullet was electrum-plated."

Electrum plating was a relatively inexpensive method for rendering ammo more effective against beings like shifters. Injuries caused by it were slower to heal. Evina had been feeling grateful the shooter had been too cheap to buy a full metal jacket. Nate, apparently, didn't see it that way.

"Oh my God," he repeated, his voice spiking high enough to crack.

Sitting on the floor now, Jonah began to laugh. "Man," he said, "I'd feel sorry for you if you hadn't nearly broke my arm. Wolf-boy's got cat-scratch fever bad."

"Jesus," Evina swore, horrified at him.

"Sorry, boss." Jonah creaked to his feet, where he rubbed his elbow and winced. "Shit. I got to ice this thing."

Freda had by this time finished sauntering down the open stairs, looking sexier in her dark blue EMT shirt and trousers than any woman had a right to. She smiled knowingly at Evina. "Since you seem to be in good hands, I'll be going. Nice meeting *you*, Mr. Dark and Lethal."

Nate wrenched his worried gaze from Evina's. "Uh," he said to Freda, not his usual style at all.

Freda laughed. "No driving until tomorrow," she tossed over her shoulder to Evina. Grumpily, Evina noticed her walk exhibited more wiggle than usual.

Nate mostly seemed confused as he watched her go.

"She's a friend," Evina sighed. "And, yes, she's available."

"What?" Nate turned back to her. Evina didn't feel like repeating her answer. His eyes cleared after a moment of gazing into hers. "She said no driving. Do you need a ride home?"

"Actually . . . I could use a ride to St. Aelfryd's. I want to check in on Christophe."

Nate's warm hands were wrapped lightly around hers. How long had he been holding them, and why did they feel so good? "I can drive you."

"I might be a little while. If you drop me, I can take a cab home from there."

"I don't have plans. I'll browse the gift shop while you visit."

His irises were starting to glow a little, turning their coffee color gold. Evina's breathing deepened against her will. Watching him fight had done a number on her libido. She couldn't forget how quick he'd been . . . The way he moved to take his bigger opponent down . . . She knew her pupils were expanding with arousal, because the room was suddenly brighter. Nate wet his fascinating lips, his nostrils flaring like hers were.

"How did you get shot?" he asked, his voice a caress trailing down her spine.

"Some teenager got caught holding up a convenience store. Decided the best way to evade the police was to set the Quik-Mart on fire. He'd trapped himself in the back by the time we got there."

"Did you get him out?"

"We got everyone out. Owner. Customers. Even a pet lizard."

Remembering, Evina broke into a grin.

"A good day then. Despite being shot."

Oh, Nate got it, maybe as much as her fellow firefighters. Her body grew even warmer, positively aching to let that powerful cock of his shove in it. She could practically feel him thumping her body into the nearest wall.

"Nate," she said, soft as smoke.

Her tone was too bed-friendly, considering where they were. Realizing this, Nate cleared his throat and stepped back. He released her hands grudgingly. "I'll bring the car around. You—" He paused to look at her, more fire kindling in his eyes. "Just grab whatever you want to bring with you."

Right that moment, the main thing she wanted to grab was him.

~

The gift shop at St. Aelfryd's Hospital held the usual flowers, magazines, and baby-strength amulets for invoking deities. Heavy duty magic was left to the elfin and human healers who ran the place. Nate bought an imported copy of the *Sports Illustrated Swimsuit Edition*. The Outsider publication was popular here. Then, unaccountably restless, he followed his nose to find Evina in Christophe's room.

He wasn't trying to rush her. He simply didn't have the patience to sit in a waiting room.

When he caught up to her, Evina sat by Christophe's bed, the steel and vinyl chair crowded close to him. Her senior man was yet another huge tiger—older than the others Nate had met, though that was hard to tell. The cat was in bad shape. The parts of him that weren't wrapped up like a mummy looked red and raw. Clearly, he wasn't healing the way a shifter should. Evina had told Nate the doctors were trying to adjust his pain medication. Too much and he'd be too doped up to change. Too little and his physical distress would interfere. Right then, they seemed to have underdone it. Christophe was hurting enough that he shook with a fine tremor.

Nate totally understood why Evina was crooning to him and gently stroking the unburned bend of his right arm. Her touch wasn't as soothing as it should have been. Christophe's brow remained puckered, and Nate got the impression worry was partly responsible. He and Evina looked around when Nate stopped at the doorway.

"Hey, man," he said. "Sorry to interrupt." He held up the *Sports Illustrated*. "Thought you might like a magazine."

In spite of his discomfort, a naughty smile stretched Christophe's face. When he spoke, his voice was smoke-roughened. "You must be the dirty dog the other guys were griping about."

"Ah." Nate scratched the side of his mouth. "I suppose tigers gossip as much as wolves."

"Sometimes we gossip, and sometimes we stick our noses in the air like we're above noticing."

Nate laughed, but then Christophe coughed, the movement evidently painful inside and out. Nate rushed forward to the other side of the bed to help Evina steady him.

"Fuck," Christophe gasped when the fit was over. "This seriously sucks."

"Just hang in there," Evina said. "The doctors say your body is bound to shift before much longer. Your tiger half wouldn't let lasting harm come to you."

"From your mouth . . . to the ear of the Tiger Queen," Christophe said, almost too tired to speak.

A nurse came in: a young gold elf with a serious face. "You should probably let him rest now. The doctors are making the rounds with sleep charms."

Nate and Evina helped Christophe sink back into the pillows. Seeing how weak he was, an odd sensation ran through Nate, an almost physical tug to take action. Though this man was a stranger, it was as if something inside Nate *needed* to assist him. He let go of Christophe's arm with an effort.

Evina bent to her beta, pressing her lips to a safe spot on his temple. "Rest up, partner. We miss you at the station."

"Not . . . as much as I miss . . . being there." Christophe looked at Nate, his gaze measuring. Careful not to set off another cough, he pulled in a steadying breath. "Don't be a dog to her."

Nate could have turned the warning into a joke. Instead, he met Christophe's stare head on. "I won't. Not if there's any way to avoid it."

Christophe nodded and closed his eyes. The nurse shooed them out into the hall. The shutting of the door left them together in silence. Evina looked at her feet with her hands shoved into her pockets, mute testimony to her worry over her crewmember's condition. It was an alpha's nature to want to aid her people, the attribute as much instinct as basic shifter decency. Nate knew she couldn't like feeling helpless. He gave her shoulder a little rub.

"Come on," he said. "I'll get you home."

He drove her to her townhouse, a touch of that same helplessness chafing him. Evina was a good person. How could it be wrong for him to admire her the way he did?

He pulled into a parking spot by the curb, tempted to shut off his Goblinati's engine but wondering if this was presumptuous.

He turned to her on his seat as she turned to him. It seemed a sign that he ought to speak. He cupped her ear with one hand, his thumb stroking a path around it as if he'd been touching her all his life. Evina smiled at him. His cock tightened and grew hot. The mist was thicker in her neighborhood, like a fog machine had been turned on.

"How's the arm?" he asked, noting she'd stopped poking it to test.

"I think it's healed now. I hate having the kids see me hurt."

Nate hadn't liked it much himself. "Do you get hurt often?"

"Firemen aren't hotshots," she said with a smile to suggest maybe she thought cops were. "Despite being shifters, we always try to work safe. We use our protective gear, and we keep up with the latest techniques. What happened to me today . . . what happened to Christophe . . . is unusual."

He nodded, unsettled by his own relief at her reassurance. Part of him wished she'd never be in the thick of things. She was a gifted astral projector. She could have stuck to that. But no alpha could command respect from her crew if she didn't share the same dangers. That's how it worked with wolves anyway. Adam didn't molder behind a desk.

"So," Evina said, starting to reach for her door handle. He couldn't just let her go, not with what he was feeling.

"I want to come in," he said.

"My mother's watching the twins."

"I like your mother."

Evina laughed, kneeling up and leaning forward to drop a kiss on his nose. "Wait here. I'll check if the twins are in bed and report back to you."

"I wouldn't mind meeting them as well."

He hadn't planned to say that. Evina's eyebrows rose. He set his jaw and didn't retract the statement, though he wasn't certain what he'd meant to imply. Evina didn't seem prepared to ask. She cocked her head but didn't press him to explain.

"Wait," she repeated, swinging out of the car. "I'll be back as soon as I can."

~

Evina tried to recall if a man had stirred Nate's mix of perplexity and attraction in her before. Everyone liked her mother, so that claim was no surprise. Him wanting to meet her kids, however, knocked her off balance. He'd be good with kids, she was sure. He could charm anyone, young or old. She just wouldn't have expected her grocery store Romeo to be into the idea.

Of course, she also wouldn't have predicted she'd go warm and gooey at his interest. Whatever he'd meant, that couldn't be smart.

The house was in a state inside. Rita was great about babysitting, but she drew the line at tidying up. Evina found her perusing *Magical Antiques Monthly* in the den, probably imagining what she'd like to buy for her shop. Seeming tired, Rita took the back way out, across the development's shared stretch of grass to her own townhome. Quickly disposing of her bandage, Evina stuck her head in each twin's room. They were sound asleep. Abby sprawled in her bed face down, while Rafi curled up in his cat roost—in boy form, thank goodness.

Because there was too much mess to tackle without a backhoe, Evina shook her head, sighed, and went to wave for Nate to come in. She consoled herself that at least the lights were off.

"Sorry about the tornado," she said as he looked around.

"These things happen," he said diplomatically.

Evina had to chuckle.

"What?" he asked, following her up the narrow toy-cluttered stairs.

"Well, 'these things' don't happen at your place, do they?"

"A little mess is homey," he said, his night vision sharp enough to spare him tripping over Elf Barbie's Dream Garage.

Evina snorted under her breath.

"It is," he insisted.

They'd reached her bedroom on the second floor. Elf Barbie's pink convertible was parked outside the door, but thankfully hadn't been driven in. Evina's room was no worse off than when she'd left it this morning. Bracing herself, she shut the door behind Nate and turned on a bedside light.

"Sorry I didn't make the—"

Nate silenced her apology with a kiss.

It wasn't just any kiss, but a deceptively lazy demonstration of his ability to seduce. Slow and sweet, the kiss melted her from the inside out. His arms came around her as she leaned into and up to him, his warm palms cruising from her shoulder blades to the lower curve of her butt. She obeyed their urging to rock her hips closer. His cock was rising beneath his jeans, its solidity increasing by the second. As they kissed, he rubbed the ridge in a slow rotation against her stomach. The heat that had been simmering inside her grew heavy.

When he drew his head back, her eyes didn't want to open.

"I take it tonight's activities need to stay quiet?"

"What? Oh. Yes. My kids . . . I don't want them to be confused."

"I understand." His fingers drew figure eights on her bottom, making her want to push back to them. His eyes were slumberous, his gaze focused on her lips. His black expression-concealing lashes inspired tremors in her sex. "Where's your bathroom?"

Bemused, she pointed it out.

He disappeared inside, the sound of him doing personal things in there weirdly appealing. This wasn't a fling-your-partner-down-and-take-her encounter. This was almost domestic. Evina sat on her rumpled bed—whose memory foam thankfully didn't squeak—and took off her shoes. Nate washed his hands, then rummaged for who knew what in her medicine cabinet. Extra toothbrush, she realized as she heard him brushing his pearly whites.

Evina peeled off her top and caught herself smiling. She tried to erase the expression, but her lips curved again. She unzipped her jeans, stood, and pushed them down her legs. Her underwear was nothing special, just what she'd grabbed from her everyday drawer when she got up. Deciding it wasn't worth leaving on, she'd tossed it toward the closet when Nate prowled back into the bedroom.

He was bare-ass naked, his skin toasty brown all over, his erection shooting high and thick from the hair at his groin. Bouncing a bit with his strides, his glans shone with excitement.

"Yum," she said, the first word that came to mind.

He grinned slyly, remaining where he was so she could circle him and admire. He didn't seem to know what shyness was. His glutes tensed for her, the layered muscles of his back and rear truly a sight to see. Reluctantly, Evina came back around to his front.

"Should I feel objectified?" he teased.

She balanced her fingertips on the light furring of his chest, enjoying the feel of his life pulsing under his skin. Their thighs were inches apart. "Maybe."

"Do you have something in mind you'd like to do to me?"

The playful way he put this seemed to give her permission for anything. "Do you trust me?"

His eyes searched hers, his amusement deepening. "More than you might expect."

That delighted her so much she had to bite her lip.

Both times they'd been together he'd overwhelmed her. She'd enjoyed that surprisingly much. This time, though, she wanted to show him her alpha tigress claws.

Grinning, she went down on her stomach to wriggle under her queen size bed.

"Not that I'm complaining about the view," Nate said from above her, probably because her butt stuck out, "but I don't think I can fit with you under there."

"Ha ha." She emerged, breathless and dusty, with her prize.

Nate's brows drew together when he got a look at it. "Extra sheets? Shouldn't we save those for after we've dirtied the ones you've got?"

"You forget who I live with. This only looks like linens fresh from the store." She held out the package. Nate undid the plastic flap.

"Aha," he said, pulling out the wooden box that was cleverly concealed between pillowcases. He set the box on the bed and opened it carefully.

As the lid came up on its hinge, Evina's private toys were revealed. Nestled in rich red velvet were a small and extremely quiet vibrator, a dildo, a silver butt plug with an extra curve to the tip, a cock ring, lubricant, and a pair of padded leather cuffs.

To Evina's pleasure, Nate smiled at the contents. His fingertips stroked the leather cuffs. "I must admit, you've taken me by surprise. I wouldn't have pegged you as being quite this adventurous."

"Do you object to anything in that box being used on you?"

His gaze shifted from the case to her, the asymmetry of his lower lip making his smile slant even more to the left. "The dildo doesn't look comfortable."

"But other than that?"

"No, no objections." His eyes were twinkling, maybe a bit too amused.

"Will you need a gag to keep from shouting? I can fashion one from a scarf."

His humor dialed back a notch as he realized she was serious. Evina meant this exchange to have a genuine edge. He appeared intrigued rather than disturbed, which she was happy for. Nate wouldn't fear a challenge that she could tell.

"I like to talk," he said, "as you might have noticed, but I do promise I can keep quiet when there's a need."

"No matter what?"

A sharper sort of humor narrowed his eyes. "Bring it on, Evina. I'd *love* to have you pull out your stops for me."

Her fierce feline grin made him blink, exactly as it was supposed to. She gestured to her headboard, which was framed on either side by a short post and finial. "On the mattress, please," she said. "On your knees, with one hand on each bedpost. I'd like *you* to present for *me*."

He knew what she meant; she saw that from the subtle erotic shudder that rolled through him. When his hands were where she wanted—not a problem, given how tall he was—she crawled onto the bed and attached his wrists to the posts with the padded cuffs. Nate tugged once to test the restraints, the combination of the leather and his muscles made him seem gladiator-like. Once he'd established her knots would hold, he looked back at her over his beautifully developed shoulder. Something in his eyes excited her very much. He was struggling with this a little, wanting to warn her not to push him too far, but also not wanting to miss out.

"A weretiger could snap those ties," she informed him. "I assume the same holds true for werewolves."

"In tiger form, your kind has more strength. In human form, studies show we're neck and neck."

His voice was breathy, which sent a thrill zinging to her sex. She pulled the clasp from his ponytail, parting his straight black hair to fall to either of his neck. She stroked the vertebrae she'd bared with the backs of her knuckles. "Do you remember how you bit me here the other night?"

"It's instinct for male wolves to do that."

She trailed her hand to his tailbone, loving how his skin shivered. "It's instinct for male cats too. No male wants his mate to escape when he's shooting his seed in her."

"Christ," Nate said, letting out a brief pant.

Evina smiled and nipped the ball of his shoulder. He wasn't the only one who knew how to talk in bed. She moved behind him, her knees digging into the unmade covers outside his calves. Because they were there, right in front of her, she wrapped her hands around his butt cheeks and gave them a good squeeze.

Something dripped to the covers that she didn't think was sweat.

"Has a man ever taken you like this?" she asked. "From behind?"

Nate craned around to her again. "No." He pleased her by not sounding offended. "That's not a kink of mine. Is men doing it together something you enjoy thinking about?"

Evina drew her tongue around her upper lip, appreciating the way his gaze followed it. Her hands continued to knead and circle his butt muscles. "I don't dislike the idea, but I have one problem."

"Which is?"

"That I'd rather *be* the man doing the taking, instead of watching it. When you're a woman, even if you're alpha, sometimes men treat you as if you aren't as tough as they are."

"Physically, you're not."

"Perhaps. But toughness has to do with more than the physical."

"So . . ." Nate wet his own lips. "You want to take me the way a man would."

She smiled. "I want to do more than to take you. I want you to feel ravished."

~

Nate didn't think a woman had ever spoken to him like that. Certainly, none had gotten her results. His cock stiffened beneath him as if it meant to break records for steel-hard rigidity.

"I suppose . . . everyone deserves to feel ravished now and then."

She laughed as she kissed his back, then retrieved the lube from her box of tricks. She held the tube between the globes of her breasts, warming the gel it contained. Her lack of self-consciousness implied this wasn't her first ride on the carousel. He *thought* he didn't mind that. Considering what she planned to do, probably it was best to be in experienced hands.

Lubricant warmed, she squeezed two lines of gel up her fingers and another down his crack. She rubbed her now slick fingers along that line, stirring subtly pleasurable sensations everywhere she touched. "You can relax. I'll be careful I don't hurt you."

He believed her but tensed when she pushed two fingers into his orifice. This was an intimacy he wasn't that familiar with. Sensing he needed time to adjust, she left her fingers unmoving inside him. The nerves in his outer reaches tingled enjoyably.

"Can you sink closer to the bed?" she asked.

He could and he did, shifting his knees farther up the bed. Keeping the hand that speared him in place, she moved over him, folding her body around his to blanket him. He'd done this to her, more or less, though he was sure she felt different. Her breasts were warm, their softness flattening against him. With a crooning murmur, she began moving her fingers in and out. He wasn't prepared for that. Pleasure lashed through his lower body in red-hot waves.

He bit his lip to prevent himself from groaning.

"Good?" she whispered.

He nodded and arched his back, helpless not to invite her to rub deeper. She slid her other hand down his chest, skirting past his penis to palm his balls. Nate sucked in air, his death grip on the bedposts helping to support both of them. She squeezed him gently, testing how much force he liked. Nate ground his teeth together. Hard or soft, everything she did felt amazing to him.

She, however, was a perfectionist.

"I need lube," she decided after a few trials.

Oh God, was all Nate could think.

Somehow she managed to get the gel on one-handed. When she cupped him again, her hold was slick. She used it to stretch his testicles, the repeated tug and release inspiring increasingly powerful sensations, heightening the ones that built in his back passage. Her hands were hot, her naturally warm temperature rising as she got more into what she was doing. Soon her nipples were burning pebbles against his back—exciting all by themselves. He was glad she wasn't pulling on his cock. He'd have blasted off in seconds if she'd been doing that.

Of course, part of him thought blasting off right then would have been fine. His cockhead pulsed so sharply it felt like someone was tapping it.

"God," he hissed between his teeth. "This is making me crazy."

Evina released his scrotum. "Hold on," she said. "I've got something that will help."

Her hand came back to push the rubber cock ring down his erection.

"Shit," he said, because even that stimulation was a tad too good.

"Is it too tight?" she asked. "It's elf made. It's supposed to adjust to the wearer's size."

He couldn't speak. The cock ring's charm had activated, and the rubber was constricting on his root. The resulting pressure was perfect, snug and thick, providing an odd combination of reassurance and frustration. The ring would keep him from ejaculating. He'd stay hard and ready until she decided to let him off the hook.

That knowledge was exciting too.

Her other fingers continued to move, slowly fucking him from behind. It was as if she controlled him from all directions, as if she really were taking charge of him. That she could, that she didn't *hesitate,* blew his mind.

"I'm okay," he gasped, forcing it from his throat. "The ring is . . . doing what it's supposed to."

Evina dragged the tip of her tongue between his shoulder blades.

It was a simple enough caress, but it arched his head back with desire. His hands tightened on the two wooden balls they held, the movement reminding him the leather wrist cuffs were there.

To his surprise, they cranked his lust up another notch. This was going to be some climax when it finally won free of him.

"I'll get the other toy," she said, easing her fingers out.

Bereft of her digit's skill, pride was all that kept him from whimpering.

Thankfully, the other toy was the silver butt plug. She lubed it but slid it into him unwarmed. The contrast of his sizzling insides with the cool smooth metal drew a low moan from him. He'd tried anal play before without it turning him on like this. She seemed to be the magic ingredient: her interest in doing this, her understanding of men's bodies. The plug was thicker and harder than her fingers, stretching him more than they had.

"*Now* I'm taking you," she said as she breached him with it. "Now I'm making you mine."

Her voice was breathless with arousal. The sound nearly pushed him over—never mind the cock ring. He felt the extra curve at the metal phallus's tip searching out his prostate. Craving that like he wouldn't have believed, his eyes began to sting with sweat.

"Tell me when I hit it," she whispered.

She'd bent herself around him again, leaving only enough room between them for her hand to manipulate the toy. Her heart was pounding, her hot skin soft against his. The curve of the butt plug found the spot she was looking for.

The effect was like a gun's hammer striking sparks. A spasm bulleted from his prostate and up his cock, electric fire licking all the nerves. He couldn't have stopped the climax to save his life. He gasped, coming without a drop of seed shooting free.

Evina knew what was happening. She kept the tip locked on his joy trigger, rubbing back and forth at shifter speed, her weretiger dexterity allowing her to maintain the pressure on the exact millimeters that lusted after it. He whined in reaction, unable to keep it in.

She liked that, all right.

"Nate," she breathed, his name a gift coming from her lips. She stretched up, mouthing the back of his neck.

He'd suspected she meant to do this, and yet it shocked. Her incisors lengthened. She bit his nape and held on.

She was taking the man's position with him.

89

Switches flipped inside him, primitive reactions he didn't know he had in him and couldn't hope to repress. She dominated him, and the pleasure of that swamped him. She felt like his alpha, protecting him, making sure he was happy and satisfied. For once, he experienced no urge to throw off the subordinate mantle. She did this *for* rather than to him. The only mystery was that surrender could feel like an action and not the lack of one.

But maybe that was because he'd chosen to let her master him.

He muffled his cries on his own shoulder, not wanting her to stop as his body strove to ejaculate. It couldn't do it. The rapture inside him simply spiraled higher without breaking. Finally, it grew too intense to bear.

"Enough," he rasped.

Evina released him immediately, her hand coming to a halt behind him. Nate was breathing so hard he lifted her up and down.

"Take off the cock ring," he commanded. Inexplicably, that felt as natural as her controlling him.

She removed it with trembling hands. His cock felt strange without the constriction: fuller and not as safe.

Then again, he wasn't in the mood to be safe right then.

"Come under me," he ordered.

"Do you want me to remove the cuffs?"

His claws had extended and were dug into her bedposts.

"No," he growled, because he didn't want them dug into her.

She scooted under him, her curly head on the pillow, her wide and glowing eyes meeting his. She didn't look afraid but as if she worried she'd gone too far. He wasn't sure how to tell her she could have pushed him anywhere she liked, and he'd have gone happily. Come to that, he wasn't sure he wanted her to know. He liked her niggle of insecurity. Given how rocked he was, it was only fair.

"Has it happened for you like this before?" he asked gruffly.

She didn't deny their exchange had been intense, shaking her head tight and quick. "No. I never had the nerve to ask anyone to play like that."

"Good." The word resonated with satisfaction. Her hands came up to his chest, kneading him just a bit.

"Nate . . ."

"No," he said at her cautioning tone. He wanted no reminders they weren't supposed to be serious. "Let me enjoy being the only one."

~

He dipped his head to kiss her while she was still startled by his possessive tone. It occurred to her that Nate hadn't been threatened by her playing dominant, not like her ex used to be. Considering how easily Nate assumed the leading role, this was ironic. She'd have thought about that more, because the idea of being able to be herself with a man seemed sort of important. Nate's kiss didn't give her a chance to follow the thread. Those lips of his were addictive: their smooth warm firmness and their agility. His tongue slipped inward—stroking, sucking, luring her to forget everything but him. Her knees drew higher, her thighs contracting to hug his narrow waist. She was wet, and the upward roll of her pelvis pressed the moisture against his skin. He let out a hum of pleasure at feeling it.

He continued to grip the bedposts, the stretch of his arms preventing the weight of his upper torso from sinking onto hers. Taking advantage of the extra access, she ran her hands up and down his front. Because she was so excited, kitty claws lightly raked his lean muscles. This didn't bother him. His breath came faster, his mouth changing angles to go deeper. Wanting to purr at how good he tasted, Evina wrapped her clawed thumb and finger very carefully around his throbbing cock.

That broke him from the kiss.

"I'll come this time," he said.

"I want you to," she answered.

His face flushed darker, and probably hers did too.

"You have to scoot down so I can enter you."

She scooted, not letting go of him.

"Just place me," he said. "I'd like to push in myself."

She didn't know why him saying that was a turn-on. Maybe everything he wanted was going to be one for her. She brought his tip to her, squirming as the satiny crest parted her swollen folds. More cream welled up in her, a longing sound breaking in her throat.

"Do you need a gag?" he teased even as his cock jerked and trembled against her. "You really shouldn't. You're the one using all the toys."

She growled at him, though she was amused.

"Ready?" he asked, lifting one dark eyebrow.

"Do it or I will," she warned.

He smirked and pushed from the hips and, oh, he went into her like a dream. He was just right—his thickness, his length, the little grunt he made when he was in all the way. He might have lost control in the cock ring, but he seemed to have recovered it. She rubbed her hands up his back, groaning with the sheer tactile pleasure of their contact.

"Sh," he cautioned. "You need to be quieter than that."

He drew back within her, biting his lip when her muscles tightened around him. The flare of his rim stretched the nerve-laden area near her gate. He forged in again slowly.

Evina's hands curled into almost-fists on his back. "I'm going to scream if you don't go faster."

He laughed as softly as she'd spoken. "I love how wet you are," he crooned, repeating his pelvis's wavelike motion. "My dick could drown in that amount of cream."

Evina crossed her ankles behind him, trying to pull him in harder. "Good thing your dick doesn't need to breathe."

This time he laughed silently. "You know what else I love?"

"No," she said, miffed she wasn't strong enough to shift his pace.

He dropped his mouth to her ear. "I love that your pussy muscles could crack a nut."

"I'll crack your nuts if you're not careful."

He nipped her earlobe and stirred a shiver. "That butt plug is still in me. Maybe you should use it to speed me up."

"Promise it will?"

He kissed her deep and intimate in reply. If that was meant to distract her, it only worked for a few heartbeats. She glided her hand down to grip the ring at the base of the polished toy.

"Shit," he broke free to gasp when she gently rotated it. A second later, his hips rotated too.

"Like that?"

His eyes flared at her. "You know the answer to that."

To her relief, he took a tighter grip on the posts and began to sling harder into her. He used good long strokes—steady, strong. They pressed into her at their culmination, his pelvis grinding her clit. That didn't make her come straight off, but it certainly pulled her closer, obliging her to bite her lip against a nearly uncontrollable urge to groan. His expression grew more determined, though his face went dreamy each time she stroked the toy over his prostate.

"Mmm," he hummed, changing thrusting angles inside of her.

He hit an unexpected sensitivity in her pussy, some happy net of nerves concentrated in her right wall. Evina gushed, and arched, and suddenly he really went at her. He wasn't groaning, but he was panting hard.

"Come," he huffed, his body focused on executing this new stroke. Sweat glittered on his face, the muscles in his outspread arms bulging. His pelvis slammed into her. "Come for me, Evina."

She knew she was going to. All those delicious feelings were gathering low and heated inside her sex. God, she wanted to go over. Playing with him before had gotten her so worked up. She tightened on him, loving how that made him gasp. His cock jerked inside her, and abruptly he felt fuller, like he'd gained some impossible inch of girth. Hissing, he rubbed the fuller bit harder against her, his shaft continuing to angle to the right. Her orgasm spiked into existence, gone from almost to completely there. With the last of her brainpower, she remembered to rock the butt toy inside of him.

He grunted, his head flung back and his lips pulled into a snarl. His upper and lower canines glinted in the light from the bedside lamp, reminding her how animal men were when they climaxed. She knew the extra stimulation was bringing it out in him. He was powering into her, ejaculating so strongly she felt the heat of it.

The orgasm she'd thought was *there* suddenly proved it could double.

She started to moan and heard a snap. He'd broken free of one wrist cuff. His palm slapped over her mouth, muffling the sound she couldn't help making. Her body jerked, the partial restraint exciting her. Her orgasm thundered higher, points of hot sensation marking her tightened nipples, her clit, the arch of her curving feet. Nate must have liked her reaction.

"Unh," he grunted into her pillow, shooting hard into her again. "Unh."

Wetness spilled thickly out of her.

Jesus, she thought, the climax finally ebbing for them both. Nate slowly relaxed on top of her. He moved his hand from her mouth.

"Christ," he sighed, and it was like he'd finished her mental curse.

He snapped the leather ties on the second wrist cuff, demonstrating how voluntary his bondage was all along. His newly freed hand stroked her ribs. "You okay?"

She nodded, breathing too hard to speak. He rolled without warning, pulling her on top of him. She wriggled, testing him out as a mattress. He was certainly warm, and she liked the way his arms circled her. Though he couldn't quite comb her tangled hair, he did pet it down her back.

"You're amazing," he murmured.

"You too," she mumbled, ear pressed to his heartbeat.

Then, without a second thought for consequences, they sank under together.

❧ CHAPTER EIGHT

NATE couldn't move his feet.

He knew he'd been sleeping—and not in his own bed. Evina lay behind him, her hand flopped lax and warm on his back. Her scent was nice to wake up to, a mixture of peppery and sweet spices. Because of her position, she couldn't be the weight immobilizing his lower legs.

Knowing he had to face it, Nate opened reluctant eyes.

His heart nearly stopped. Lit by a square of sun from the window, a tiger the size of a German shepherd sat staring solemnly at him.

"Um," he said, grateful sheets covered them. "Are you Abby or Rafiq?"

The tiger blinked. Within the orange and white and black patterning its face, its eyes were a startling blue, like the crystalline waters of a sheltered Caribbean cove. Nate cleared gravel from his throat.

"I'm Nate," he ventured. "Perhaps your mom mentioned we were friends."

The cub yawned at him, displaying teeth and tongue. The reaction seemed relaxed rather than insulting. As if to confirm this, the tiger dropped its furry head to its sphinxlike paws. A smile tugged the corners of Nate's mouth. Coming up on one elbow, he stretched out an arm carefully to scratch the cat behind one round ear, working his fingers into soft thick fur. Fortunately for those fingers, the tiger didn't object.

"I think you're Rafiq," Nate said. "You feel like a boy to me. I bet your mother would like you to change for breakfast. Not to brag, but I scramble a mean egg."

A muffled warble issued from the tiger's throat, more like a bird sound than a cat's purr. The cub tilted its head for a last good scratch, then pushed to its feet and thudded softly onto the floor.

"Bye," Nate said as the little tiger paused to glance back. "See you in a bit."

Perhaps this at last made the tiger shy. Evina's son streaked off in a sudden bound.

"Mmph," Evina said, burrowing her face into the pillow. Though she was two-legged, Nate reached to scratch her behind the ear as well. Still drowsing, she hunched her shoulder and smiled.

"Better get up," he murmured. His mood was oddly elated, considering this wasn't his usual morning after—alone in his own home. "I promised your son I would make breakfast."

That bolted her up wide awake. "Rafi was here?"

"Rafi was sitting in his tiger form on the foot of your bed. I'm not sure how long he was there."

Evina pressed both hands to her mouth.

"We were covered up," Nate assured her. "And he didn't seem upset."

"Crap."

Nate rubbed her bare shoulder. "He'll be okay. He must have been curious who was in here with his mother. I don't think it's possible to hide everything from kids."

"No," she admitted ruefully.

"I'll make you breakfast too," he coaxed. "Assuming you have eggs."

That pulled a small catlike smile from her. "I have eggs *and* sausage."

"Well," he said, "good thing I know what to do with both."

~

The weather had cleared overnight. The bright cloudless sky matched Nate's mood perfectly. He sang opera to himself on his drive into work. His Italian sucked, so it was just as well he didn't have company. Breakfast at Evina's had gone swimmingly. Every scrap he'd prepared had been eaten, including two rounds of toast. Rafi was quiet but smiled more than once at Nate's silly jokes. Quicker to relax with a stranger, his more outgoing sister Abby insisted Nate watch her operate the little hydraulic lift for Elf Barbie's Dream Garage.

When he asked why she didn't have Tiger Barbie, she primly informed him Tiger Barbies didn't look any different from human ones. "They only wear stripey clothes," she said. "Elf Barbies have pointy ears at least, and they come in blue and gold. The toymakers should figure out how to make shifter Barbies change."

"They could give them tails," Rafi piped up to say.

His sister considered this. "Yes," she agreed. "That would be better."

Privately, Nate found both six-year-olds hilarious.

Once the twins had been walked out to their yellow school bus and kissed before clambering in, Nate told Evina about the arrests they'd made at the bogus adoption agency. She'd been glad to hear the news, but understood why he was concerned. Though she saw some aspects of the case differently, that sat okay with him.

It was funny, since she was alpha, but she never made him feel he wasn't her absolute equal.

By contrast, the first words out of Adam's mouth when Nate arrived at work were, "You're back on the Galina case. No more monkeying around." Due to the magical removal of evidence linking Ivan the Terrible to the murdered accountant's corpse, the investigation had stalled out.

"We need to find the girlfriend," Adam said, his feet stacked on Tony's desk. He had his hands laced behind his head and his elbows stretched. Because they were powwowing in the squad room and not his office, Adam had commandeered their lowest ranking pack member's chair. Tony sat backwards in a guest chair, which he didn't seem to mind. "Supposedly, Ellen Owen is the reason Ivan and Vasili fell out in the first place. Where has she been since we started full-court pressing her new boyfriend?"

"Hiding," Rick suggested, his pose behind his desk nearly identical to Adam's. "Waiting for the dust to settle."

"Sure," Carmine said. "But where? And why doesn't she care enough about Vasili to check on him?"

"Too smart?" Rick said. "Maybe she's not the brainless bimbo she's been painted."

Nate was resting his hips on the front of Rick's desk, which faced Tony's across five feet of dull brown tile. He had to admit tracking down the girlfriend was an angle worth following.

"I'll go back to the smoke shop," he volunteered, then smiled at the blank looks he got. "You know, the store we spotted Vasili coming out of before we dragged him in for questioning? Didn't surveillance say Ellen Owen's cousins ran it? Maybe they'll let something slip about where she is."

Adam dropped his hands from behind his head. "Convenient that the smoke shop is in the same area as the factory used by those doctors we arrested."

Nate shrugged. "Doesn't mean the owners aren't worth questioning." He grabbed his leather jacket, prepared to go then and there.

"Take Tony," Adam said.

"Two cops will put their guard up. Besides which, I don't need a babysitter. I said I'd go to the smoke shop, and that's what I'm intending. No hidden agenda."

Adam met his stare with thinned lips. Nate ordered his body language to remain calm and non-rebellious. Challenging Adam would only make him dig in.

"Fine," Adam relented. "Take an earpiece and stay in touch through Dana."

Nate hid his resentment as well as he was able.

~

He took the earpiece. In fact, he wore it all the way to Quince Street.

"I'm here," he murmured to Dana before pulling out the bud and shoving it in his glove compartment.

That counted as checking in, didn't it?

He'd stopped at his place after leaving Evina's so he could dress. As a result, he was now too crisp for the neighborhood. He tugged his tie down, opened his collar, and rolled up his shirtsleeves.

You're a stockbroker, he told his reflection in the rear view mirror. *You're here on your morning coffee break.*

He stashed his police ID behind the visor and got out of the low-slung car. He didn't like leaving the Goblinati, but it fit who he planned to be. He sent a prayer to St. Michael to look out for it, then did his best yuppie jog across the steep warehouse district street.

One reason he hadn't wanted Tony around was that he was far more apt than Nate to be pegged as a cop. Today's strategy depended on being seen as a civilian.

The River Smokes Tobacco Shop was a narrow storefront next to a nondescript factory. No other businesses were nearby, giving it plenty of privacy. The inventory on its shadowy shelves was legal, but maybe not everything it sold. A bell jangled as he entered. Nate didn't go looking straight for service. Taking his time, he studied the water pipes in the window display. A prickling between his shoulders assured him he was being watched. The hookahs were beautiful, handcrafted with colorful braiding on the hoses. He lifted a smaller double-stemmed example in what looked like real silver. A quick glance at the eyebrow-raising price told him, yes, it was. He held onto it anyway, browsing his way toward the back and the register.

Whatever their actual trade, shop owners tended to warm up to people who bought things.

Judging a few more items would add authenticity; he grabbed a pack of clove cigarettes and an herbal cure for allergies. Shifters rarely suffered from them, but he thought a stockbroker might. That took him to the rear of the store. Behind the slightly grubby counter, with a camera peering over their heads, stood a pair of men so androgynously gorgeous Nate wondered if they were part fae. One clerk had long hair and the other short. Both sets of locks gleamed the pinky-red of a young sunset. Their eyes were a glacial green, their shoulders disproportionately broad for their slender frames. Their matching T-shirts, which bore the River Smokes store logo, seemed cut purposefully to show them off.

Now Nate was really glad Tony wasn't here. He'd have been drooling, and these two—despite their unimpressive profession and apparent youth—gave off the vibe that they could eat nice guys like Tony for breakfast.

Their close resemblance to photos of Vasili's girlfriend didn't escape his notice. Nate set the cigarettes, the herbal cure, and the expensive silver hookah on the counter.

"Nice," said the longhaired guy. "We don't sell a lot of these."

His voice was California surfer lazy, his eyes cool and sharp.

Nate pulled out his electrum ResEx card. "Got a vacay coming up with my girl. We could do with some unwinding."

"I hear you," said the longhaired guy.

Nate put one forearm on the counter and rested his weight on it. The cashier was part fae, all right. This close, the air hummed with his magic. "Actually," Nate said, "I was hoping you might sell me something more under-the-counter, if you know what I mean."

Nate cast a significant glance toward the security camera. He didn't see the cashier press any buttons, but the camera's recording light suddenly flicked off. Possibly he'd worked it telekinetically.

"Damn things," said Long Hair. "Always cutting out on us."

"You got cash?" Short Hair asked, speaking for the first time. His voice was the aural equivalent of butterscotch. Nate didn't bat leftie, but it made him think of hot seduction poured over cool ice cream.

"I do," he said, straightening.

Short Hair pinned him with his green gaze. Like most RPD detectives, Nate was charmed twice a year to prevent him from being identified as a wolf, which too frequently equaled "cop" to criminals. He prayed Short Hair didn't have enough fae magic to see through it.

"We've got faerie dust-laced Marlboros," Short Hair said.

"Mm," Nate responded unsurely, because this might have been a test. Dealing faerie dust carried a hefty mandatory sentence. Most Vice detectives wouldn't have been able to resist grabbing for that collar. "That's a bit more *oomph* than I'm looking for. My girl's kind of a lightweight. I was hoping you had some of the Outsider weed I've heard about. You know, that Royal whatsis from Canada."

"That's special order," Short Hair said, "but we've got a decent strain on hand from Virginia."

He quoted a price that Nate accepted, which led to Short Hair disappearing into the back.

"You know," Nate said, leaning on the counter again, "you guys look really familiar. My cousin used to go to high school with this serious babe, Ellen Something. Man, you should hear him talk about her still."

Long Hair shot him a sharp look Nate pretended not to see. "Where did your cousin go to school?'

"St. Dunstan's in Little Jersey." Nate knew this was the school Ellen Owen had attended from reading up on her in the Galina file. "I doubt she noticed my cousin. He was a big ole nerd. He's a chemist at Killburn-Waring these days. Heads some development whatsis or other."

Long Hair was as aware as Nate how useful a highly placed employee at a pharmaceuticals firm could be—especially to a pair of enterprising drug dealers.

"One of my cousins is named Ellen," Long Hair admitted, "though I couldn't swear it's the same girl."

"Really." Nate pretended to be amazed. Short Hair came out with a small neatly wrapped package. Nate sniffed it appreciatively. If the smell could be trusted, the weed was more than decent. Surer than ever he'd chosen the right approach, he counted out the requested bills and passed them over. "I don't suppose your cousin would want to meet mine for coffee. Tad would so owe me if I hooked that up for him."

"I couldn't answer for her," Long Hair said.

"I understand." Nate pulled a seemingly genuine brokerage card from his wallet, one he kept for this sort of situation. The front listed a generic-sounding firm and a fake personal line. On the back, he scribbled *Tad Montoya* and another of the numbers the RPD kept to shore up aliases. "Maybe you could give her Tad's number, in case she's feeling curious. He looks better than he did in high school, and he's a steady guy. Maybe they'd hit it off if they actually talked."

Long Hair took the card without promising anything. His perfect face could have been carved from ivory.

"Well, okay," Nate said, putting on a hint of embarrassment. "Thanks for, uh, selling me the stuff."

He took his brown paper bag and left, unsure he'd hooked his fish but hopeful. He'd give it a day or two. See if they decided their cousin Ellen could spin some pharmaceutical gold out of seducing the fictional Tad. If they did, it'd pull her out of hiding. If it didn't, the buy Nate had made was sufficient cause to get the pair in for questioning. They probably wouldn't nark on family, but that too would be worth a shot.

He looked up at the blue sky outside. Those two for certain weren't amateurs, what with the faerie dust and the special order ganja. The average street dealer couldn't supply either. He wondered if they worked for Ivan the Terrible. Galina business included drugs, but part fae could be as elitist as purebloods, and they wouldn't like answering to shifters. He decided he'd mull this over with Adam—as a peace offering.

A contrary impulse led his feet around the corner to the old blanket factory. Seeing the building in daylight did it no favors. The crime scene tape remained on the door but was badly sagging, as sad and abandoned as the rest of the place. Was it really coincidence these seemingly disparate cases had ties to the same two-block stretch? The River Smokes dealers were part fae. Did they know who'd spun the stay-away spell around the metal room? Could the same individual have erased the trace from the accountant's corpse? Carmine and the uniforms had probably questioned the smoke shop owners during their canvas, but they'd have gone as cops. Two sharp tacks like Long Hair and Short would be careful not to send up red flags.

Nate shook his head and forced himself to walk away. For the time being, until something happened or he knew more, he'd have to drop the mystery.

Something happened sooner than he expected. He'd been in his car maybe fifteen minutes when it occurred to him to pop his earpiece back in. The moment he did, Dana their dispatcher started yelling at him.

Needless to say, her calling him a dickhead wasn't SOP.

"Jesus, Dana," he said. "What crawled up your butt?"

"Get your ass to 122 on Park. Ivan the Terrible is dead."

"Dead," he repeated, his brain refusing to compute this. He couldn't be dead. They were still trying to put him in jail.

"That isn't all," Dana told him, her upset causing her to be voluble. "Vasili slipped his minders at the safe house. He's unaccounted for at the time of his brother's death."

"They didn't notice him leaving?"

"Apparently not. What's more, Vasili claims to have found the body."

"Crap," Nate said. When this got out, the RPD would look as competent as gnats. "Adam's on scene, I take it."

"On scene and wondering where the eff you are. You were supposed to leave that earpiece on."

Nate decided it wasn't worth pretending it had malfunctioned.

"I said prayers for you," Dana reproached. "I asked three saints and an angel to steer you back onto the right path."

Dana was notoriously superstitious, her tech-laden cubicle at the precinct scrawled so thickly with good luck spells that the squad sometimes wondered how the various powers she was importuning knew who she was talking to.

"Thank you," Nate said, because right then wasn't the time to tease. "I'm sure the praying helped."

~

Ivan's mansion at 122 Park Avenue looked like an embassy and was probably even more secure. Located across from Resurrection's sprawling version of Central Park, the residence hearkened back to the days of carriages and top hats. A wrought iron fence girded its sliver-wide front grounds, safeguarding it from curious tourists. They frequently mistook it for a museum.

At the moment, tourists weren't getting anywhere near the place. Half the RPD's black and whites appeared to be surrounding it. Nate squeaked his vehicle into a clear spot and ID'd himself to the uniforms. Though he was in no rush to collect his dressing down, he sprinted up the carpeted double stairway in the front hall. To judge by the thickest clustering of police personnel, the second floor was where the action was.

A roped crystal chandelier hung from the foyer dome. It cast an undiscriminating glitter onto the many living and the single dead.

Adam gave Nate a cool look when he saw him, not bothering to wave him over. Rick and Carmine had corralled Vasili at the end of the long landing, away from his brother's body, which the Crime Scene guys were still swarmed around. Nate approached carefully, stopping when he'd reached Adam's side at the edge of activity. The evidence techs were muttering to each other in a way that didn't sound happy. Nate had a sinking feeling this corpse had received the same magical cleaning as the accountant's.

Nate pulled his focus together to study it.

Ordinary dirt and gore were clinging to Ivan fine. He'd been a big wolf: tall, muscular, with a peppering of gray in his beard and at his temples. He was just starting to get jowls and deeper wrinkling around his eyes. He looked the seventy years he was—seventy for a wolf anyway. Rumor had it that early in his career, Ivan had strung up one of his lieutenants on four meat hooks. Because the man was a were, his dangling body had torn and healed, torn and healed until he confessed . . . to whatever Ivan wanted, Nate assumed. In death, the crime family's leader looked strangely ordinary—tired perhaps, but not capable of infamous cruelty.

Vasili was twenty years his brother's junior. Their parents had died young, so Ivan had filled the role of father and sibling. An old-fashioned dagger with a gold-encrusted hilt appeared to have severed both relationships. Thrust between Ivan's ribs and into his heart, the murder weapon looked like it had been twisted for good measure, allowing more blood to gush from the wound than would have escaped otherwise.

The blade must have been electrum. Ivan's wound showed no sign of having started healing before he died.

"That's a helluva personal way to go," Nate observed. "Face to face. Stab *and* twist. The killer had to be someone close to him."

Adam grunted grudgingly. "Someone close and someone angry."

"Not too angry, or there'd be more than one stab wound. We're looking for someone with strength, aim, and emotional control." Nate wasn't sure Vasili qualified—his lack of alibi notwithstanding. Maybe Adam was thinking along the same lines. He glanced at the apparently distraught man Rick and Carmine were restraining. Then he looked back at Nate.

"Where do you want me, boss?" Nate asked.

"I *should* tell you to interview the staff with Tony."

"But?"

"But Carmine's better with domestics, and you have damn sharp eyes. Join me and Rick in the dining room. We're going to give Vasili a little squeeze."

Adam collected their weeping suspect from Rick and Carmine, steering him gently but firmly by the elbow. Vasili stopped struggling the moment

Adam took him in hand. Though the wolf might not realize it, his brother's death left him vulnerable to any strong alpha's influence.

"Ivan's gone," he choked out as Adam guided him to sit on one side of the long polished table. He was handsomer than his brother but not as imposing. The tip of the hawk-like nose they'd shared was pink, the rims of his leaf-shaped brown eyes reddened from crying. His grief seemed sincere, but Nate had seen other murderers spout tears after killing relatives.

One thing he hadn't noticed genuine mourners do was shoot the cuffs of their tailored shirts the minute they sat down.

"Ivan is gone," Adam agreed. He took the seat next to Vasili. Its tall carved back and deep blue embroidered velvet testified to Ivan's fondness for pretending he was a duke. When Rick sat on Vasili's other side, his six-four frame made the grand chair look normal sized. Nate remained by the door as if he were guarding it. In actuality, it was in the perfect spot from which to observe.

"We have to find who did this," Vasili pleaded, clutching at Adam's arm. "Ivan was my only blood."

"We'll catch the murderer," Adam said. "First, though, we need to clear up a few inconsistencies."

Vasili's expression rippled with annoyance. "I told the others. Those men who were guarding me fell asleep."

"But why did you leave, Vasili? You knew your brother wanted you dead. Why not stay where you were safe?"

"I was climbing the walls!" he exclaimed. "You know what it's like for wolves when we're cooped up. I wanted to get some air."

If Vasili hoped to help his cause by reminding Adam he was a fellow wolf, he was barking up the wrong tree. Adam thought worse of the Galinas for choosing the path they had. His features hardened, though probably not intentionally.

"Why did you come here?" he asked. "Is the 'air' better in Ivan's house?"

"It's my house too," Vasili said. "And I wanted to talk to him. I thought if we spoke face to face, maybe we could reconcile. My brother . . . loved me before all this."

"Before you stole from him, you mean."

"That was a misunderstanding!" Vasili's back was up, his defenses beginning to stiffen against his questioner.

"Where's Ellen?" Rick asked, smoothly distracting him.

Vasili twisted around to him. "Ellen?"

When he said her name, a different note vibrated through his energy. The change yanked Nate's wolf's ears to attention, though it took a moment to identify the younger Galina's emotion.

Pride, he thought. Winning his brother's girl was a source of pride to him.

"Ellen doesn't have anything to do with this," Vasili said. "I haven't seen her since you people took me into your supposed protective custody. Ellen is a sweet girl. She's not cut out to be in the middle of this mess."

Vasili's body language indicated some or all of this was a lie. Adam opened his mouth, likely about to press him for the truth. Nate had a feeling this would simply make the wolf clam up.

"Ellen's fae, isn't she?" he interrupted from the doorway.

"What?" asked Vasili, seeming to notice him for the first time.

"Ellen Owen has faerie blood."

Again, irritation flicked like lightning through Vasili's red-rimmed eyes. "She's only a sixteenth fae. She doesn't make a big deal about it. It's not enough to give her any special magic juice."

"She's pretty, though," Nate said. "I've seen pictures. She's got that glowing skin part fae have. And those green eyes that shine like jewels. Nice hair too. Ordinary people don't get that shade of red naturally."

"Sure," Vasili said, not quite selling his casual shrug. "She's beautiful. You got a thing for fae?"

"Doesn't everyone?" Nate asked. "They're Resurrection's royalty, our very own magical golden boys and girls. A man would do quite a lot to keep a female who was even a teensy bit faerie tucked up safe in his bed."

Vasili stared at him openmouthed, too dazzled by the pictures Nate was painting to follow his full meaning. Evidently, just thinking about his girlfriend caused his brain to slow down. When it finally caught up, he shook his head like a dog flinging off water. "You think I killed my only brother for my girlfriend? Why on earth would Ellen want me to do that?"

"Maybe she wanted to be a boss's girlfriend again. Maybe she figured you'd take over with him out of the way."

"Right." Vasili was bitterly amused. "I'm going to take over from Ivan."

The ridiculousness of this suggestion was immediately obvious to everyone. Vasili didn't have it in him to lead, even with his brother out of the way.

His subordinate's theory wilting, Adam decided Nate had wandered far enough off script. He pushed up from his tall carved chair. "You mind if I visit your brother's kitchen? I'm gonna rustle us up some sandwiches."

"I don't think I could eat," Vasili said.

"Sure you can." Adam dropped his hand to their suspect's shoulder, his hold visibly heavy. "We're wolves, right? We'll think more clearly once we've seen to our stomachs."

Him assuming a paternal pose was no accident, no more than the warning look he shot Nate. Reading its implicit order, Nate followed him from the room.

Adam preceded him into what Nate supposed had been a salon. The furniture was as grandiose as that in the dining room. A huge still life of a dead deer hung over the fireplace's onyx mantel. Nate thought the painting might be a real Landseer.

In case the testosterone wasn't thick enough, the walls were painted tobacco brown.

Adam faced Nate with his back to the hearth, crossing his arms as he did. "Tell me you've got a decent reason for grabbing control of that interview."

Nate wasn't convinced Adam would approve of his reason, but he shared what he'd discovered at the smoke shop. Adam was quiet for half a minute after he'd finished. Nate doubted this was a good sign.

"You bought marijuana from them," he said at last, his manner icily sardonic, "which you didn't get on tape, because you decided to leave your fucking earpiece back in your car. The earpiece I told you to wear for your own safety, because it's not like investigating Russian wolves might get dangerous. Oh, and let's remember you specifically asked not to have Tony back you up."

"Uh," Nate said.

"'Uh' isn't going to cut it, Nate. Given the cockamamie story Vasili is trying to peddle, this is looking increasingly like a coup and not a falling out. What do you want to bet Ivan's corpse has been charmed to remove evidence? We can't prosecute Vasili. We can't shut down the Galina organization. We've got nothing to show for our efforts but a dead mobster.

"Basically, this is a cluster fuck. The Police Commissioner already called me twice, threatening to sic the media dogs on me. You had a bird in the hand with Ellen Owen's cousins. You could have salvaged a scrap of progress from this shit heap, but you fucking *let them go.*"

By this point, Adam's chill had turned to fire. Nate set his shoulders into a straighter line. He didn't see how it was his fault that Vasili's minders had screwed up—or that the PC was on the warpath. With an effort, he kept himself on topic. "With the information I had at the time, what I did was strategic. And it might still bear fruit."

"Jesus, Nate." Nate had been hoping to keep the tone of this reasonable, but Adam shoved his hands through his hair the same as if Nate were an irresponsible idiot. "This isn't the Wild Wild West, where you're the only law in town, and you make it up as you go along. You're supposed to be a part of a team, a team I'm the boss of. You need to run these things by me before you hare off."

A starch Nate knew he ought to suppress surged into his spine. Sadly, knowing he ought to didn't mean he could. "I did better on my own than I would have with Tony. Plus, I'd have been in a helluva lot more danger if that damned receiver had been spotted in my ear."

Adam's eyes glowed with anger. "Are you trying to make me pull the pin on ousting you from the pack?"

"You do what you have to do," Nate clipped out. "I'm not a fucking kid."

They both knew this was too much defiance. "Nate . . ." Adam said, more than a bit of a growl in it.

Nate didn't know what would have happened next, only that his heart pounded like a jackhammer. A vein ticked in Adam's temple, like a clock counting down his doom. Carmine stuck his head in the door, sparing him from finding out what that was.

"Boss," he said. "You really want those sandwiches?"

Adam sighed, letting some of the tension run out of him. "Yes," he said. "I want Vasili nice and relaxed before we question him again. First, though, send an unmarked unit out to that smoke shop. Actually, make it two. I don't want the owners sneaking out the back."

"We're taking the owners in?"

"We are," he confirmed. "Nate here made a drug buy from them."

"Boss—" Nate began.

"Don't." Adam cut him off with a chopping motion. "Do not tell me you don't think this is the right approach."

Nate clamped his lips together, though this was exactly what he thought. In the end, it didn't matter whether he stuck to his guns or not. When the unmarkeds pulled up at River Smokes, it wasn't simply closed; it was shut down, its dubious inventory absent, its glamorous-grungy owners off in the wind somewhere.

This, of course, was too easy to blame on him.

The others seemed to think it was his fault too.

"Kid," Carmine said, wagging his curly head the moment they were alone. "You need to watch your step."

If Nate had been a fraction more childish, he'd have said Adam needed to watch his.

❧ CHAPTER NINE

IN return for the babysitting her mother did, Evina sometimes ran errands for Rita. Today, she was dropping off two of Rita's business suits at her old dry cleaners. Back when she and Paul had been together, he'd sworn it was the only place in Resurrection that got the starch in his shirts just right. Rita concurred, but Evina had switched cleaners after Paul's marriage to Liane, because he'd trained his wife to go there too. Running into her beautiful younger replacement on a regular basis was more than Evina was up for.

It's not cowardice, she assured herself as she pulled into the small shopping center. *You see Liane when you have to, and you're perfectly nice to her.*

If Evina preferred to skip the reminder that Liane—and not she—was marrying material, well, even alphas had weak spots.

This afternoon she was spared the trial. The dry cleaner's had no line, and she finished within minutes. She checked her watch, gauging how much of her break remained. She could drive to the little park near the fire station, maybe sit on a sunny bench and daydream about Nate. She smiled, unable to recall when she'd last done something that frivolous. He'd been so sweet and funny with her kids this morning. She could tell he liked them. He wasn't putting it on. Just maybe it wouldn't be the stupidest thing in the world to allow herself to indulge in a fantasy.

Ahead of her, on the shopping mall's uninspired sidewalk, a man emerged from a Postboxes Unlimited. There were other people around. He didn't stand out especially. Evina wouldn't have given him a second glance except that every hair on her arms suddenly stood up.

She didn't know him, or not that she could tell from behind. He was of average height and build, with short, neatly cut brown hair. His suit was well made but unexceptional. His stride was more confident than average—brisk, she'd say, with a smidgen of impatience. He stepped off the curb toward a new-looking black SUV. She recognized it as a converted Cadillac Escalade, too rich for her blood but very nice. As he turned to open the driver's door, she caught sight of his profile.

Still, she didn't know him. He was handsome in a stern sort of way. Then, as if he felt her staring, he twisted to look at her.

The chill that went through her was like nothing she'd ever felt. She knew those eyes. The last time she'd seen them, they'd been above a surgical mask. She thought she hadn't noticed, but now she wondered how she'd forgot. Their irises were a gray so clear they could have been made of glass.

This was the head doctor from the blanket factory.

Except he couldn't be. Nate said the trio had been arrested and, due to the seriousness of their crimes, weren't eligible for bail. Evina looked at the Cadillac owner's hands. She could have sworn they were the same that had smothered the werefox boy with the small pillow. His fingers were long and bony, their nails buffed to a soft sheen. The RPD must have arrested someone else. Perhaps the scheme had involved more than the three men she saw in her vision. Nate hadn't asked her to identify them. Neither of them realized she could.

The doctor's glass-gray eyes narrowed. No doubt he was wondering why she gaped at him.

Go up to him, Evina ordered herself. *He doesn't know who you are. Pretend you're flirting. Get his name and number the way Rita would.*

She couldn't make her feet unstick from the sidewalk. Her skin was clammy, her muscles rippling with shivers. Her fear triggered her impatience. If he'd been on fire, she'd have chased him across the city until she put him out. The reminder of her training let her take a few steps forward, let her paste what she hoped wasn't a sickly smile on her face. *Just do what your mother would,* she urged.

The man's lips formed words she wasn't close enough to hear. The movements were too rapid for normal speech—more like a chant, she thought. Her terror increased, freezing her in place.

Crap, she thought, powerless to budge. Was he putting a whammy on her?

He moved, getting into the SUV and slamming the door. He started the engine, swiftly reversing the shiny black vehicle. The windows were tinted so she couldn't see inside.

Get the license plate, she ordered.

When she tried to, her eyes refused to focus on the numbers. Some power outside her was blurring her vision. Her growl of frustration caused a young woman with a baby stroller to veer away from her. At least her anger broke her paralysis. She dug in her purse for her phone, intending to report to Nate what she'd seen. The number he'd given her rolled to voicemail. She growled again, then left a message for him to call her as soon as he was free. She debated dialing 911, but didn't know what she'd say.

Nate was the only cop she had a shot at convincing she wasn't imagining things.

~

Embarrassed, unhappy, and a breath away from driving his fist through the nearest wall, Nate returned to the squad room to go through the Galina file again. He had the place to himself. Adam didn't come back to yell at him. Tony didn't rap on his desk to see if he was hungry for take-out. Now that his initial defensive anger had guttered out, Nate felt the pack's disapproval like a hunch he couldn't get out of his shoulders. He'd screwed up. Rebelled against the way things were supposed to be. He'd wanted so badly to be the one who was right he hadn't thought through what he was doing.

Nothing he found in the files helped him make up for that.

He gave up when his eyes got tired of him rubbing them. He drove straight home in his Goblinati. He didn't stop in a bar or pick up a fifth of scotch. In his current mood, he'd have overdone it, and that wouldn't help either. He was so deeply into his pity party he didn't immediately notice Adam's wife sitting on the floor outside his condo. Ari's eyes were closed, her head bobbing to the music playing on her ePod. She didn't look much like a mother in her ripped jeans and gray hoodie. A half-full liquor bottle sat beside her hip: Tullamore Dew, unless he was mistaken—Adam's special occasion indulgence.

"Ari," he said, stopping in his tracks in surprise. "What are you doing here?"

She looked up and took out her earbuds. "Good. I was hoping you wouldn't be too long." She got up before he could help her. "Come on then. Open the door."

Bemused, he let them both in and turned on the lights.

"This is for you," Ari said, gesturing with the bottle as she headed for his kitchen. "You're helping prevent my darling husband from drinking any more tonight."

"Adam's drinking?" That wasn't usual, not hard drinking anyway. Was his alpha upset about their fight too?

Ari pulled a pair of Irish crystal tumblers from a shelf. She poured Nate two fingers and herself maybe half of one. She sipped hers, squinched her face, and set it back down again. "Ugh. Whiskey is disgusting. I swear I don't know how you men drink it."

To prove he could, Nate tossed his back in a single gulp. The ensuing burn rose from his belly into his eyes. "What are you doing here?" he asked again in an unavoidably alcohol-roughened voice.

Ari covered the hand he'd laid on his counter. "You know what I'm doing. I'm playing peacemaker. Adam doesn't want to lose you, but you're triggering his alpha instincts. You're making it hard for him to be reasonable."

"Did he send you here?"

"No, but when I told him I was coming and shoved the baby into his arms, he didn't say a word in protest."

Nate snorted. He could imagine her doing that. Ari wasn't cowed by Adam at all.

Seeing he was amused, she rubbed his hand. "He loves you, Nate. Everyone does. No one wants you to end up pushed away."

"I don't want that either. I just . . . There's something prodding me inside lately. I mean to back down, I swear, but somehow I never can."

Sympathy filled Ari's Iowa-blue eyes. "When the people you work with are also family, the chain of command thing doesn't always sit well."

"It's supposed to," Nate said. "I'm supposed to know my place in the pack and feel comfortable in it—just like Tony and Carmine do."

"But for you it's work," Ari said softly. "For you not being Number One feels unfair."

What she said was so true he teared up. Ari saw it, of course. "C'mere," she said, holding out her arms.

She was a shrimp and only had a human's strength, but she hugged pretty well. He felt better as she held him; she had enough pack essence in her for that. After a bit, she sighed and pushed back from him. "You're a smart man. So is Adam. Sometimes, though, neither of you are very good at not thinking like your wolves."

Nate tugged one spike of her strawberry colored hair. "We are what we are."

"Oh blah-di-blah," she scoffed. "Thinking like that is defeatist."

He shook his head, and she raised her eyebrows. Then, probably considering this as good as getting in the last word, she craned around him to peer at something in his living room.

"Your message light is blinking," she informed him.

Nate loved high tech gadgets. He had his virtual answering machine set up to display on his wide screen TV. Six messages showed there now, all from the same number.

Heat rose into his cheeks as he recognized whose it was.

"Why, Nate," Ari teased, "I do believe you're blushing."

"It's just a woman I've been seeing."

"The tigress." Ari wagged her eyebrows meaningfully. "Believe me, I heard an earful about that too."

"Evina is a really nice person."

"I'm sure she is, considering you like her enough to blush." She cocked her head, still amused by this. "I'd like to meet her some time, if it isn't too soon for that. You know I don't give a hoot about the supposedly deathly important cats and dogs conflict."

Nate supposed she wouldn't, given that she'd grown up Outside. He tried to imagine Ari and Evina enjoying a girl's lunch together. It made for a strange image. Though they both were mothers, Ari still reminded him of a street kid sometimes. He wouldn't lay odds as to whether they'd hit it off.

"That's nice of you to offer," he said cautiously.

Ari punched his arm like the tomboy she used to be. "Get your voicemail. I know you're dying to. Besides which, I believe I've accomplished as much of my peace mission as I can."

"Thank you," he said as she swanned comically to the door.

She stopped there to grin at him. "Call your love interest, lady-killer. Someone has to distract you from getting into more trouble."

Rather than listen to six messages, as soon as Ari was gone, Nate dialed Evina on his cell. Evina answered on the second ring. She must not have had caller ID service on her phone. "Mohajit residence," she said in a harried voice.

"It's Nate."

"Oh thank goodness. I was hoping you'd call me back tonight. I'm sorry to bother you—" A thunderous noise interrupted her, not unlike a stampeding herd of cows. "Abby! Stop chasing your brother down the stairs while I'm on the phone. Can you come over? I need to talk to you, but I can't leave the kids."

"What's the matter? You sound upset."

She blew out a gust of air. "Maybe it's nothing. I thought I saw the head doctor from my vision at the dry cleaners, the one who smothered the little boy. Also, he—"

"I'll be right over," Nate said, having heard enough.

"But I—"

"I already have my car keys," he said, which he did. "Lock the doors and keep the kids inside."

"I don't think that's—"

"Please, Evina." He was halfway down the stairs by then. "I don't want to talk and drive. Just stay put and wait for me."

His palms were sweating, his body energized—adrenaline and other things goading him to get to her without delay. His instinct to protect her was as impossible to mistake as it was to ignore.

"Okay," she said, sounding less certain than he was. "But I warn you, it's a bit of a madhouse here."

"No worries," he said grimly, swinging into his car. "Someone recently told me I'd benefit from a distraction."

~

The idea of Nate rushing over to keep her safe made Evina almost as nervous as her memory of the murderous doctor. She grabbed the fifteen minutes she thought she had to tidy up, a task her hyperactive kids weren't making easier.

"*Please* change into your boy form," she pleaded with Rafi.

"We're playing, Mommy," Abby protested. "I'm Daniel, and Rafi's being the lion."

The lion let out his scratchy cub roar to demonstrate.

Great, Evina thought. This is what her children picked up in All-Faith Sunday school.

Nate must have driven from his condo with his foot on the floor. No more than ten minutes later, his inimitable police knock thumped at the front door.

Evina threw one last toy into the box in the living room and went to answer it.

She really, truly didn't expect the relief that flooded her when she saw him. "Hey," she said, and he smiled at her.

It was a tired smile, but in that moment, he was the best-looking man she'd ever seen. His crooked grin was enchanting, his lean build perfect, his crinkling eyes as welcome as a hot cup of coffee first thing in the morning. She wanted to give him a giant hug, but didn't quite know how to initiate one.

"Hey," he answered and bent to do it himself.

They both held on a little longer than they had to. Abby spotted them from the foot of the stairs.

"You're back," she said with obvious surprise. Though she was only six, she sometimes shared her mother's slightly cynical view of men.

"I am," Nate agreed.

He stepped inside and shut the door, giving it the extra hip shove it always took. He locked it before Evina could. The presumption should have made her bristle, but for some reason it didn't. Come to join his sister, Rafi plunked down in the entryway. His tiger mouth gawped at Nate, his striped tail curled around his haunches.

"Hi again," Nate greeted. "Shall I shake your paw, or would you like to change into boy form and say hello."

Rafi's response was to turn and bound up the stairs.

"He's shy sometimes," Evina said.

"Can I watch *Mini-Dragons to the Rescue*?" Abby asked.

"Sure," Evina consented. The cartoon was her kids' favorite. She'd be surprised if they didn't have every DVD of them ever made. "One episode, okay? Bedtime is pretty close."

"And don't leave the house," Nate added.

Abby's eyes went round at being given an order from a near stranger. She shot a look at her mother, who could practically hear her quick little mind figuring angles. "What if Rafi wants to run on the grass?"

"Not tonight," Evina said. "Grandmom's not around to watch you."

With her kids dispersed, Evina and Nate went to the couch in the living room. Telling him what happened turned out not to be difficult. The way he laid his hand on her knee and kept it there while she spoke calmed her nerves wonderfully.

"You're sure he spelled you?" Nate asked.

"Pretty sure. I mean, no one's ever done it to me before, but it felt like people describe. I literally was too afraid to move."

Nate squeezed her knee and mulled this over, staring at the wall opposite the couch. A length of traditional Indian fabric hung there in lieu of art. She wondered what he thought of her low-budget decorations, but told herself just because he had good stuff didn't mean he was a snob.

"Do you think he recognized you?" he asked.

Evina forced herself not to shiver. "How could he? I only saw him in a vision. He couldn't have seen *me*. Maybe he's paranoid and spells everyone who stares at him."

Nate gave her an amused but dubious look.

"Well, I don't know why he did it."

"You said he didn't look like an elf, but did he seem human?"

She considered this. "You mean a human sorcerer? I don't think he could have been, because they draw on their own energy, and the spell didn't weaken him. I suppose he could have been a natural human Talent, but then why would he have chanted? Talents don't use rituals. He'd just *think* me into being afraid."

"Could he have been part fae?"

That hadn't occurred to her. "I don't know. I'm not sure I'd spot it. My ex's wife is one part fae and three parts shifter. Apart from being unfairly gorgeous, she seems normal."

Nate rubbed his chin with the fingers of his free hand, the other now entwined with hers. "Is your ex's wife a redhead, by chance?"

Evina grimaced at being obliged to answer this. "She's a silky sunshiny blonde, like a princess from a story. Natural too. Never had a root in her life. Also, her thighs are thin."

"Hm," Nate said distractedly. She'd expected him to laugh.

"Why is this important?" she asked.

"I'm not sure. My gut tells me this fake adoption case is linked to the Galinas. I just haven't figured out how the two intersect."

"I saw on the news today that Ivan Galina was murdered."

"Yes. Probably by his brother, though—thanks to me—we can't prove that."

"How can it be thanks to you?"

He shook his head; shook himself, in fact. "It isn't. I'm feeling sorry for myself. I spooked some people of interest I thought I had on a hook, and things got . . . tense today at work."

Evina wouldn't let him turn away. She took his angular and wonderful face between her hands. "Nobody makes the right choices every time. That doesn't mean you aren't good at your job. If you weren't passionate about doing it well, you wouldn't be here now, trying to keep me and my family safe."

He rubbed her wrists, holding her clasp to him. Looking into his eyes, seeing his affection and wry humor, Evina began to melt in a whole new way. This wasn't a crush. This was a once in a lifetime emotion she was feeling. The embers that began to glow in his gaze said maybe he felt the same.

"Evina Mohajit," he murmured, "you are one in a million."

Perhaps she'd have joked that he'd known a million, but then an idea hit him.

"He didn't ask for protection."

"Who didn't?"

His hands chafed her forearms, like maybe touching her helped him think. Evina dropped her palms to his hard shoulders. "Vasili Galina. He's not an alpha, but at least on paper, he's Ivan's heir. The first thing any of his more ambitious lieutenants are going to do is eliminate the chance Vasili will claim the empty throne. But Vasili wasn't afraid of that. Mostly, he was annoyed at us."

"Maybe he's too stupid to see the danger."

"He's smart enough. And he's canny, which sometimes matters more. When we first arrested him, he seemed relieved to go into protective custody. So what's making him brave now?"

"He must have a partner."

Nate smiled at her. "Yes. He must have a partner shoring up his nerves, someone who was also afraid of Ivan but not his underlings."

She smiled in return, pleased she'd helped him figure this out, if only by accident. "I'm sorry I didn't get the SUV's license plate," she said, remembering her own brush with fear.

"You did better than most people would. I'll run the Escalade's description. Maybe narrow it down to vehicles with 'MD' on the plate. Doctors like those vanity things."

"Smart," Evina said.

Nate wiggled his brows at her. "I'm not just charming and good-looking. I also have a brain."

"Sheesh." Evina laughed, happy to see the shadows in his face fading.

Nate stroked her cheek, then cupped her chin and kissed her. Heat sluiced through her body at the first slick touch of his tongue. She gripped his shoulders, pulling herself to him.

He hummed, his hands sliding to her waist. He pulled back as if he didn't intend to do so for long. "How is it you taste so good to me?"

"Mommy," Rafi said from the open arch to the living room. "Is Detective

Rivera going to help you tuck us in?"

They'd jolted apart the instant his voice rang out. Evina saw her son was in his Spiderman PJs. From the minty smell he was wafting, he'd also brushed his teeth. Miracles didn't cease, apparently.

"I changed," he said. "So I could say hello."

Nate let out a snort that was probably a laugh.

"That's good," Evina said. "I guess . . ." She looked at Nate, at a loss.

"I'd be happy to help tuck you in," he said. "There's a boy in my pack I get to practice on now and then. Ethan's only a little younger than you."

"Is he a wolf?"

"He is."

"They only change when the moon is full."

"That's generally true."

"I can change anytime."

"I've noticed that," Nate said with a half-smile.

"Mommy!" Abby wailed from upstairs. "My one episode is over."

"Hm," Nate said. "Sounds like you have two cubs to tuck in."

"You don't have to," Evina said, awkwardness rising inside her. "I didn't call you over for this."

"I want to." Nate's eyes were warm on hers. "This is exactly what I needed tonight."

~

The process of tucking in tiger cubs was neither more nor less involved than Nate's experiences with Ethan. He helped Evina serenade them with all three verses of the Mini-Dragons theme song, checked under the beds for monsters, locked the windows, and made sure each child's covers were arranged as they preferred. He left the forehead kissing to Evina, deciding hair mussing was more appropriate for a visitor.

"You're nicer than Gretel Newman's mother's boyfriend," Abby mumbled sleepily. "Even if you're a wolf."

"Sorry about that," Evina said once they were alone in the hall.

Nate shook his head. His hands slid naturally down her arms to weave their fingers together. "Kids pick up things from each other."

Evina pulled a humorous face. "I'm afraid that 'even if you're a wolf' stuff came from her father. My crew told him about you."

Nate was amused. "They must think there's cause for worry."

"Nothing but." Evina smiled back slyly. "You're a dangerous man."

Their hands swung together like teenagers on a date. "I should stay tonight," Nate said. "Until we find out what's up with that doctor."

Evina's golden eyes turned so molten they should have set him on fire. He hardened in a surge that left him pounding in suddenly snug trousers. Her next question tightened them even more. "How do you feel about going to bed early?"

He felt good about it; so good he took her three times in the next half hour. They both were keener to have sex than he expected, and it was quiet but vigorous. Nate punched a few new claw holes into her headboard, and Evina lost control enough to rake his back.

He'd thought that would be it, but she squirmed out from under him and sat on top of his butt.

"Nothing you can do from there," he teased drowsily. "Unless you're planning to dig out your boy-toys again."

"Ha ha." Evina bent to kiss one of the scratch marks she'd left on him. The tip of her tongue curled out, trailing up the short score line. The moisture tickled, but the sensation turned to an itch as the injury healed. She repeated the lick on the next two scratches.

The sweetness of the gesture threatened to close his throat.

"You could leave me one," he suggested lightly. "As a souvenir."

"You'd like it if I marked you then?"

"Maybe."

"Your packmates won't tease you in the locker room?"

"They tease me as it is. On account of my sharp wardrobe."

She laughed, and he shifted around under her, wanting to see her face. Her braid had fallen forward over her shoulder, its disheveled length curved between her breasts. Nate reached to pet it even as her hands slid up the sides of his ribs. They were sharing a supremely lazy state, practically drunk from their orgasms. Nate's cock stirred between them anyway.

Evina gave him a look like, *You're kidding me. You want to go **again**?* Nate knew she wasn't complaining. Her nipples drew tight as he stroked her hair.

"I've had daydreams about this braid," he confessed.

"Oh really?"

"Yes. It's Rapunzel-long, and it winds around my naked body to tie me up."

"Ah. That sort of daydream." She smiled, hands drawing to his hips where her thumbs pushed through the curls of his pubic thatch. Nate's cock stirred more energetically.

"You're very cruel in my dreams," he went on, taking her nipples between his fingers. "You keep me prisoner and have your way with me."

Since her nipples had beaded up, he pinched them. Evina sucked in a breath, her hold tightening on his hips. Warmth and wetness welled from her body onto his. Nate's cock finished stiffening in one quick punch.

"My hair isn't long enough to tie you up," she said.

She'd seen the idea he'd painted, and she was digging it. Her voice had the husky edge that meant she wanted him.

"You could let it down," he proposed. "You could ride me and I'd pretend."

Their gazes connected, their imaginations mutually inspired by the fantasy. Evina began to unbind her hair, the motions of her fingers causing his blood to heat. He didn't want to speak for fear of breaking the spell. She parted the plaits that made up her hair . . . halfway, then all, combing the ripples and shaking her dark curls free. Her nipples peeked through the strands like an X-rated fairy tale.

Nate's hands still cupped her breasts. She took his wrists in her hold, her grip cuffing them. He knew what was coming, and it excited him all the same.

Slowly, firmly, she pulled his hands away.

He resisted, but only enough to give her something to work against. This was a demonstration of tiger strength, and he was enjoying it. By the time she'd forced his wrists down against the pillow, his cock was as hard as stone. He tightened his buttocks to push his hard-on up at her.

Getting what he wanted wasn't going to be that simple. Rather than take him, she dragged her creamy labia up his length.

He gasped, nerves jangling wildly at that treatment.

She bent to kiss him, her curls spilling around them. Her mouth was tender and forceful at the same time. When he struggled, she clamped his wrists harder.

The tip of his penis began to leak, the drops falling onto his stomach.

"You're my prisoner," she whispered against his lips. "You're not getting out of here until I have my way with you."

She made a game into something real, rubbing her pussy along his shaft in increasingly gentle rolls. He couldn't come; she'd lightened the pressure too much for that. This didn't mean her actions weren't pleasurable. She was sleek and soft and her folds clung to him wetly. The contrast between this and her iron grip on his wrists sharpened his perceptions of both places. His spine felt like a wire was tightening inside it, starting in his tailbone.

"Please," he said, giving in. "Take me inside you."

He must have liked pleading when it was to her. Odd little sparks sizzled through his groin as he said the words. Evina wet her wine-red lips and rolled her hips up again. "Please means nothing to me. I'll fuck you when I decide."

She yanked his arms wider. The abrupt jerk shocked him as much as her saying *fuck,* though the shock was hardly a bad one. A throb shot up his penis, an ache of want so intense he couldn't tell if it was discomfort or pleasure. Suddenly, her gentleness was gone. Her hips ground over the ache—the friction almost too hard, almost too sweet—and then she tipped and moved and the crazily pulsing head of his penis was sliding into her.

He nearly bit his tongue at how incredible that felt.

She took him: her strength, her power, her thigh muscles cording beautifully as she pushed down his length. Heat licked down him inch by inch. She wriggled him deeper when he was seated, just as he would have done to her.

"You're mine," she said, growling it.

Somehow this didn't sound like playacting.

"I am," he growled back in the same maybe-I'm-serious spirit. "And I'm not going to let you forget it."

Her pupils flashed, the alpha in her resisting his warning. Nate didn't care. If he was hers, then certainly she was his. He twisted his hands, and her wrists were the ones that were cuffed. Evina yanked, but couldn't free herself. Nate didn't think she minded. Despite the sparks her eyes were shooting, her sheath alternately quivered and clamped around his cock.

"Ride me hard," he dared, low and dark. "Prove to me you're in charge."

She tossed her hair and did her damnedest.

Nate loved every second: every bounce of her gorgeous breasts, every curve and muscle she showed off. She was his tiger queen, putting her slavish mount through his helpless paces. She rode him so well he needed years of tricks to stave off coming. He wasn't surprised when his bulbus gland activated; that primitive part of him couldn't help but give its all for her.

Its engorgement warned him tricks wouldn't help him now. He released her wrists to grab for her hips, needing to add his strength to hers for the final thrusts. She gripped his shoulders, her tiger claws digging in. She pumped herself on his cock so fast he had to bite his lip to keep from shouting.

Glorious was the only word to describe how she looked when she flung back her curls and came. Her abandon awed him, the passion she seemed to have no fear of expressing. As her pussy compressed around him in orgasm, he doubted his cock had ever been so hard. The tightening of her walls on his swollen gland was exquisite—and more than his control could stand. The pressure in his groin hit flashpoint. His orgasm crested, the pleasure so powerful he put bruises on both their thighs from bucking into her like a fiend.

He assumed Evina liked it. She let out a strangled sound, like she could hardly bear how good it felt. The throbbing contractions of her pussy told him she was coming again.

At last, they settled on their backs on her very rumpled bed. Their ribs went in and out as they tried to catch their breaths. He wondered if she'd bring up the fact that she'd called him hers—or that he hadn't protested.

"Whew," she said, her hand squeezing his. "You are a good workout."

He guessed she was going to let it lie for now. That was okay. At least, he thought it was. If all she'd been doing was role-playing, he suspected he might be ticked.

"I hope you're ready to sleep now," he said aloud. "You wore me out good that time."

She rolled up on her elbow to study his slight smile, her right index finger tracing the sweaty hollow beneath his eye. The light touch felt nice to him. "You looked tired when you showed up tonight."

Nate really didn't want to get into that. "I *was* tired. Now I'm also satisfied."

She laughed, though concern remained in her eyes. "Sleep, little wolf," she crooned. "I'll watch over you tonight."

Nate's grin fought through his weariness. "Will you sing *me* the Mini-Dragons' theme song?"

She snuggled down against him, her cheek on his chest, her upper arm hugging his ribcage. "I'll sing you *Bohemian Demon Rhapsody* if you want, though I warn you I don't really know the tune."

"Don't care. Love means never having to apologize for being off key."

He didn't care that she jerked at his use of the *L* word. Let her wonder if he meant it. Let her get used to the idea. For once, Nate Rivera was happy to have a woman think he was serious about her.

❧ CHAPTER TEN

BECAUSE the contents of Evina's fridge had dwindled to pitiful, Nate called his favorite grocery delivery service first thing after he woke up. The smells woke Evina's son sooner than the others. Silent but interested, Rafi hopped onto his chair at the kitchen table mere minutes after Nate began cooking.

Since his feet didn't reach the floor, he had no trouble swinging his legs. He watched Nate work with great attention.

"That's steak," he said. "For breakfast."

"Yes, it is. Don't you like steak?"

Nate had never met a predator were who didn't. He wasn't surprised when the boy nodded emphatically. "Is it your birthday?"

Nate was realizing the Mohajits' budgetary belt was a few holes tighter than his own. "It's not my birthday. Sometimes treats are for no reason."

"That's what Mom says. And then she says don't get used to it."

Nate felt like a crossbow bolt had struck him in the chest. He looked at the boy. Rafi's blue eyes were huge in his narrow face, his black curls resembling something that came from sticking your finger in a light socket. The boy wasn't complaining. He seemed to want to know the rules for this new visitor's behavior.

"Are you sad?" Rafi asked. "Your eyes look funny."

Oh boy, Nate thought as his heart gave another lurch. He accepted he was probably falling for Evina. Falling for her kids he hadn't prepared for.

"I'm thinking about cutting onions," he told Rafi. "I like them in my eggs."

Rafi's giggle was infectious. "You must be thinking about them hard."

Knowing how much growing weres could eat, Nate scrambled an egg for Rafi, then set up Evina's stovetop grill. As that heated up for the meat, he made coffee, proud of himself for juggling tasks and amounts so well. Two-person dinners were more his usual. Everything was going perfectly until a tall broad shadow appeared outside the kitchen door. Evina's townhome was an end unit, or it wouldn't have had this entrance. As a key slid into the lock, Nate wasn't glad for the perk.

He flicked off the burners and pulled his ankle piece in nearly the same motion. Rafi gasped in shock, which Nate took a second to feel bad about.

"Don't move," he ordered the intruder. With a small corner of his mind, he noticed the man had two women behind him.

"That's my Daddy!" Rafi said. "Don't shoot him!"

The man had his hands up, an instinctive reaction that showed he had some sense. His expression, on the other hand, was surlier than Nate would have recommended, considering which of them had the gun.

"What are *you* doing here?" Rafi's father demanded.

Built on the same huge lines as Evina's crew, his azure eyes matched the twins'. His hair was honey-brown and wavy, and his jaw was square. Movie heroes had looks like his, though his obvious ego spoiled them some.

Play nice, Nate reminded himself. *There's a kid in the room.*

"I'm cooking breakfast," he said as mildly as he was able. Though Evina's ex seemed to know who he was, he introduced himself anyway. "I'm Nate Rivera, with the RPD. I'm sure Rafi would run upstairs and get Evina for you."

This made the man—*Paul,* Nate thought he was called—frown harder.

"Actually," he said, "we . . . we were hoping Evina could put us in touch with you."

Nate lowered his gun and stuck it in the back of his trousers, though his wolf half didn't want to be civilized. This was Evina's ex-boyfriend, the father of her children.

Nate wasn't convinced he'd deserved either of those honors.

But perhaps Paul wasn't at his best. He looked ragged, like he'd been on a bender and hadn't slept a wink. A quick glance at the women who hovered together at the open side door confirmed something was going on. Both females were slender, fair-haired, and beautiful. Though repairs had been made, he saw signs of worry and weeping—more in the woman he suspected was younger. She was slightly shorter than her companion and was clinging to her as if afraid she'd blow away without an anchor. Her pretty flower-bedecked cardigan was buttoned crookedly.

"Why do you want to talk to me?" he asked, having observed all this in a few seconds.

Paul and the younger blonde drew breath to answer, but the sound of feet coming down the steps stopped them. Dressed in a button-down yellow oxford and khaki pants, Evina was hurrying to join them.

"What's going on?" she asked, her gaze going around the kitchen. She stopped on her ex's face. "Paul, what's wrong?"

The tall strapping tiger burst into tears. "It's Malik," he said, struggling to speak clearly. "Someone kidnapped him."

"Oh my God." Evina's eyes filled with horror, suggesting her imagination was going the same place as his.

"Malik is your son?" Nate asked.

Paul nodded jerkily. "He's barely two," added the woman Nate assumed was Paul's wife. "Please help us get him back."

"Did you get a ransom call?"

"Yes." Paul wiped his face and tried to pull himself together. "It woke us up this morning. They want sixty thousand dollars. Until we heard, we had no idea Malik was missing. Liane and I ran to his room, but his crib was empty."

His voice broke, the memory overwhelming him. Nate looked at the wife. Liane was crying as well, but seemed better able to speak. Unfairly gorgeous was a good way to describe her. Her teary eyes were the blue of violets, her skin like rose powder mixed in cream. With her delicate frame and features, she gave off an impression of fragility, the sort of woman most men felt compelled to protect. When her petal pink lips parted, Nate had to struggle to focus.

She smelled like a spring meadow.

"Did you contact the police?" he asked. "Apart from me, that is."

"No," she said in a soft sweet voice that made him think of kittens—anxious kittens, at the moment. "The kidnappers said they'd kill Malik if we went to the cops. I didn't want to come to you at all, but my mother and Paul thought we should talk to someone with experience."

"We knew Evina and you were friendly," Paul said, a hint of sourness returning to his tone. Nate fought the smile that wanted to rise at this. "We figured you could help us quietly."

"I could help you better with my whole team."

"Please don't tell anyone," Liane begged. "We took a risk coming here. If the kidnappers found out . . . Malik is so little, and he's . . . special."

She didn't say *special* like her son was the destined savior of his people. She said *special* like he had some weakness. Nate shot a glance at Evina and back to Paul's wife. "Mrs.—"

"Liane," she corrected. "And this is my mother, Iseult Fionn."

Both nice fae names, he couldn't help noticing. Iseult inclined her head to him coolly. In contrast to her daughter's misbuttoned cardigan and jeans, she wore a crisp cream-colored pantsuit with a pale blue satin shirt. Worried or not, she was perfectly accessorized. Solitary rose-tinted pearls gleamed at her ears and in the hollow of her elegant throat. If she'd been expected to pay the ransom, Nate had a feeling the kidnappers could have asked for more.

Filing this away, he returned his attention to her daughter. "Liane, I know this is a personal question, but does your son have trouble shifting into his tiger form?"

"What the fuck, Evina!" Paul snapped.

"I didn't tell him," Evina denied hotly. "Though maybe I should have!"

"Maybe you—"

"*Stop*," Nate said, hard and low, before the exes could get into it. "Liane, are you the person who answered the ransom call?"

Her eyes were round, both her arms hugging one of her mother's. "My mother answered the phone, but then she got me. Mom's been staying with us to help with Malik." She paused, seeming to decide whether to say what she did next. "I remember every word the kidnappers said. It's one of my few gifts. I'm a quarter-faerie on my mother's side."

Her mother stroked her flaxen hair, presumably to comfort her. Her face showed less emotion than her daughter's, but that could have been due to her being half faerie. Faeries didn't believe in displaying feelings in front of inferiors. Oddly, considering she had more fae blood, Iseult seemed less beautiful to him than Liane. Maybe her coldness was the reason. Nate had never gone for icy blondes.

"Can you help us?" Iseult asked Nate. Her voice was warmer than her expression, though he wouldn't call it sultry. The observation was trite, but she and her daughter could have passed for sisters in age.

Nate suspected Iseult didn't mind that at all.

"I hope I can, Mrs. Fionn," he said, aware he wasn't going to be asked to call her by her first name. "Perhaps you could keep the others calm in the living room while Evina and I have a quick discussion. Do you have a phone the kidnappers can reach you on?"

Paul pulled a 4G Elfnet Galaxy from his pants pocket. His hand was shaking, but he was calmer. "I had our other line forwarded."

"Good," Nate said. "If they call again, please send Rafi up to get me."

When Nate looked at the boy, the six-year-old nodded that he could do this. Nate smiled at Rafi's wide-eyed readiness to help. Throwing appropriateness to the wind, he bent to kiss the curly top of his head.

"You're a trooper," he whispered.

"I like Malik," he whispered back. "Thank you for saving him."

Nate hoped this nice expression of faith didn't turn out to be misplaced.

Aware that nothing but sharp ears surrounded them, Nate led Evina to the upstairs bathroom. There, he shut the door behind them and turned the taps on full. She sat on the edge of the tub while Nate leaned against the savannah-themed wallpaper. He was sorry the space wasn't bigger. He would have liked to pace.

"We have to do something," Evina said. "Whatever is going on, we can't let those butchers cut up another child and sell it for parts."

Nate was glad her mind had followed the same track as his. He only wished his own would work faster. He crossed his arms and drummed his fingers on one elbow. Clearly, the powers behind the bogus adoption scheme, the ones they hadn't discovered and arrested, had decided he was too close to unmasking them. Otherwise, why choose a kidnapping target so likely to involve him in the rescue? Paul and Liane might or might not have been steered into contacting him. The baby sellers could have relied on natural association suggesting the path to them. What he had trouble guessing was what he'd done to set these particular wheels in motion. Was the final straw the search he'd phoned in about the black SUV? His visit to the smoke shop for the Galina case?

Until Ellen Owen's cousins had turned off their camera, his image had been on it. They could have discovered he'd spearheaded the shutdown of the poorly named Wings of Love agency. Someone might be afraid he'd find the pivot that linked the two cases. Unfortunately, he didn't know what he knew. If he had, choosing his next move would be easier.

"Nate." Evina reached out to clasp his forearm. "I thought we came up here to talk."

Nate uncrossed his arms and cupped her cheek instead. Her face was turned up to him, shower spray pounding the plastic mini-dragon curtain behind her head. Her corkscrewed curls were springy against his fingers, her skin warm velvet under his palm. Normally, Nate would have been revved by this stage of an investigation. Motion wasn't that different from progress. Today, he was simply praying he could keep these people he cared about safely out of it.

"It's some kind of trap, isn't it?" she asked, her shoulders bracing for his answer. "Malik being taken. You being asked to help."

"It seems likely. Ivan Galina dies, and the following morning, another shifter child who can't change disappears. That can't be happenstance."

"Malik is older than the others, and this isn't being disguised as an adoption."

She was grasping at straws, hoping he'd say this could be a regular kidnapping for money. Nate understood, but wouldn't give her false hope.

"We shut down the fake agency," he said. "Possibly the people behind this are desperate to fill orders."

Evina shuddered. "Orders. Like those children were groceries."

"I know." He stroked her hair behind her ear. "I don't like to ask this, but could your ex-boyfriend be involved?"

"No," she said, quiet but definite. "Not Paul. He has his faults, but he's dedicated his life to rescuing people, not putting them in danger—and certainly not his own cub."

"And Liane?"

"I don't think so," she said less surely. "I've seen her with Malik. She adores him, just as Paul does. I know they probably wish he was normal, but they'd never wish him gone. That's why I didn't warn them to be careful earlier. They'd never give him up for adoption. Overprotect him, maybe, but not that."

Nate folded his arms again to think, rubbing his chin this time. He remembered the werefoxes' embarrassment over their imperfect son. Could similar emotions have influenced Paul and Liane? Nate respected Evina's judgment, but couldn't substitute it for his own. Evina might be trying to be *too* fair to Liane, because she knew her position as the replaced girlfriend created a natural bias against her.

Her next words didn't erase that possibility. "I don't know about Iseult," she said. "I've only met her twice, when I was dropping the kids at Paul's. As you can tell, she's a cold fae fish. From what I've seen, she doesn't mind cowing her daughter, though Liane seems attached to her. I suppose if there were a ring of part-fae criminals no one knew about, she might be willing to help it out. I don't think she likes non-fae much."

Nate drew his hands down his face. Him agreeing with this assessment didn't mean it was true.

"What are you going to do?" Evina asked.

"The only way to see where this leads is to play along."

"You'll tell your squad, though. You wouldn't play along that far."

Her dismay warmed him. "I don't think I can tell them, Evina. I don't know where the involved parties are getting their information. I trust my pack members, but they could be being watched without knowing it. Adam never liked me pursuing this case. He kept his focus and the others' on bringing the Galinas down."

"Your alpha won't like you doing this alone."

"Even so."

"But you know it's a trap!"

His reaction to her outburst strengthened his sureness that this was the right option, no matter what it cost him. "Whether it's a trap or not, that two-year-old was taken. Are you willing to bet they're not going to hurt Malik because—maybe—Liane's mother is their ally? I need them to believe this trap is unfolding the way they want."

"Crap," Evina said.

The word held such surrender and frustration Nate smiled at her.

"My kids love Malik," she admitted. "I worried they'd be jealous about their father starting a new family, but them having a little half-brother is the one nice thing to come out of me and Paul breaking up."

"Just the one?" Nate teased, loving how she scowled at him in response. *She* certainly wasn't going to blow away in a wind. He chafed her shoulders to bolster them both for what he had to say. "I want you to call your mother. Don't send the kids to school. Stick together somewhere other than here. It shouldn't seem out of character if you want to pull close today."

"I hate this," Evina huffed. "I want to fight this with you."

His chest couldn't have ached more if she'd said *I love you.* "You need to keep your family safe," he reminded. "And yourself. I think you know that matters to me."

She stared hard at him, not happy but not putting up a fight. "Give me your alpha's direct phone number."

"Evina . . ."

"That's my condition for going along with this. I know I'm trained to fight fires and not criminals, but if this goes wrong, someone has to be able to call in the cavalry."

"Fine." He told her the number, trusting her to remember it. Chances were, if he needed the cavalry, Evina would have no idea until it was too late. If she got into trouble, better she could reach Adam. Despite the strain between them, his alpha could be counted on to come to her rescue.

Not wanting to leave the others alone any longer, Nate left the bathroom and trotted down the stairs. Liane was in the kitchen with the twins—Abby having finally woken up. Liane earned at least one point with Nate for taking over preparing the children's steaks.

Seeing they were fine, and knowing Evina was calling her mother, he stepped into the living room. Paul and his mother-in-law were on the couch. A space the width of Liane's bottom separated them on the cushions. These two weren't sharing comfort in their time of need. Iseult's spine was so ramrod straight she could have been planted on a stick. Nate reminded himself she must have let her hair down with a full shifter once, or her daughter wouldn't exist. Iseult couldn't be as bloodless as she seemed.

She and Paul turned their heads to him when he entered. Iseult smoothed the perfect knees of her cream pantsuit. Her hands were breathtakingly graceful, perhaps her loveliest attribute.

"Here's how it's going to be," Nate said, deciding to let Liane stay where she was for this talk. "I'll accompany Paul to the bank to facilitate him withdrawing the sixty thousand without trouble."

"The kidnappers said they'd call me with directions for the drop."

"All right," Nate said. "If it's you they want to make the delivery and not Liane—"

"Liane!" Paul had the decency to look horrified.

"You wife might seem less threatening than a man. In any case, whoever they choose, I'll follow him or her to the drop off point."

"If they spot you . . ." Iseult said, lovely hand to her throat.

"They won't spot me. I know how to blend in. Anyway, I'll follow Paul or whoever. The place for retrieving Malik will probably be somewhere else, though I'll coach you on how to negotiate the same drop off and exchange point."

"You mean they could take the money and not return Malik." Not as calm as he was trying to sound, Paul wet dry lips.

"They could. You'll want to ask for proof of life. A video sent to your phone or the sound of your son's voice. He can talk, yes?"

Paul's mouth twitched with an ironic smile. "Malik's a terrible two. He can be very expressive."

"That's good. He'll understand you. If you get a chance to speak to him, say whatever you can to soothe him."

"What if I get nervous?"

"The kidnappers will expect you to be. We'll go over this again. Just do the best you can."

Paul looked at him, and Nate saw a normal scared civilian behind his eyes.

"I'll do my best to get your son back safe," Nate promised.

Paul nodded and dropped his gaze, probably embarrassed for needing reassurance from a man he didn't approve of.

Nate patted his trouser pocket to make sure his keys were there. He realized he couldn't take his Goblinati if he was pretending to blend in. Evina's Camry would be better, but the converted model was a for-shit car. The last thing he needed was for his ride to break down. That left Rick's Buick among his options, though he'd have to borrow it without permission.

"Give me your bank address," Nate said. "Wait in the parking lot until I text you. The people who have Malik may be watching what you do. I'll go in first and badge the manager for you."

Paul rose stiffly from the couch. He swiped his palm down his shirt before offering it to Nate. His tiger strength was apparent in the squeeze. Nate didn't think he was being macho so much as earnest.

"Thank you, man. This is decent of you."

"It's my job," Nate said. "Just like saving people from fires is yours."

Iseult stood a moment later, more gracefully. "You'll keep this quiet, won't you? You won't risk my grandson's life by going to your pack." She held the pink-tinged pearl pendant that hung at her throat, a nervous habit, he guessed. Her irises were pure silver, as if strands of that precious metal had been set to radiate around her jet-black pupils. He saw her appeal then. She was a cool calm lake among icy mountains, a respite from the heat and jangle of normal life. Other women's beauty was crude compared to hers. Most men would consider it an honor to do as she asked them.

"You can count on me," he said. For at least three heartbeats, he meant exactly that.

~

Nate's motto was: if you don't know what to expect, expect everything. Paul's bank seemed innocuous enough. It was a small Resurrection Savings and Loan, a suburban style one-story with a drive-through. The drive-through wasn't going to cut it for a sixty thousand buck withdrawal. As he strode across the grass-rimmed parking lot, Nate saw Paul sitting in his car. He was alone; Liane was being excluded from the proceedings for as long as possible. Paul looked nervous, but no more than he ought to be. A florist's van parked half a block down could have been surveillance—as could any of the five customers inside.

When he'd let himself into Rick's apartment to take the keys to his car, Nate had liberated a few items from his ammo closet as well. He had six electrum throwing stars in his leather jacket's pocket, a tiny canister of knockout gas, and fresh clips for his ankle gun. Anything bigger was likely to be spotted. As it was, he was counting on an old obfuscation charm to confuse the bank's weapons detectors. The bag of pre-spelled herbs had been gathering lint in Rick's catchall drawer, saved for a rainy day that had finally come.

No alarms went off as he entered, so he could check off one worry box. Badging the oldest of the four tellers also went smoothly. Her brows shot up, but she closed her window and went for the manager. A brief discussion with that gentleman reassured Nate he could text Paul to come in. The teller would direct Paul to the manager's office, where Nate and he would be assembling the not-new, non-sequential bills—just as the kidnappers had instructed. Paul wasn't on as tight a budget as Evina, but he wasn't rolling in dough either. The money would have to be drawn from Paul and Liane's accounts, including their 401k—no easy task on short notice unless the cops were involved.

Once again he noted how neatly the necessity for his presence had been arranged.

The bank's offices were small, arranged in a line at the rear of the building along a narrow hall. The manager's office was the last. Paul joined them a few minutes later, carrying the gym bag he'd been told to bring. He seemed surprised to see them counting money already.

"That's it?" he said. "You're just giving us the cash?"

The manager, an older human with short white hair, slid him some forms. "You understand if something happens, we can't reimburse your accounts."

"Sure," Paul said dazedly, sitting down to sign.

A polite knock sounded on the door. "Excuse me, Mr. White," said the original teller. "Your ten o'clock has arrived. Shall I ask him to wait?"

"Tell him I'll be free in fifteen minutes," he said.

There was nothing odd about this conversation. Both their voices and manners were perfectly normal. Nate's objection was that they were *too* normal. The teller didn't bat an eye at the sight of her boss dropping stacks of rubber-banded twenties into a black gym bag. No matter how well trained she was, she wouldn't see that everyday.

Fuck, he thought. *They're in on it.*

Small though the movement was, the bank manager saw him stiffen. A semi-automatic Ruger flashed into his hand, drawn from behind the machine he was using to count the cash. Nate had a millisecond to decide on his reaction. Let himself be taken and see what happened next, or grab one of them to question while the odds against him were relatively low. The female teller was near enough to subdue. Nate slammed her into the wall with his forearm against her neck.

This required more force than he'd intended to use. For a human in her sixties, the teller had fight in her.

Then again, maybe she wasn't as human as she looked. As she struggled, her age-seamed skin began twinkling.

It took quite a bit of his strength and quickness, but Nate got one of his razor sharp throwing stars up against her neck.

"Drop the gun, Mr. White," he ordered, "or I puncture your friend's esophagus." Wolves were known to be hotdogs. They might believe he'd do it.

"Jesus," Paul breathed, half a step behind.

"Drop it!" Nate repeated.

"That's not necessary," said the teller with a slight smile. "Not when I can so easily drop you."

She had her hands up against his chest. She whispered a word, and her fingernails grew longer. They weren't animal nails. From the glimpse he caught, they seemed to be made of brass. Their tips were sharp. Two broke through his cotton shirt to pierce his skin. Blood welled up in hot drops.

"Sleep," she said.

Nate dropped like he'd been hammered.

❧ CHAPTER ELEVEN

NORMALLY, Evina's kids would have been delighted to spend the day in their grandmom's shop. Rita's Treasures was filled with mazelike aisles of treats—including vintage toys.

Today, Abby and Rafiq had caught their mother's restlessness. Necessarily in protective mode, Evina was jumping at every jingle of the door or shift in the light. Not wanting to ruin her mother's sales, she'd shooed the kids and herself into the children's corner in the rear. There she took up a post at the start of the hall that ran between Rita's storage room and office. The position provided a view of the front and back exits. The back was the door to the alley, where Rita accepted deliveries.

Twice since they'd arrived, Evina had checked that it was locked.

Unaware what was going on, Abby and Rafi shared a two-bottomed wicker chair. Together, they flipped the pages of their favorites from Rita's collection of picture books. Though Abby was a better reader than her brother, she didn't seem in the mood to read to him.

"Why can't we go to school?" she asked.

Rafi looked at her like she was crazy.

"I told you," Evina said. "We're taking a family day off today."

"Then why can't we go to the movies or the zoo?"

"Maybe we'll do that later. Right now Grandmom is working." Evina swept her watchful gaze to the front of the store. Two display windows framed the entrance, the little stages behind them arranged around themes that struck Rita's fancy. On the left, she'd set up an assortment of quilts and blankets, which she'd draped over colonial style furniture. On the right, two mannequins in 1950's dress drank tea at a chic brasserie table.

Evina had an uncontrollable urge to confirm once again that the back door was secure.

"Mommy," Rafi said in the piping tone all adults learned to fear, "is Detective Rivera your boyfriend now?"

"I don't know," she said without thinking.

"Why don't you know? Didn't he ask if he could be?"

Evina looked at her son and smiled. "Maybe he'll ask me later."

"Could you ask him?" Rafi suggested hopefully. "I think he's nice."

"That's girl stuff," Abby scolded, shoving him with her shoulder. "First Mommy has to decide how much she likes him."

Rafi shoved her back harder, the pair of them threatening to tip the light chair over.

"Settle down," Evina said, scanning the store again. Her mother was at the counter, bringing out trays of costume jewelry for a pretty female elf customer. Evina bit the side of her thumbnail. The mention of Nate had snarled her nerves. He'd said he'd call when he got a chance but couldn't predict when that would be. To her, not knowing when she'd get news was worse than it being overdue.

"To hell with it," she muttered, rummaging through the purse that hung on her shoulder for her cell. The digits she punched into it weren't Nate's. He'd warned her he was turning off his phone.

"Damn it," she said as the line she'd dialed rang and rang. "Don't you wolves ever pick up calls?" Voicemail activated, telling her to leave her name and a brief description of her business. *Fine,* she thought, fed up with being civilized.

"This is Evina Mohajit, calling for Adam Santini. I've been dating your packmember, Nate. I know he hasn't been your favorite person lately, but if your head isn't shoved too far up your fat alpha ass to listen, he could use your help today. He's going after the rest of the bogus adoption ring. You know, the ones you were too pigheaded to look for? Oh, and if protecting the people you're responsible for isn't enough of an incentive, he stole someone named Rick's car. If nothing else, you might want to find Nate to get it back."

Sorry her cell phone didn't have anything to slam, she pushed the 'end call' button.

Rafi and Abby were staring at her like owls.

"All right," she said, forcing herself to calm. "Mommy lost her temper a little bit. She knows she shouldn't talk on the phone that way."

To make matters worse, Rita had heard the outburst too. Her well-plucked eyebrows were raised as her high heels clicked crisply to the back of the store.

"Darling," she said sweetly, causing Evina to wince inside. This was the tone Rita used to keep her in line as a teenager. "You know I'm happy to have you and the kids with me, but maybe you could try not to scare away customers? That lovely elf *was* going to buy the thank you presents for her bridesmaids."

"Sorry," Evina said. "Maybe she'll come back later?"

Rita rolled her eyes as the bell on the front door jingled. "Behave yourself, Evina-Monster. I don't want to ground you."

Evina grinned at the dredging up of her old nickname. Her amusement didn't prevent her from checking out the new customer. When she did, her pulse started thudding with something other than anger. The man in the suit might look like he was browsing for silver spoons, but she'd know that arrogant profile anywhere.

She yanked her mother out of the evil doctor's view.

"Mom," she said as quietly as she could. "Do you have a key to your news producer friend's apartment?"

"Yes," Rita said, thankfully just as hushed. "Why do you want to know?"

Evina met and held her gaze, aware she was about to ask a lot of her. "I want you to take the kids out the back door and drive to his place. Wait. Make them change in your office first. If anyone tries to stop you, I don't want them to be defenseless. As cubs, they'll have teeth and claws."

Rita's beautifully made-up face was truly worried now. "Darling—"

"Please, Mom, just go as fast as you can."

"But, sweetie, what are you planning to do?" Rita was already pulling Abby and Rafi gently from their chair. They behaved like tiger cubs in the wild in the face of danger, not uttering a peep, though their eyes were big. Evina knew she'd never loved her mother or her children more.

"I'm going to cover your getaway," she said.

~

The doctor smiled at her approach—just a little smile, too smug to show his teeth. His glass-gray eyes gleamed with enjoyment beneath his plain brown brows.

"How nice to see you again," he said. "I'm so glad I have different instructions for dealing with you today. My name is Clarence, by the way. Clarence Beaumont, M.D."

He held out his hand. The air around it shimmered like a heat mirage from the power he'd fed into it. Evina kept her hand behind her back. She had better uses for it than falling for his trick.

"What do you want?" she asked flatly.

"Merely to invite you to a party we're throwing." His offer to shake refused, Beaumont examined his fingernails. "You've been quite the little thorn in our sides, Evina. First that vision, then recognizing me at the strip mall. I'd say you have a knack for sticking your kitty nose where it doesn't belong."

He knew about the vision? Only the cops in Nate's squad should have known about her report of that. Had she screwed up by calling Nate's alpha?

"I'm not really a party girl," she said.

She heard the sound she'd been waiting for, the quiet click of her mother and the kids closing the back door. She prayed Dr. Beaumont was too much of an egotist to think he needed reinforcements in the alley. He certainly didn't seem to understand what an alpha tigress could do.

She flexed the hand she was holding behind her back. "Maybe you should go."

Beaumont smiled more deeply and began whispering.

He didn't get past the first two words of his chant. Evina lashed out hard, raking four long tiger claws down his face. She gouged him deeper than she ever had a human being, actual bone scraping her claw tips. Beaumont cried out as blood flew.

He didn't cry out loud enough for her. The wounds she'd made were filling with light so thick it resembled glowing gelatin. Evina gaped in dismay as the rips sealed themselves.

"That," he said coldly, touching fingertips to his cheek, "wasn't a smart thing to do."

She wouldn't allow herself to run; she had too much to stand and fight for. She leaped at him, growling for courage, her left hand clawed now as well. Beaumont didn't crash over like she expected. To her amazement, he braced and shoved and she went flying through the air instead.

She landed on a collection of bentwood chairs, their legs snapping like kindling under her. Mostly unhurt, she jumped upward onto her feet. Beaumont was already on her, his speed as fast as a shifter's, though his energy signature wasn't animal. She tried slashing his face again, but he caught her swing with his arm.

Hitting something so unmoving sent a reverb along her bones.

Wishing she had more training, she kicked out as hard as she could with her sneakered foot. He went sailing this time, the front display case shattering under him as he fell. Shards of glass bristled from his face and neck like a horror movie, bleeding some but not much. Also like a horror movie, she hadn't knocked him out. At least his movements were sluggish as he began yanking out slivers.

More glowing light filled the injuries.

Knowing she'd fight better in tiger form, Evina closed her eyes and ordered her fear to settle. She needed to change fast, or she'd lose her advantage.

She didn't calm fast enough. The energy of her beast had just begun to brighten when Beaumont started up his blasted chanting again. Her eyes snapped open. He was up, attacking her too fast to evade. He slapped his left hand around her wrist. His right—the one she'd refused to shake because he'd pumped it full of magic—took hold of her clawed middle finger. Evina panted as he whispered faster, her inner tigress beginning to panic right along with her. She wasn't an expert, but she thought he was speaking High Fae.

She struggled to get away, but his grip was iron. He pulled her finger like he meant to wrench it off, his clear gray eyes blazing white fire at her.

In the end, it wasn't her finger he ripped free; it was her tiger claw.

Her tiger's power ran out of her like water, her hands immediately reverting to human. The finger whose claw he'd yanked off dripped blood from its bare nail bed. It throbbed like a mother, thought that didn't especially matter.

Beaumont curled his fist around his grisly prize. "Thank you," he said, only a bit breathless. "I could have done without the fight, but this is exactly what I needed."

Clearly, he'd stolen more from her than a claw. Evina was almost too weak to stand, as dizzy as if she were about to faint. He pulled a pair of electrum-plated handcuffs from the jacket of his bloodied Brooks Brothers suit, the metal spelled so that a shifter—no matter how strong—wouldn't be able to break them. Her strength was hardly an issue. When she tried to tug from his hold, her knees gave way and she fell over.

"Now, now," Beaumont said, crouching down to snap on the cuffs. "You have to know there's no point in resisting."

~

Nate didn't know how long he was out. He woke groggy and stark naked in some kind of metal container. There was enough room for him to sit up but not to stretch his legs. As he pushed onto his butt, he recognized the enclosure as a dangerous animal crate, the sort Shifter Control used to transport weres who, for whatever reason, weren't mastering themselves. The front of the crate was an electrum-plated grill, very likely enchanted to prevent him from busting out. The view through the bars was of a quiet forest. The trunks were as tall as redwoods, isolated splashes of scarlet declaring autumn was on its way. Muted sunbeams angled through the leaves, adding to the sacred feel. Nate had been set down on mossy ground in a glade of trees. Wind whispered through the branches, and somewhere not far away a stream clattered over stones.

He wished the stream were closer. He was thirsty. Unable to do anything about that, he sniffed at his surroundings. Though he couldn't see them in his restricted field of view, people were around, their scents mingling too much to pick out individuals. The composition of the earth smelled familiar—the minerals that were in it, the plants it supported. He thought this might be Wolf Woods, a game preserve outside the city limits that had been established for werewolves to hunt in. If this was true, it was good news for him. Years of running here with his pack when the moon was full had acquainted him with the terrain.

More because he had to try than because he believed it would do any good, Nate braced his back against the rear of the crate and kicked out at the grating. Pain shot up his legs at the force he used, but the charmed metal didn't budge.

"Well," said a female voice he didn't recognize. "Our special guest is up."

A young woman crouched in front of his crate, joined a moment later by two very familiar men. All three had the same pale red hair and creamy skin, all the same jewel green eyes. They might only be part fae, but seen together, in this naturally magical setting, they rather stole his breath. None of them seemed put off by his nakedness.

"Ellen Owen," he said huskily.

"On the nose," she agreed, tapping her delicate proboscis. "And these are my cousins Blue and Brone, whom you've already met."

"I'd offer to shake," Nate said. "But you'd have to open this door."

Ellen Owen's smile bared small and twinkling snow-white teeth. "I'm glad you've kept your sense of humor. You've no idea how amused I was when you showed up at their shop, trying to lure me into the open. How is your cousin Tad, by the way? Still mooning over me from high school?"

"Ellen," the voice of Vasili Galina interrupted. "Come away from there. It isn't safe to tease him."

The annoyance that simultaneously crossed the trio's faces, as if scorn could be synchronized, didn't bode well for Vasili's future happiness. Ellen rose, leaving her cousins where they were. Light as a feather, she pattered across the mossy ground to Vasili, twining her slender arms behind his neck. The invitation to kiss her was clear. Vasili accepted with an enthusiasm that made Nate uncomfortable. As if he couldn't get enough of her, the Russian's hands slid down her back to pull her hips up and against him.

His girlfriend wore a white silk kaftan—not exactly stylish but pretty enough on her. The shimmery cloth was embroidered with woodland flowers and belted at her waist by the sort of girdle princesses wore in fairytales. Hers was fashioned from fine chainmail links, its three dangling tassels finished off by pink pearls. As Vasili groped her and groaned, it became apparent she wasn't wearing underwear.

Ellen pushed back from him before he seemed remotely ready to let go. She touched his lips with her fingertips. "You're sweet to be protective of me," she said.

Nate half believed she meant it—and he knew better. Vasili had no problem at all. "You're my most precious treasure. You gave me the courage to dream bigger."

If Nate had ever doubted Vasili killed his brother, he gave up doubting then. He also stopped wondering why Vasili's minders at the safe house had conveniently slept through his departure. The bank teller had demonstrated how easily Ellen and her cohorts arranged such things.

Vasili must have decided he could fill that alpha throne after all.

Blue and Brone were smirking at Vasili's declaration of devotion to their cousin. They stopped, wiping their faces clean, when Ellen turned to them. Nate assumed she wasn't jailbait, but she looked like a teenage sprite. She had her hands on Vasili's shoulders and hovered on tiptoe. "Have we heard from Clarence and the others yet?"

Her cousins stood. Though Ellen seemed younger, it was clear—at least to Nate—that she was in charge of them. "On their way," Blue said. "Clarence completed his job without a hitch."

A groan jerked Nate's head to the left. Another crate like his sat there.

"Fuck," grated a voice he recognized as Paul's. As big as the tiger was, he had to be squished in the carrier. His body bumped its walls as he squirmed around to sit up. "What the hell is going on?"

Nate supposed this settled the issue of whether Evina's ex was involved.

"Lovely." Ellen Owen beamed, ignoring his question. "All our ducklings are lining up."

Her face was so beautiful with happiness shining from it that Vasili's eyes weren't the only ones to blink.

"She doesn't mean you well," Nate said calmly, pitching his words to carry to the besotted man. "If you think she does, you're a bigger fool than you look."

Vasili gawped like he was speaking an extremely foreign tongue.

"Oh, tut," Ellen scolded sweetly. She waved toward her tall redheaded relatives. "Give Detective Rivera a shock with the cattle prod. In fact, give both of our guests one."

Neither Nate nor Paul enjoyed that much.

"You're her stalking horse," he panted once he'd recovered. "You're going to take the fall for killing your brother so that her crew can step into the power vacuum his death left."

"Don't be stupid," Vasili said down his nose. "Ellen is just a girl. She doesn't have a crew. She's helping me take over from Ivan."

"Really? Didn't *that girl's* people remove the evidence of you killing your brother and the accountant? Don't you think they'll put it back if you being blamed becomes convenient? Wasn't it her idea to embezzle from Ivan in the first place?"

Nate's guesses would hardly hold up in court. They were, however, accurate enough to narrow Vasili's eyes. Observing this, Ellen grabbed the cattle prod from Blue—he of the longer hair and the surfer drawl—and poked the business end into Nate herself.

The zap she gave him was twice what the others had. He was lucky he was a shifter and resilient. Otherwise, she would have stopped his heart.

When she pulled the prod back, she tossed her head loftily. "Dogs like you don't understand true love."

Nate saw that her using *dog* as an insult startled Vasili, considering he was a wolf himself. "I understand that being part fae doesn't make you any less of a two-faced ho."

Ellen's growl of rage gurgled in her throat.

"Uh," Paul said from his neighboring crate. "Maybe you should shut up."

His comment gave Ellen a chance to pull herself together, sparing her from betraying more of her character. "Yes," she said coolly, satisfying her temper by rapping his cage's grill. "Maybe you should shut up."

Since his heart was still skipping beats, Nate decided to comply. Convincing Vasili to switch sides had been a long shot at best anyway.

Brone and Blue went motionless—listening, he thought. "The others are near," Brone said.

Focusing his own ears, Nate heard the sound of approaching feet. They were too noisy to belong to weres, snapping twigs and scuffing leaves as they went. An energy that was almost fae preceded them. The current wasn't steady, seeming to surge and ebb unpredictably. Despite the danger from the cattle prod, Nate pressed his face to the grate to get a better look.

Perhaps a dozen people tramped into the beautiful dappled glade. Mr. White and the bank teller, whom Nate hadn't noticed there before, greeted them. The newcomers were strangers. If he hadn't sensed their group power, he'd have sworn they were human. They looked like any suburban dweller's neighbors. One wore a postman's uniform, another a waitress's stereotypical white shirt and black trousers. They weren't ugly, by any means, but none displayed a tenth of Ellen Owen's beauty or glamour.

Interestingly, though not surprisingly, they inclined their heads to her.

Nate saw Vasili notice. The Russian gangster gave a little start. Maybe Nate's accusations hadn't fallen on totally deaf ears. Ellen must have marked the reaction too, because her manner turned sugary again.

"How kind of you to come!" she exclaimed, clapping her hands girlishly. "Vasili and I really appreciate your help. Now we only need the last two."

Nate's chest grew very tight. He suspected he wouldn't enjoy discovering who the last two were.

He smelled Evina before he heard her: that beloved scent like Indian spices and woman. A man in a blood-spattered suit led her by the elbow into the clearing. One of her fingers bled, which increased his uneasiness. The injury didn't seem to be healing. When she shoved a few errant curls from her face, he couldn't help noticing how shaken and tired she was. Though not as gory as her captor, her yellow shirt had spots of blood on it.

"Beaumont," Ellen said in a lower, richer voice to the new arrival. *Sleeping together,* Nate thought immediately. "Congratulations and welcome."

Beaumont grinned. "Tigress put up a fight. Happily, thanks to some excellent spellwork, I set her straight about who's in charge."

Ellen's part-fae suburban groupies—Nate wasn't sure what else to call them—chuckled in appreciation of Beaumont's wit. The trick the teller had pulled on Nate at the bank had been impressive. He could be wrong, but none of these folks gave off a sense of being on that level. So why would they laugh with Beaumont as if they were equal powers?

A terrible idea occurred to him. What if this gang was organized around more than acquiring and selling magical baby parts? Maybe money wasn't the main motivation. Maybe they were sampling the goods.

If you'd been born with a little fae blood but not enough for power, you might think you were entitled to steal some.

He let out a sound of dismay. The sound was soft, but Evina's head swung toward the crate that held him. She gasped, recognizing he was in it.

Hang in there, sweetheart, he thought, not daring to speak to her.

Paul wasn't so restrained. "Evina?" he asked from the carrier next to Nate's. "What the fuck is all this?" Understandably confused, he rattled the bars that kept him imprisoned. "Where is my son, bitch? What did you do to Malik?"

This was demanded of Ellen and not his ex.

Ellen still held the cattle prod. Seeming not to view Paul's outburst as worth responding to, she resting its tip in the dirt like an elegant walking stick. Her cousin Blue kicked Paul's cage on her behalf.

"Thank you," she said as the firefighter fell quiet. "Shall we get on with the ritual? Blue and Brone, you handle the tiger. Beaumont, perhaps you and Mrs. Norman would be good enough to take charge of our guest from the RPD."

Mrs. Norman was the bank teller. Nate was grateful to be free of the box but less so to be in her care again. Beaumont shifting to him left Evina unguarded. Mr. White, the bank manager, assumed the empty place at her side. Was White as juiced as his teller? Could Evina overpower him and escape? Nate met her weary gaze. Why was she so tired? What had Beaumont done to her?

At Ellen's mention of a ritual, all the part fae's excitement shot up a notch. It jumped again when she began drawing magical symbols in the soil with her cattle prod. The symbols circumscribed a circle, which she gracefully stepped inside. The faces of her gang grew avid, not so innocuous then. She held her slender hand out to Vasili, who stepped into the ring with her. He seemed dazzled, his earlier doubts forgotten. Ellen's fair skin was sparkling nearly as much as a true faerie. She was so lovely it hurt to look at her. When she spoke, her voice was as clear and cool as brook water.

"Take your places, you who have sworn to me."

Everyone who wasn't engaged in guard duty stepped to one of the runes she'd drawn.

"From where does our power come?" Ellen asked.

"From the blood," her acolytes answered in unison.

"And who channels that power to you?"

"You, Mistress," they all said.

"Fuck," Nate muttered under his breath, disliking the way the air beneath the trees was thickening and buzzing. Sensing he was going to try something, Beaumont took a tighter grip on his right elbow. On his left, Mrs. Norman's bright brass nails slid out from their sheaths, pricking his arm in warning. A bead of blood welled as she broke skin.

"Hush," the teller said, compelling him as she had before.

Ellen drew a small jeweled dagger from a hidden pocket in her silk gown. Apparently, she had similar taste in knives to Ivan the Terrible. This one could have been taken straight from his collection—and perhaps it had been. Its three-edged blade shimmered silver and gold: pure electrum from the liquid look of the reflections. "Is the sacrifice prepared?"

"It is," said her followers.

With a tiny smirk, Vasili looked straight at Paul.

Given what he so obviously expected Paul's fate to be, Nate shouldn't have felt sorry about what happened next. Vasili stood to his girlfriend's left. Ellen held the gaudy dagger in her right hand. She put her left hand on Vasili's shoulder, holding him in place as she turned to him. He smiled down at her like she'd hung his personal moon . . . right up until the moment she slid the blade butter-easy between his ribs.

She shoved it deeper as he fell to his knees.

"Ellen?" he said as if begging her to deny what she'd done.

Silent, she twisted the blade just as he'd done to his brother.

The light ran out of his eyes as the heart blood ran from his chest. He toppled onto his side, soaking the earth beneath.

Shit, Nate thought, because he couldn't say it out loud.

Aside from being slightly out of breath, the delicate murderess appeared unmoved by what she'd done. She straightened, turning away from the fallen body to face east again. She closed her eyes and steadied her breathing by filling her lungs with air. She stretched her arms slightly outward from her sides. Her right hand kept a grip on the knife, her fist coated in red as if she'd dipped it to the wrist. Her left hand caught the tails of her chainmail belt. Her thumb ran up the rings to the three pink pearls, very much as if the chain were a rosary.

Nate had witnessed a pureblood fae doing magic on a previous case. When Ellen began her chant, her High Fae sounded as good as his. If what Vasili believed was true, and Ellen Owen was only a sixteenth fae, she'd taken her self-improvement seriously.

His mouth went dry as power drew to her, seeming to funnel upward from the blood darkened soil. The cornsilk strands of her pale red hair lifted in a breeze that blew on no one but her. The breeze grew stronger and stronger, until her hair sailed nearly straight behind her.

Nate's eyes sought Evina's on the opposite side of this wild display. Her expression was as dismayed as his. He remembered stories he'd heard about Wolf Woods: that back when their fae forefathers created Resurrection, these giant trees had grown up overnight. Supposedly, their roots ran so deep they took their sustenance from Faerie itself. He'd thought being here would be an advantage, because his beast knew this place so well. He'd forgotten the local enchantments might have their own agenda. From what he knew, Faerie wasn't a land of sweetness. In that realm, blood sacrifice earned rewards.

Ellen was about to reward her followers. She thrust out her hands, fingers spread, killing knife dropping to the ground. Light shot out from her like the spokes of a wheel, each ray terminating at one of her acolytes. Their bodies jerked, and a chorus of moans ran around the circle. The suburban gangsters' expressions were orgasmic.

For about five seconds, all of them sparkled from head to toe.

Then Ellen dropped her hands. To judge by the way she continued shining, this divvying up of power wasn't meant to be equal.

Her gemmy green eyes opened, her attention zeroing in on Paul. He tried to shrink back in his minders' grip. Nate didn't blame him. The part fae smiled like she knew a joke that wasn't going to amuse him.

Without warning, her aura flared as bright as a camera strobe. Caught unprepared, the flash momentarily blinded Nate. When his vision cleared, a different person stood where Ellen Owen had. This new person was taller, blonder, and more imposing, though she wore the same clothes. Despite the differences, she was familiar. Nate and Evina sucked in matching gasps of shock.

The new priestess rolled her shoulders, the glow in her cool blue eyes deeply satisfied. "That's better," she commented. "Glamours get so sticky after you wear them for a while."

"Iseult?" Paul said, evidently having trouble processing his mother-in-law's presence. "What— Why are you— Jesus."

He shut his mouth and swallowed. Enjoying herself, Iseult laughed huskily. "Really, Paul? You had no idea I was playing a double game?"

Paul shook his head. "Is . . . does Liane know?"

Iseult didn't like that question. Her merry expression cooled to that of the very controlled woman Nate had met this morning. "Liane rarely knows what's good for her."

The answer seemed to hearten Paul. He appealed to her as the more ordinary female who'd shared a house with him. "Iseult, please don't hurt Malik. I'll do anything you want. He's your daughter's son. He's your own grandchild."

It occurred to Nate that maybe little Malik wasn't the grandson Iseult wanted. To her, a handsome alpha firefighter might not have seemed a catch, not when it meant Liane's offspring would have even less fae blood.

Chances were, she regretted her own past dalliance with a cat.

Her lips thinned as she considered Paul. "Put this one back in his cage," she said to Blue and Brone. "We'll save him for later."

"Don't!" Evina burst out, unable to help defending the father of her children.

With an air of amusement, Iseult turned. "Very laudable. Speaking up for the man who threw you over for my daughter. I'm sure you'd laugh if you knew how many times she confided her jealousy to me. 'Evina is so strong, Mother. She's not afraid of anything. Sometimes I have no idea why Paul traded her for me.' As if Liane being weaker didn't explain it very well!"

Evina grimaced. Possibly, Iseult's theory struck too close to her own. "Liane loves Paul," she said. "She won't thank you if you harm her husband."

"She won't thank me if she *knows*," Iseult said. "If she doesn't, she'll recover. In time, I'll steer the poor grieving child to a more beneficial match."

Nate sighed inside himself. Iseult had covered her bases quite neatly.

❧ CHAPTER TWELVE

AS a tiger, Evina had never been to Wolf Woods. They'd passed the sign for the preserve when Beaumont drove in, her presence hidden behind the tinted windows of his black Escalade. Because the moon wasn't full, the rutted dirt parking lot was empty. She remembered hearing other races could use the grounds when wolves weren't hunting, so perhaps Beaumont and his cohorts had spelled the entrance to repel them.

There wasn't anyone to yell to for help, even if she'd had energy.

In an odd twist on gentlemanly behavior, Beaumont took her cuffed hands to keep her from falling from the tall vehicle. The moment she was out of the SUV, she felt the area's Otherness. Her skin prickled with it, but not unpleasantly. The place smelled like Nate—woodsy and mysterious. Evina wasn't sure when it had come to pass, but for her Nate represented comfort and safety. She felt steadier as soon as her sneakers hit the ground. She wasn't up to her usual self, but she no longer felt in danger of crumpling.

Because it wouldn't do to let Beaumont know that, twice she tripped and fell sprawling. The second time, she worked a few I'm-a-helpless-little-woman tears into her eyes. Rita would have been proud. Though Beaumont cursed, he unlocked the cuffs, figuring they weren't helping her balance and probably not in the mood to keep hauling her onto her feet.

"Don't make me put these back on," he warned.

Maybe she should have tried to run. Instead, she rubbed her wrists and nodded a curt thank you. She'd been infected by Nate's play-this-out attitude. If she had a chance to rescue Malik or just find out where he was, she'd hightail out of these woods then.

With a plodding gait to show Beaumont she was harmless, she preceded him down the paw-marked path into the forest without further assistance.

Seeing Nate held captive was a blow. Privately, she'd been counting on him rescuing her. Seeing Paul as well . . . and then *Iseult* had her brain spinning. If the Easter Bunny had hopped into the clearing, she wouldn't have batted one eyelash.

She wondered if Nate had a plan. Somehow, she didn't think she should hold her breath. When his eyes met hers, they were shadowed like they'd been that night in the pie section at Holy Foods. But maybe she didn't care whether he knew precisely how to get them out of this. She felt better with him around anyway.

She hoped he didn't mind that she'd spoken against Iseult hurting Paul.

Her objection hadn't done any good. The two redheaded men stuffed Paul back into the animal crate, jolting him with a cattle prod when he fought. She winced but didn't know how to stop it. Paul was alpha. Of course he resisted.

"Not to be trite," Nate said to Iseult with amazing calmness, "but you won't get away with this. Harming a cop or anyone a cop cares about brings a world of hurt crashing down on people's heads. My pack is just the beginning of what you'll have to worry about. The entire RPD will be up in arms."

The stir of discomfort that ran through some of the others didn't touch Iseult. "You've gone rogue," she said serenely. "That gets the RPD up in arms as well."

"Excuse me?" Nate responded.

"Everyone in your precinct knows you haven't been yourself lately. You've been at loggerheads with your alpha for some time now. Defying orders. Sleeping with tigers, for goodness sake! Your quirky dispatcher Dana filled me in on the scuttlebutt."

Nate was too shocked to hide his horror. "She wouldn't."

Iseult stroked the dangling tails of her chainmail belt. "Of course she would. Her little secret makes her so lonely. I took her to dinner and then to bed. She told me everything I wanted to know. Someone should tell her all those anti-hex spells she uses cancel each other out. I barely had to charm her."

Nate shut his gaping jaw. "My pack will figure out I was working your kidnapping plot."

"What kidnapping plot?" Iseult pouted prettily, looking for the moment more like her youthful alter ego. "Mr. White doesn't know about any kidnapping plot. Neither will Paul soon enough. My daughter I can handle, and you were kind enough not to inform your lieutenant, just as requested."

"You spelled me," he said flatly.

Iseult shrugged. "Not very hard. You were disinclined to turn to him already. No, I'm afraid you bringing Evina here, to your traditional hunting grounds, will look like more of your rogue behavior. I suppose your pack will be surprised about you changing without a moon, but there are indications you have latent alpha tendencies. Dana certainly thinks so, and it would explain the trouble you've been having fitting into your place. Mrs. Sand here is a psychologist." Iseult waved toward one of her female cronies. "She's convinced that sort of stress could drive a wolf right over the brink of sanity. I find it . . . elegant that everything you've been working on will be discredited."

A muscle in Nate's cheek bunched. A second later, he wrenched against the hold Beaumont and the woman with the brass claws had on him. The attempt came without warning, and Nate was powerful. The woman was stronger than she looked. She was able to hold Nate almost without Beaumont's help. Nate kicked at Beaumont's legs, but aside from earning him a curse, that didn't gain him ground either.

The straining of his muscular body reminded Evina—and a few of the other women, apparently—that Nate was naked and very nicely put together. Iseult seemed to like the visual too, though for different reasons.

"Just look at you," she exclaimed. "Who could doubt you'd turn killer?"

Her comment put an end to his struggling, if not his defiance.

"If I turn killer," he growled, the sound low enough to stand hair on end, "I think you know whose throat I'll clamp my jaws on first."

Iseult laughed, seeming not to mind the threat. "You hold onto that belief. It will make all of this easier. Brone?" She turned to the shorter-haired redhead. "Could you collect Evina's gift for the detective from our good doctor?"

Her *gift* was the talon Beaumont had ripped from her. As Beaumont dropped it into Iseult's palm, its edges began to glow. Evina swallowed queasily. The claw was pink from her blood smearing it.

Brone and Blue must have known what was coming next. Without requiring an order, they helped Nate's guards force him into Iseult's circle. As he fought, his bare feet scraped through her markings. The magic she'd put into them was so strong they immediately reformed. Once he was in front of her, the guards shoved Nate onto his knees. This wasn't enough for Brone. His big hand pushed Nate's head into an attitude of respect.

"Be still," Iseult snapped, a strong pulse of power in it.

Nate grimaced but could only strain in place.

"Now," Iseult said, "we're going to put a little part of your lover into the heart of you."

Chanting rapidly again, she held up the claw like an offering to the redwood's gods. A beam of sunlight fell through the branches onto her palm—not by accident, Evina thought.

Faeries drew power from nature, so she supposed this was appropriate. Iseult closed her eyes. As if the claw were a mirror, the sunbeam bent, striking Nate dead center in his chest. He twitched, his aura igniting the way her followers' had earlier. Whatever sensations this inspired, he didn't welcome them. He groaned, his body straining the few millimeters her compulsion allowed it.

The light disappeared, sucking abruptly into his center.

He shuddered like this had hurt. His claws and both sets of canines were distended. His eyes glowed so brightly the radiance lit his face.

He glared at Iseult like he hated her.

Her hand was now empty.

"Stay," she said, giving him the same signal one would a dog.

She and the four who'd dragged him into the circle stepped out of it. Nate and the fallen corpse remained in there alone. Evina looked at Nate, not understanding what had been done to him, only that it wasn't good. He'd begun to tremble, his hands dropping to the ground a few feet before his knees. The earth his fingers sank in was muddied by the Russian's blood.

"I'm going to . . . kill you," Nate swore through gritted fangs.

The others were filing out of the clearing. Two stooped to grab the handles on Paul's carrier, their shoulders straining at his weight. Evina didn't know where they were going; they took a different path from the one she'd been led in on. Perhaps they didn't want to be around when whatever was happening to Nate finished. Perhaps they had more nefarious deeds to see to today.

Evina didn't think she cared as long as they left her and Nate alone. That they were a team, and maybe had been one from the start, she sensed in her soul. If the Tiger Queen of the Universe had offered to find her a bondmate, Evina would have accepted none but Nate.

Liane's mother was the last to leave. She looked back at Evina over her shoulder. "You can run," she said, "but it won't matter. He'll hunt you down no matter where you go."

"*You* run," Evina retorted, anger stiffening her. "Nate isn't the only one who'd enjoy ripping you limb from limb."

Iseult's hooded smile of enjoyment wasn't comforting.

Comforting or not, as soon as she was gone, Evina ran to Nate. She touched his shoulder, which was now slick with sweat.

"God," he said, his back contorting uncomfortably.

"Nate," she crooned, trying to soothe him. "Sweetheart, how can I help?"

"Maybe you should go."

"I won't! Not when they were stupid enough to leave us alone."

He laughed shakily. They both knew Iseult being stupid was unlikely. When Nate looked up, his eyes were gold, their normally dark color bleeding into his wolf's. "Honey, she gave me your power to change without the moon, and she charmed me to use it. I don't think I can stop myself from shifting. She expects me to kill you."

"Then she's doubly stupid. Werewolves aren't mindless beasts. Your human consciousness is the boss. It would never let your wolf hurt me."

Swallowing a cry, Nate reared back onto folded legs. Wolf hair rolled in a wave down his chest. In this new position, she saw he had an erection, which disconcerted her. She shook off the distraction. The shift affected hormones, and his had to be haywire.

"This . . . doesn't feel like a normal shift," he said, speaking with difficulty around his changing teeth. "She sent me mental pictures when she put your power into me. I don't think I'm going to be able to hold onto myself. I can sense the human in me fading."

He panted, doglike, bones popping in his face and arms. "Evina, you have to change into your tiger. Your cat is bigger than my wolf. It can face it down. It can stop me from hurting you."

Evina didn't want to tell him the truth, but she had to. She cupped the misshapen structure of his cheek. "I can't change, Nate. That's why Beaumont stole my claw. I'm stuck in human form until it grows back."

"How long will that take?"

"I couldn't say. Nothing like this has happened to me before. I do know my power to heal myself is linked to my power to shift."

"Crap." The word sounded strange in his lengthening muzzle. He was right about this not being normal. She'd seen footage of wolves shifting. When the moon was full, it happened like it did for tigers, in a quick and painless wave of light.

Nate fumbled in the dirt around him, searching the mud until his fur-covered fist came up holding the knife Iseult had used to kill Vasili. Despite knowing how much Nate cared for her, the intensity with which he gripped it, blade pointed straight at her, sent a spurt of alarm through her.

"She wants this to look as if she has no hand in it," he said. "As if I went crazy, and hunted my girlfriend down. Take the dagger, Evina. I don't want your blood on my hands."

"I'm not going to kill you!"

Another spasm of pain gripped him. He groaned as he fought the advancing transformation. The spasm passed, but not before altering him even more. "Do it for your kids," he gasped, barely intelligible. "They need their mother."

He folded her fingers around the hilt a second before his hands finished shifting into paws. He fell onto them, a monstrous half-wolf, half-man creature. He shook his furry self as if he were wet. When the shaking finished, he was completely wolf. Evina scrambled backward instinctively. Nate's canine eyes had an instant to plead with her. Then, like a curtain dropping, all the human awareness slipped out of them.

His wolf was staring at her now.

Its lips pulled back, its hackles rising in a clear threat display. It seemed huge, like maybe her tiger wasn't that much bigger.

Her fist tightened on the knife. Carefully, so as not to make his wolf think she was attacking, she pushed onto her feet.

Nate's ears flattened, his growl trailing down into decibels only a beast could hear.

Evina's heart pounded with a complicated panic. She couldn't end his life, not on the chance that he might kill her, maybe not even if his teeth had been at throat. Her attitude might be ill considered, but he was still Nate to her.

"I love you," she said, far from sure he could understand. "I hope you'll forgive me if this turns out badly, but I just can't kill you."

His golden eyes held no comprehension, only a predator's sharp focus. Unable to choose differently, Evina did the very thing she knew was a bad idea. She spun around and ran, instantly turning herself into prey.

~

Adrenaline was an amazing bracer. Though she couldn't change, it pumped Evina up to nearly her normal vigor. Firefighters trained to stay in shape physically. Evina was glad for that, though—admittedly—most of her running on two legs was after the twins.

She also didn't spend much time leaping over fallen trunks or ducking low branches. *I should,* she thought, trying to hold onto her sense of humor. *This is an amazing cardio workout.*

The thought of putting her crew of macho tigers through it cheered her up a little.

Nate's wolf seemed to follow her without effort. Wolves loped, she remembered, covering ground steadily rather than at a run. Because of this, Evina could get ahead of him, though he always caught up again. He never seemed winded when he did. In truth, his wolf appeared to be enjoying the pursuit.

Evina was pretty sure he could keep it up longer than she could.

She tried disguising her scent along the path of a brook. All she accomplished was giving him a chance to slake his thirst. The part of him that was Nate remembered her smell too well not to pick it up again.

Evina's weary legs began to scream at her. She considered climbing a tree and trying to wait him out. Maybe someone would find them, or Iseult's spell would wear off. Then she discovered she couldn't change even enough to extend her remaining claws. Without them to dig into the bark, she doubted she'd haul herself very far. She was too tired now to do it with human hands.

She didn't bother cursing herself for not getting the idea sooner. She just wished Nate wouldn't look at her like he was checking an oven's window each time he caught up to her.

Piping hot cherry pie wouldn't have distracted him from her now.

She thought she heard him in the distance, his paw pads not quite silent on the forest floor. Tigers liked to lay in wait for unsuspecting prey, hoping for a chance to pounce onto it. Wolves used surprise as well, but were just as good at chasing an animal until they exhausted it.

That thought pushed Evina from her latest breath-catching pause. At first, she'd tried to run toward the parking lot. Each time she had, Nate's wolf had steered her deeper into the woods. Now all she knew was that she was heading generally north.

She couldn't remember how many acres Wolf Woods enclosed. Thousands, she had a sick feeling.

A small bird startled from the thick undergrowth, brown wings whirring as it took flight. Evina stumbled but caught herself on a vine. The sound of Nate's paw strikes suddenly thudded faster, like he'd decided he'd tired her out enough, and it was time to close in.

When she tried to put on a burst of speed, her trembling thighs simply refused her.

Come on, she exhorted. *Do this for Rafi and Abby. Do it for Nate, if it comes to that.* She couldn't imagine how he'd live with the knowledge that he'd eaten her. He'd go mad, precisely as Iseult hoped.

Before the pep talk had a chance to help, the forest parted before her, taking her and her shaky muscles by surprise. She skidded to an awkward halt on the gritty shore of a dark green lake. The lake wasn't big, maybe a hundred feet in diameter. Trees enclosed it, pines and redwoods, their canopy broken up by patches of velvety blue sky.

Goosebumps rolled across Evina's otherwise overheated skin. In the center of lake sat a large white boulder. It looked like raw marble, its sugary surface unstained by the water's rich green algae. She half expected to see Excalibur sticking out of it. This wasn't an ordinary swimming hole in the woods. This was one of those spots where the veil between Resurrection and Faerie thinned.

Can you help me? she asked whatever deity ruled the place.

She certainly needed help. Stumbling onto this little lakeshore left her with nowhere else to run.

A quiet thrashing from the ferns behind her warned her Nate's wolf had arrived. In spite of everything, when she spun around to face him, she found him beautiful.

His beast froze where it was, perhaps fifteen feet from her. It seemed wary, maybe waiting to verify how worn out she'd become. She was on two feet, and that made her taller. Height intimidated tigers. In the wild, they usually only attacked humans who were bent over or crouching. She didn't know if the same held true for wolves.

She had the knife Nate had forced on her. She'd tucked it, jeweled hilt down, in the back pocket of her now-filthy khaki pants. Left with little choice, she pulled it out and showed the blade to him.

"I can hurt you with this," she said as steadily as she could. "It's sharper than teeth, and it's electrum. You won't like the feel of it."

Nate's wolf cocked its head to the side as if wondering what to make of her strange noises. Reminding herself to show no fear, Evina took a step forward.

Nate's wolf skittered exactly one step back.

With that small reaction, everything clicked for her.

She was alpha to him. Even exhausted, even unable to change into tiger form, her will had the power to master his. Both sides of her nature knew how to dominate, not just the furry one.

The ability was what had driven Paul away, and likely other men in her past as well. She'd learned to soften it, to keep her superiority under wraps unless she needed it for her job. Right then, she didn't have the luxury of pretending to be one iota less than she was.

She stepped toward Nate again.

This time his wolf growled at her, hunkering down on its forelegs. She locked her eyes on the beast's, pushing her resolve at it. Nate's wolf wriggled as if it were going to spring.

"Stay," she said, low and hard.

The wolf snarled out a protest but obeyed, its dark gray hackles puffed up around its neck. Drawing her confidence together, Evina kept the knife up in front of her. This was her claw. She'd cut him with it if she had to. Perhaps Nate's wolf sensed her seriousness. It whimpered and laid down on its belly.

Evina continued stalking toward it, and it continued cowering. Though her heart thumped in her throat at its more-than-natural wolf size, when she reached it, she put her sneaker on top of its neck and pushed.

She didn't do this gently. She shoved the wolf's head into the bracken with all her weight and strength. It tried to move, but she wouldn't let it escape her pin.

"You're *my* wolf," she said, the words coming out as harsh as any she'd ever spoken. "You follow *my* lead, and you do what I say."

The wolf rolled one worried gold eye at her. It would fight her if she gave it an opening, and it had the strength to win. Nate had proved willing to switch roles in bed, but that was play, and his human had been in charge. Even as a human, Nate had issues about other people exerting authority over him. Would his wolf recognize her as someone worthy of dominating him?

She thrust her doubts from her awareness, ignoring the possible cost of succeeding. Doing this was the only option for both of them.

"Change," she ordered, channeling everything within her that had been born to lead. "Walk on two feet again."

Her will rushed out of her like a sold thing. She felt it shake her stomach, felt it shoot down her arms . . .

He shuddered.

And then he changed the way shifters should. A ring of radiant light rolled down him from nose to tail, like a magician's hoop being waved over him. Nate was back, folded up on the ground with his face hidden on his outstretched arms. His naked skin shone with perspiration, his ribs going up and down with hard breathing. Evina removed her foot from his neck.

"Nate?" she said, because he wasn't getting up.

He moaned, a soft, lost sound she didn't know how to interpret. She knelt beside him and laid her hand gently on his spine. Scratches and stains covered her fingers, but all that marked him was sweat. The contrast between her dirt and his cleanliness couldn't have been plainer.

"Nate," she said, bending to kiss his shoulder blade. "Please tell me you're all right."

His laugh sounded dangerously like a sob. "Please tell you *I'm* all right. Evina, I was hunting you. My wolf wanted to eat you."

She hadn't been certain he'd remember. "You didn't let it," she said, rubbing his hunched-over back. "You let me control you."

This seemed a better way to phrase it than saying she'd forced him to submit.

Nate sighed and sat up slowly. His face was his face, his eyes returned to their normal black coffee brown. They were guarded, but she supposed that was to be expected. He touched her cheek with his fingertips, dragging them gently to her jaw. Her hair had to be holding a few birds' nests worth of leaves. By this point, it was more clumped than it was braided. Nate's mouth curved sardonically. "Christophe will be happy to hear you've learned to make shifters change."

Evina supposed this was true. At the moment, she was more concerned with whether Nate was okay with it.

"We should probably try to find our way back to civilization. Iseult still has Paul and Malik. Your alpha will help us if we ask, won't he?"

Nate dropped his hand. "Yes, I . . . I think I can retrace our path. We'll find a phone and call for backup."

She flung her arms around him. She didn't know if he wanted a hug right then, but she couldn't help herself. After a couple seconds, he held her back as tightly. She didn't have words for how good that felt.

"It's going to be all right," he said against her tangled hair.

He was shaking, but she didn't say a word about that.

❧ CHAPTER THIRTEEN

WITH seriously uncomfortable emotions, Nate retraced the path along which he'd hunted Evina. His wolf had been in charge, obviously, but he was inside there too, helplessly observing everything his beast thought and did.

Wolves were intelligent predators. Evina had been unnervingly interesting for his to chase. If she hadn't thought to use her alpha power at the end, he knew what it would have done. His wolf had been strategizing which part of her to eat first—and this was *after* she'd said she loved him.

Shame didn't cover what that memory stirred in him. Left to himself, he wasn't certain he'd ever change into his wolf again.

He took grim satisfaction in Evina trailing more than one stride behind him. If he'd been her, he wouldn't have felt safe with him at her back.

"Nate," she said as he waded across the stream where she'd tried to confuse her scent. "You can't beat yourself up about this. I'm a predator myself. I knew what instincts I'd trigger when I ran. I couldn't think how else to buy time."

"Don't—" *try to make me feel better,* he began to say, but under the circumstances, that seemed churlish. He stopped in the brook to look back at her. Her worried face struck him like a blow: the exotic beauty no amount of exhaustion or dirt could dim.

"Don't what?" she asked.

He put his hand on her shoulder. "Nothing." His throat was thick. "Am I going too fast for you?"

She shook her head. "I just can't smell right. Losing that claw screwed me up. Other than that, I feel a lot better. I'm glad we're together."

He was too, crazy as that sounded. He rubbed her shoulder, about to say he didn't think they had much farther to go. Before he could, a different scent caught his nose.

"They came this way," he said.

"Iseult's crew?"

"Yes, but they weren't moving toward the parking lot." He stepped out of the brook to get a better whiff. Iseult's people had crossed the stream directly, rather than walking along it. "They went south and east, toward the cabins some wolves rent to stay overnight for the moon."

Evina stopped at his side, her arm brushing his warmly. "Do you think, maybe, they're keeping Malik there?"

He and Evina looked at each other. "We've only got a few more miles. I know there's a pay phone near the park gate."

"What if Malik can't wait for us to contact your squad? Iseult spent a lot of power back in that clearing. What if she . . . uses him to recharge?"

Us, she'd said. Nate fought against that sounding sweeter than sunshine. "You could go on without me and make the call."

Evina smiled, sly and small. "Can't. My sniffer is wonky. Nate, I really am better, even if I can't change." Her smile twisted into a rueful shape. "I think channeling my inner alpha gave me a second wind."

"You're sure?"

"I'm sure," she said. "And I'll follow your lead, I swear."

His brow wrinkled at the way she said this, but now wasn't the time to probe.

"All right," he said and turned to guide her down the new trail of smells.

They'd loped along for about ten minutes when they came across the remnants of Paul's carrying crate. The steel looked like the Hulk had ripped it apart. Even the electrum grill was twisted out of shape.

Evina gasped, then crouched to examine the pieces. "No blood," she said quietly. "Paul must have changed inside the box."

Her ex could have crushed his tiger attempting this, but as far as getting free went, the risk paid off. Nate's head came up. An odd crackling noise tore the air, like a really big transformer spitting electricity. It sounded like it came from where Nate thought the cabins were.

He and Evina broke into a run, their hands reaching naturally for each other. To Nate's surprise, the clasp didn't slow them down. They leaped obstacles together, suddenly as nimble as if this were the start of their day. They reached the edge of the cabins quickly, dropping as one behind a dry woodpile.

To their amazement, Paul—in his tiger form—was doing a fair job of holding off Iseult's contingent by himself.

Nate whistled in his head at the tiger's size. Ten feet long and easily six hundred pounds, the striped orange beast was making his stand before the open door to one of the half dozen log cabins. The arcing sound they'd heard was Iseult throwing lightning balls at him.

She resembled a vengeful goddess, her fair hair blown back, her eyes glowing with grief and rage. Blue and Brone lay on the gravel drive to either side of her, the savaged state of their intestines telling a gory tale.

Nate didn't know if they'd truly been her cousins, but he guessed she'd been fond of them.

The rest of her people huddled behind a light blue pickup, probably thanks to Paul's fear-inducing weretiger roars. Of course, they also might have wanted to stay out of Iseult's way. Beaumont and the bank teller—clearly the coolest heads in the bunch—were firing semiautomatic pistols, their hands and wrists braced on the pickup's hood. Thankfully, neither was a sharpshooter. Iseult appeared to have done most of the damage to the furious tiger.

Why he was furious soon became apparent.

A small blond head poked into the doorway behind him—Paul's two-year-old son Malik, Nate assumed. The youngster's head jerked back when Iseult's next crackling electric orb singed his father's rear left paw.

"Oh my God," Evina breathed in a wondering tone.

Nate thought she must have spotted Malik, but she pointed toward what she wanted him to see. Nate's heart nearly turned inside out. A chubby baby in a onesie was crawling toward the threshold, apparently curious to see what the noise was about. A second baby joined the first a moment later, this one wearing only a diaper. With a practicality that would have been amusing if the danger hadn't been so great, two-year-old Malik darted out, grabbed each infant by one ankle, and dragged it back into the cabin.

Holy shit, Nate thought. Iseult's gang must not have killed all their fake adoptees yet. Special Crimes had taken over the search for them, but the best anyone had hoped for was to find identifiable pieces. They should have been more optimistic, or maybe realized that the best way to preserve magical material was to store it alive.

The surviving babies didn't like Malik's tactics much. They set up a wail that spurred Paul's tiger into action. He crouched and sprang, his powerful shifter's hind legs launching him toward Iseult. He would have gotten past another lightning ball, but she was too smart for that. She said a word, threw up her hands, and a shimmering shield of force appeared in midair. Paul crashed off it and fell back, lying stunned for a few seconds. When he shook himself and got up, he was limping. Nate thought he might have broken his shoulder.

"We have to stop her," Evina said, seeing as clearly as Nate that Iseult's attacks were taking a toll on Paul. "Vasili was an ordinary shifter. His blood couldn't have given her that much power. Why isn't she running out of juice?"

Nate couldn't answer that. Because theorizing seemed pointless, he took a quick inventory of the materials around them: a wall of split wood, a bottle of Jim Beam with a dribble of booze in it, a cracked Bic lighter, and a rusty bean can with its lid curled back.

"Evina," he said, "do you think you could sneak around and set that truck on fire without them catching you?"

Evina gauged the height of the end-of-summer weeds that would serve as her cover. "In my sleep," she said, grinning like the secret pyro Nate suspected many firemen were.

He wished there were time to kiss her. Instead, he handed her the lighter and the can. "Put your incendiary device together. As soon as you've thrown it, retreat out of shooting range. I'll use the distraction to charge Iseult. I expect Paul will be quick enough to join me. With her attention split, I think we can take her down."

He hoped they could anyway. He didn't have a lot of experience battling souped-up half faeries.

Almost to his dismay, Evina rigged the exploding bean can—including a fuse ripped from the tail of her shirt—in less than two minutes.

"You should take this," she said, offering him the hilt of the dagger she'd held onto all this time.

He didn't want it, partly because he thought she should keep it to defend herself. "It might be spelled. I don't think I should bring it near Iseult again."

Evina peered dubiously at him, then decided not to argue.

"See you soon," she said, and took off in a running crouch.

Tigers had a reputation for hunting like shadows. Evina didn't disprove the stereotype. Silent as a ghost, she melted into the reeds like she was part of them, her dirty yellow oxford excellent camouflage. He barely heard her toss the can underneath the car. Her targets certainly didn't. The fuse stayed lit long enough to ignite the alcohol-soaked wood chips. They burned brighter than the cotton, the twigs they were bundled with catching too. Their forking branches were designed to carry the flames upward.

Catch the oil reserve, he prayed. Cars didn't run on gasoline in Resurrection, but their gears still used lubricant. Nate hoped this one was extra greased.

Thirty nail-biting seconds later, the truck went up in a beautiful ball of fire. The blast blew Iseult's crew back like crash dummies, though Nate didn't have a chance to ascertain how badly they'd been hurt.

Here goes nothing, he thought as he vaulted over the cords of wood.

He blurred toward Iseult with all the shifter speed he could muster, not wanting to give her time to put up another shield. Paul let out a roar as Nate slammed into her, carrying Iseult and himself to the gravel drive. Fortunately, Paul figured out what was happening. Nate's hands were full enough grappling with an enraged part faerie. He didn't need to deal with the tiger too.

Whatever qualms he might have had about trying to hurt a woman he lost when he realized she had more raw strength. She made him glad for every bit of his quickness and training.

To discourage her from chanting, first chance he got, he drove his fist hard into her mouth, knocking out a portion of her pretty snow-white teeth. Iseult's head jerked back in pain and amazement. Nate had a feeling she'd never been hit like this in her life.

Then she spat blood at him.

To his relief, the blood wasn't magic and only blinded him temporarily. By this time, Paul's tiger was circling them as they wrestled back and forth. For once, the tiger's size wasn't an advantage. Paul had trouble finding an angle of attack that wouldn't result in him chomping down on Nate as well.

Iseult noticed Nate's ally closing in. She made an angry gurgling noise and started building another lightning ball in her palm.

Nate guessed she didn't need to chant for that.

Hoping to distract her again, he aimed a punch toward her nose. She wrenched away before the blow connected, kneeing him in the groin instead.

Nate saw stars—thanks to being naked—but refused to let go. Iseult's baby lightning was now as big as a golf ball. The missiles she'd lobbed at Paul had been soccer size. Preferring not to wait for that, Nate grabbed her wrist and walloped her forearm down.

Nothing happened. Her arm didn't snap, and her lightning ball didn't stop accumulating new layers of sparks. She grinned at him through her broken teeth, the smile crazy looking in the bloody mask he'd made of her face. In Nate's opinion, she should have been in too much pain for that.

Then he noticed what her left hand was doing.

She'd grabbed the triple tail of her chainmail belt, its pearl finials clenched within her fist. He remembered what he'd seen her wearing that morning: two pink pearl earrings and one pink pearl pendant.

The answer came to him in a flash. These were the same three pearls. Her power wasn't unlimited, nor was her constant rubbing of the jewelry a nervous habit. She was storing extra energy in them. She had a damn backup battery.

He wondered if the pearls were pink from being soaked in baby's blood.

"Her belt!" he cried to Paul. "Rip it off of her with your teeth!"

That made her angry. With the surge of strength her fury brought, she rolled Nate under her. Struggling against the clamp he had on her wrist, she tried to force her lightning-making hand down toward him. The crackling sphere she held might be small, but she seemed to be hoping to push it into his cranium.

Nate didn't want to discover what that would do to his gray matter.

At least the change in position, with her on top of him, allowed Paul a clear path to dart in from behind. He got his shearing teeth under her belt first try. Apparently, the chainmail links weren't ordinary steel. He tugged Iseult *and* Nate backwards in his efforts to make them snap.

Iseult tried pushing the lighting back at the tiger. Nate jerked her toward him for a head butt that should have scrambled both their brains.

"Screw you," she spat as a pistol coughed.

Beaumont and the teller had gotten back in the game.

The tiger yelped, so Nate guessed the bullet had struck him—and that it was electrum. It mustn't have done worse than crease his hide. Paul continued worrying at Iseult's belt. Convinced that getting it off her was the important thing, Nate heaved upward until he was kneeling. This positioned his back between Paul and the two shooters. Hopefully, they wouldn't target him for fear of the bullet passing through his body to Iseult's. Ammo that hurt shifters damaged faeries too.

"Pull!" he exhorted Paul. "Use the strength that broke that crate apart!"

Paul's tiger muscles bunched for one great heave. Another shot barked at them. A streak of fire licked Nate's shoulder. *Fuck it,* he thought to the pain. He sprang off his knees in a move too fast for Iseult to counter, the brief air space enabling him to whip his legs out straight. He drove his heels through the gravel and down into the earth. Braced, he pulled Iseult the opposite way from Paul, thus increasing the strain on her belt.

With perfect timing, Paul yanked massively backward.

At last, the tiger was successful. The girdle snapped, dragged from Iseult's waist and hold as the tiger tumbled backward tail over head.

The lightning ball sputtered out. Iseult threw back her head and screamed.

She did this from more than rage. Her stored-up power had been protecting her from the brunt of her injuries. Deprived of its support, her wounds turned into those a human would have suffered if Nate had used shifter strength on one. A crack appeared in her forehead from his head butt. Her lightning-throwing arm shattered even as he held it, her soft skin and lax muscles all that held it together. The punch he'd driven into her mouth caused the lower half of her face to cave. The light went out of her eyes before he could think about helping her.

Nate didn't waste valuable time mourning. Thrusting her limp body off of his, he turned and sprang over the smoldering pickup toward the shooters. Beaumont and the terrified teller got two more wild shots off. After that, he had them on the ground. Their struggles were mostly symbolic. When Iseult lost her power, it must have drained theirs too.

Evina was smart enough to dash out of hiding and grab the guns. With one pistol in each feminine fist, she ordered the rest of the cowering crew to freeze. They didn't seem inclined to run, as black-faced from the truck's explosion as coal mine employees.

"Hands behind your heads!" she barked, not taking chances. "Don't try any tricky stuff."

She uttered this with such gusto Nate thought she must have played cops and robbers back when she was a cub.

"Thanks," Nate said, hiding his amusement.

"My pleasure," she responded.

A slow clapping noise came from the nearest stretch of trees. Nate barely had strength to tense, but he did.

Then Tony stepped from the trees' shadows, bristling with assault gear and grinning like a bandit. Adam was behind him.

"Bro," Tony said with a smirk. "Naked fighting! I gotta say that is a bold fashion choice, but it looks good on you."

"Fuck," was the only retort Nate could come up with.

"Guess we missed the party," Rick added from a different direction. Tony's big brother was strolling out from between two cabins with Carmine beside him. "This all of them that you know?"

"Yes," Nate said, having done a quick headcount. He must have been tired, because seeing his pack riding in to help brought a sting to his eyes.

"Your kittycat know how to handle those?" Carmine asked, eyeing Evina and her double fistful of pistols.

"She does," Evina answered dryly, not turning from her targets to look at him.

Since she seemed steady, Nate shook his head for Carmine not to take the guns from her. "Toss me a couple cuffs," he said to Tony. "I want these two squared away."

Tony threw him the requested items, unable to resist reminding him that's what pockets were for. Beaumont and Mrs. Norman lay limp as he snapped them on, the fight literally run out of them. Seeing he had them under control, Rick and Carmine went to help secure Evina's group.

"You know," Rick said, stealing a page from his brother's book, "it looks like your girlfriend collared more perps than you."

"Jesus," Adam said—but not at their ribbing. His eyes had widened at something behind them all.

Nate turned to see and couldn't help smiling. Paul looked like a fricking fire department recruiting poster emerging from the central cabin in human form. Shirtless, he'd found a pair of too-short trousers and seemed to have healed most of his injuries. This, however, wasn't what made him noteworthy. On each of his giant arms, he carried two wriggling one-year-olds. A fifth was squished between the others, held up mostly by the fact that there wasn't room for any more on Paul's chest. Nate doubted he'd truly needed to tote them all out at once, but he understood the impulse. As if they knew they were safe, none of the babies were crying.

Though his father's arms were obviously full, Paul's son Malik appeared to think he ought to be carried too.

"I 'tected!" he yelled, tugging at Paul's pant's leg. "I 'tected good, Daddy!"

Completely charmed, Nate strode to Malik and picked him up. This startled the boy but didn't upset him. "You protected *great*," Nate said. "You should be really proud of yourself."

"Thanks," Paul said over his armload. "You probably saved our lives back there."

"I'd say that's mutual," Nate replied honestly.

Paul looked slightly embarrassed, making Nate want to laugh. Even now the tiger didn't relish being allied to a wolf.

❧ CHAPTER FOURTEEN

JOKING around aside, Nate's squad took over efficiently. Evina found herself downtown and giving Carmine a statement almost before realizing her and Nate's big quest was over.

"Couldn't I talk to Nate before we do this?" she asked the older wolf.

"He's giving a statement too," Carmine said.

He seemed good-humored and kind, everyone's favorite uncle. Evina suspected this was his best weapon.

"We didn't do anything wrong," she said. "We closed an investigation your squad didn't want to pursue."

He leaned back in his steel chair, a legal pad and mini-recorder sitting ostentatiously on the interrogation room's scribbled-on table. Evina had been interested to see the place Nate worked, but this room smelled like bad coffee and old sneakers. Thus far, Carmine hadn't turned the recorder on.

"Do I need a lawyer?" she asked tartly.

"Do you think you do?" Carmine responded.

"What about the kids we saved? At least tell me they're all right."

"Child Services is taking care of them."

As a firefighter, Evina had experience with Child Services' well meaning but occasionally idiotic employees. "What about the children's parents? Some of them may have rethought their decision to give them up for adoption. Surely those kids would be better off at home."

"Are you telling us how to do our jobs?" Carmine inquired softly.

"Well, fuck," she said, losing what was left of her patience. "Someone needs to. Nate is an amazing man—and an amazing cop. He'd have taken a bullet to save those kids, a bullet that was meant for my ex. That alone ought to earn him a medal."

Carmine smiled, his amusement seeming genuine. "You mean, we ought to give him one if we don't have our heads too far up our fat asses?"

Evina flinched in spite of her anger. She'd forgotten the angry voicemail she'd left Nate's boss that morning.

Carmine chuckled, his slightly stocky belly shaking with the laugh. "Relax. I'm not trying to trip you up. It's simply obvious there are . . . irregularities about what happened today. The criminal mastermind was your ex's mother-in-law. You and Nate are dating. All of us feel bad about Nate being left hanging out to dry—no one worse than our alpha, believe you me. We need the whole story before we can figure out how to edit it."

"You need to know everything?" Evina asked unsurely, her thumbnail finding a place to worry between two teeth.

"Well," Carmine vacillated, "no sex stuff, if that happened to happen. Bad enough I had to watch Tony ogle Nate in the buff . . ."

~

"How'd you find us?" Nate asked Rick.

Nate knew he was in Interrogation to spill his story to the squad's beta. That didn't mean Rick couldn't supply a few answers first.

This probably indicated Nate hadn't learned his lesson about sticking to his place.

Rick seemed to know this—and find it amusing. "You girlfriend informed Adam you stole my car. We tracked its GPS to the bank, where the manager and senior teller were taking a mysteriously long errand. When the black SUV you'd put a search on turned out to be one of that branch's best customers, we put the computer boys on tracking that instead."

Rick spread his hands like it had been simple.

"That was Tony's stroke of genius, wasn't it?" Nate guessed.

Rick laughed at him. "Bro, you know us too well."

It was all *bro* now, apparently.

"We're sorry," Rick said, seeing his expression. "You have no idea how much."

Nate sighed, because that didn't really matter—not compared to the rest of it. "What's happening with the tiger?"

"Shifter Counseling has him for now. He was pretty shook up after mauling those two part faeries, not to mention seeing his cub at risk. Once they're convinced he can handle it, we'll go through the drill with him."

"Counseling might want to talk to the wife as well. She's going to have a pretty weird funeral to plan."

"You could give us a little credit for having sense."

"You thought of that," Nate said.

"We thought of it," Rick confirmed. "That family isn't going to be abandoned just because a criminal made a home in it." He hesitated, then unbent. "But I understand why you asked."

A counselor would have said they were acting like grown-ups. Nate strove to keep his next question from sounding like a challenge. "Adam and Tony are questioning the people we arrested?"

"Carmine will too, when he's done with your kittycat."

He just *had* to put it like that. "Her name is Evina Mohajit," Nate said. "And she's an incredibly brave woman."

Rick smiled down at his legal pad, his well-bitten pencil tapping it.

"I could tell," he said. "She didn't once scream in horror at the sight of you naked."

~

Nate finished up with Rick in about half an hour. Until his actions could be ruled on officially, the squad was keeping him away from the rest of the interviews—which Rick trotted off to join like he couldn't wait to sink his teeth in.

Evina was still with Carmine.

Nate had a nagging urge to poke his head in on them, to reassure himself she was all right. He hadn't liked the others separating them, though he understood why they did. Looked at straight on, Nate had acted without his superior's knowledge. His pack wanted to make sure they got the whole story. They were the only people they wanted colluding to fudge the facts.

They didn't understand Nate couldn't have cared less what Evina told them—good, bad, or indifferent. The compulsion to protect her, to make up for what he'd almost done was all his instincts were locked on.

It was funny, in a sick way. Iseult had twisted his wolf's natural responses to work against its own self-interest. Mates didn't hunt each other. Mates had each other's backs.

She's my mate, he thought, testing out the words. *I love her, and I don't ever want to hurt her again.*

His stomach clenched, nerves tightening like he was gearing up for battle. Restless and with nowhere to spend his energy, he wandered to the break room.

He expected it to be empty, but Dana was in there. She'd just poured fake creamer into her coffee and was stirring it with a swizzle stick.

"Hey, Rivera," she said. "Congrats on the hero stuff. Want me to fix you a cup?"

He shook his head. He avoided the squad room's coffee whenever possible. He studied Dana, who didn't look different that he could tell. She wore her usual New Age-y clothing, complete with multiple evil eye necklaces and saints medals. She was a pretty girl under the goofiness—not a movie star but attractive. She didn't look like she harbored compromising secrets. Before this, he'd have sworn her differences were entirely out in the open.

She certainly didn't seem aware that her loose lips could have sunk his ship. Maybe she didn't know. Iseult could have glamoured herself to look like anyone when she seduced her.

Nate wondered why Dana hadn't come out as a lesbian. Tony's announcement had gone all right, maybe a bump or two on the way but nothing they hadn't gotten over. Didn't Dana know they'd accept her too? Then again, Dana was neither wolf nor pack. Had that influenced her expectations? Nate knew firsthand that feeling like an outsider might make someone hesitant to trust.

"You want a cookie?" the dispatcher asked, her elbows resting on the counter. "Rick and Tony's dad baked oatmeal raisin."

Nate started to say *no*, then realized he was hungry. Luckily, Mr. Lupone made cookies the size of paws.

"Dana?" he said once he'd polished off half of one. "You wouldn't talk about squad business outside of work, would you?"

Dana's forehead squinched up. "Of course not. Why would you even ask?"

"Because it could have repercussions. Ones you might not anticipate, even if the person's questions seemed harmless."

Dana rolled her eyes at him. "I'm not an idiot, Rivera. I know not to gossip about cases."

"Or people," he added, wanting to be clear.

"Or people," she huffed back.

Her answer stumped him. Did she not realize she'd done it? Had Iseult charmed her to forget perhaps?

Nate decided he'd better speak bluntly. "Dana, did you recently go to bed with a woman who was extra-curious about your job?"

Dana flushed and began to stammer. A second later, a look of horror chased the embarrassment from her face. "*No*," she said disbelievingly. "That woman who picked me up at the restaurant was part of this crime ring?"

Nate didn't have the heart to tell her she'd been its ringleader. "There's something else you should know. Your anti-hex charms are canceling each other out. I'm calling the precinct's magic expert tomorrow. He'll help you straighten them out."

Dana had gone pale, her hand instinctively clutching the necklaces she wore. "Oh my God." She set her coffee numbly on the Formica counter. "Oh my *God*. Are you going to tell Adam?"

"You should tell him," Nate said, knowing he couldn't keep this from him.

"He'll fire me."

"He'll be angry, but I don't think he'll go that far. Just explain everything as calmly as you can. Don't make excuses and, you know, man up and take your licks."

The ghost of a smile touched Dana's lips. "That's what you do when you're on his bad side."

"That's what I aim for, and—hey—I'm still here."

He gave her arm a pat and left the break room with two more cookies. The senior Mr. Lupone had a gift.

"Aren't you going to share?" asked his favorite voice in the whole wide world.

Evina was alone in the main squad room. Carmine had found her an RPD T-shirt to replace her bloodied button-down. She'd plunked herself at Nate's desk, mud-smeared sneakers propped on its clean surface. Normally, he'd have winced, but today he didn't care. With her sharp cat hearing, he imagined she'd heard every word he and Dana said. Her grin went a long way toward erasing the tension inside of him. Glad she was there, he sat on his desk's corner and handed her a cookie.

"You brushed your hair," he observed. "And re-braided it."

"You say that like you're disappointed."

"The uncombed version had a primitive appeal."

Evina snorted. "Yeah, like a cavewoman."

He bent and kissed her, then tucked his face against hers. They held like that, cheek to cheek, as if their beast halves needed to touch base too. Nate probably had extra testosterone in his system, left over from the fight. His cock responded to their closeness with an enthusiasm he wasn't ready to deal with then. In spite of this, when they pulled back, they were both more relaxed.

"That was kind," Evina said, cocking her head toward the break room.

Nate hitched his shoulders. "Dana didn't mean to cause trouble."

"You think like a boss, you know. A good one."

"I guess this experience didn't cure me of that."

Something flickered in her eyes. She shielded them with her lashes before he could determine what it was. "Can I ask you a favor?"

"Anything," he said sincerely.

"The hospital let Christophe sign himself out."

"He changed into tiger form?"

"No. He just healed enough that he no longer needs medical supervision. I was going to see him and . . . test out my new wings." Her gaze lifted back to his. "Could you come with me? I'm a little nervous about disappointing him."

Touched that she'd want him there, Nate caught her hand to kiss its knuckles. "Whatever I can do to help."

~

Nate seemed happy to be back in his Goblinati. Evina was entertained to see him pat the dash like it was a friend he'd been parted from.

They'd burned up the remainder of their long day at his precinct. The sun was setting as they left the city, the Friday traffic stop and start. This was date night. People were filling up sidewalk restaurants; winding down from their week in couples and groups. At times like this, Evina admitted the city was more exciting than the suburbs. She gazed longingly at the little tables, wishing she and Nate could share one. Then, because she loved watching him drive, she turned to rest her cheek on the passenger seat's leather. She could pretend this was a date if she wanted to. "Did you speak to your boss?"

"Only for a minute. He was tied up in interviews." Nate drummed the wheel and grimaced. "I guess we'll have it out tomorrow night at our traditional victory bash."

"He's going to apologize, Nate. You won't be in trouble."

He slid her an amused look. "You know that, huh?"

"It's what I'd do if I were in his shoes."

"Maybe." He unwittingly pleased her by letting the grooves on his forehead smooth. "Are the twins and your mom okay?"

"Better than okay. Apparently, Derrick Black took them to the zoo."

Nate's mouth twitched. She suspected he was imagining the driven news producer trying to herd two six-year-olds through the monkey house. "Abby must have enjoyed that."

"She mentioned they convinced him to feed the llamas. Sometimes I think she's as persuasive as my mother."

"I think she takes after you," Nate said. "Smart, bossy, and absolutely adorable."

Evina told herself he didn't mean *bossy* as an insult. "I'm not adorable."

He brushed her face with the back of his fingers. "You're adorable to me."

His voice was husky. Just like that, Evina wanted him, her body going wet and achy to have him slide in it. She dropped her hand to his thigh, rubbing the strong muscles underneath his pants leg. "Nate . . ."

"I know." He returned his gaze to the bumper that was halted ahead of them. "Now isn't the time for this."

It felt like the time for something, but perhaps the feeling wasn't mutual. She withdrew her hand from his leg. "Carmine invited me to your party tomorrow night."

"Did he?"

"I feel like I passed a macho test. Get into a fistfight, and everyone can be friends."

Nate smiled but didn't say he was glad. Ahead of them, the line of traffic moved for a green light.

"Nate," she said, lowering her voice. "I'm not sure how much I was supposed to say, but I didn't tell Carmine about your wolf wanting to eat me.

Or about me subduing you. I didn't think that was their business."

Nate scratched the bristle on his lean cheek. "I, uh, might have glossed over that bit too."

This should have made her feel better . . . except, what if he hadn't mentioned it because he didn't want them to know his girlfriend could shove his face in the dirt?

Don't be paranoid, Evina ordered herself. *He's been through a lot. He isn't pulling away from you.*

Not necessarily anyway.

~

Evina's second in command lived a couple blocks from her in the same complex of townhomes. In Nate's opinion, the dated cookie cutter structures were an eyesore. Ah well. He supposed the grassy stretches between the buildings were good for the kids to run on.

"You don't have to do this," Evina said once he'd parked and shut off the engine. "It's my problem, really."

Nate disliked hearing that more than he had a right to say. "I don't mind. This might be easier with a buffer there."

Evina blew out her breath, looking more nervous than before.

"Come on," he said, getting out. He didn't walk around to open her door for her. This was alpha business. She didn't need to be treated like a girl.

She got out and joined him on the front walk. He noticed she put her shoulders back as they strode up it together. Christophe opened the door a minute after she'd knocked.

His gray sweatpants and RFD T-shirt covered some of the damage, but his appearance inspired an inner jolt. With the bandages removed, his skin looked like a paper-mache project gone awry. The scars appeared to be hampering his range of motion. His arms were stiff as he swung the door back to let them in.

"Nate," he said, surprising him by remembering.

"Christophe," he returned, maybe just as surprised at the warmth that welled inside of him. The reaction felt like it was coming from his wolf. "Good to see you up and about."

"Well, it's better than the alternative." He hugged Evina, the gesture seeming natural and affectionate.

"You ready to try this?" she asked.

Christophe let out a sigh.

"You need to," Evina said, surprised by his reluctance. "You can't return to work as you are. You're as stiff as an arthritic."

"Maybe I'm not meant to return."

"Not meant to!" Evina's exclamation was breathless. "Chris, you love being a firefighter. Hell, in a lot of ways you're better at it than me!"

"Things happen for a reason."

"Bull," she spat back at him. She hesitated. "Is it me? Are you afraid I'm going to screw up helping you to change?"

"Of course not," he said. "If you say you can do it, I believe you."

He was afraid of something. Nate saw that shadow cross his face. He took Evina's arm before she could speak again. "You know, maybe Chris and I should have a guy talk."

"A guy talk." Evina's fists had found their way to her waist.

"Sure. In case there's anything he's too embarrassed to tell you." Both Evina and her second stared at him. "Come on, Chris," he said, ignoring how ridiculous they both seemed to be finding him. Nate had instincts, and they were telling him to keep at this. "Let's go to the kitchen and crack a beer."

Bemused, Chris led the way to his fridge. Perhaps cruelly, Nate let him fumble over opening two bottles of faerie stout with his damaged hands. Nate took one long swallow before he spoke.

"She can do it," he said quietly enough that Evina would have to strain to hear. "She might have doubts, but I don't. I'm a wolf, and she mastered me. Most alphas can only force their own pack members into a change."

"I'm not worried about that," Chris said. "We came up in the same class at the Fire Academy. Once Evina figured out how to do something, she always had it down."

"Then what's the hang up? And don't bullshit me about what's meant to be. You're afraid of something."

Christophe worried at the label of his chilled beer. "I keep thinking about that day. About how Evina warned me the room was going to flashover. She ordered me to get out of there. That's how they train us. You don't play crazy hero unless you're convinced you can make it pay off."

"You did make it pay off. You got those kids out of there."

"But I wasn't convinced I could. I wasn't even thinking. I might have been on two legs, but my tiger was in charge of me. *It* saved those kids. *It* tore off my protective gear and wrapped them up in it. I wasn't afraid at all, and that—" He gestured with the bottle for emphasis. "*That* scares the hell out of me. What if I change and it takes over? What if the impulse it decides to act on isn't benign?"

Nate couldn't speak for a few seconds. Christophe might have stolen his own terrors and put them into words. He must have been channeling Tony then, because what he finally did say was pretty damned silly.

"Cats don't wear coats."

Christophe's fire-thinned eyebrows shot up.

"They don't wear coats," Nate repeated, "and they can't tear them off. They might risk their lives to defend their own cubs, but they don't generally risk them for a stranger's. You were in there, Chris. Your cat took charge so you could do what you needed without being paralyzed. Maybe it knew you'd be successful. Sometimes our beast halves are more intuitive than our human ones. Bottom line: You're the boss of it, not the other way around."

"You really think so?"

"I really do." He felt better as he said it, not completely but enough that the knots in his shoulders let go of his trapezoids. Evina had said he'd let her dominate his wolf. Maybe there'd been more truth in that than he'd realized.

"I'll stay while Evina does it," he added. "You'll have us both to look out for you."

Nate had offered this without thinking, but Christophe wasn't offended. Though he was a grown man, relief washed visibly through him. "I'd appreciate that."

~

Evina had known Christophe would be her second before he did. The first time they teamed up for an exercise at fire school, the relationship simply clicked. The reason was more than working well together or thinking in similar ways. They had what she thought of as professional chemistry. Even at the height of her and Paul's romance, their rhythm hadn't been as smooth.

Chris had never said so, but he'd been relieved when Paul broke up with her and went to a different station. At the workplace, her ex had been the third wheel.

Her beta was in his bedroom now, laboriously undressing while Evina and Nate waited in the hall outside. That was a little weird, but not because she and Chris had ever been intimate.

"So." Nate leaned against the opposite wall. "You and Chris ever . . . ?"

"No," she said, amused by how closely his thoughts tracked hers.

"It'd be understandable. I assume he's a good-looking guy."

"He is, but we never struck those kind of sparks. We count on each other. After Freda and I guess my Mom, he's one of my closest friends."

Nate's fathoms-deep eyes met hers. Her stomach went into free fall. God, he was attractive—and for more reasons than his looks. He was brave and smart and a hundred other not-simple qualities she admired. She didn't want to think about losing him from her life any more than she did Chris. His lips tightened as if he were about to speak. Was he going to share what he and Chris discussed? Did he perhaps have something personal to say? Maybe on the topic of being her friend himself?

"Okay," Chris joked from behind the door. "I'm indecent."

They went in without laughing. Chris was in the bed, propped up on pillows. He'd pulled the sheet to his waist for modesty. Scars webbed his upper body, the hardened tissue seeming most constrictive on his right arm and face. On his chest, a couple muscles looked as if portions had melted.

The sight made her hurt inside. More than ever, she hoped she could do this, if only to restore what had been a fine example of tiger male beauty.

"Nice, huh?" Christophe said, pulling a sarcastic face at himself.

Evina sat on the edge of the bed. "Consider it a blessing. When you're healed, you'll really appreciate what a handsome stud you are."

Chris smiled at her. "I'm glad you're my boss. And my friend. No matter what happens next."

He was making her tear up. Pulling herself together, she took his right hand in hers. She held it gently against her breast and looked into his eyes.

"I'm not feeling her up, I swear," he teased aside to Nate.

"Shush," Evina said. "Focus on me right now."

He settled, letting her gaze sink into his.

"You're mine," she said much more gently than she had to Nate in the woods. "My tiger. My beta. My right hand in the pride. You've always trusted me, and I want you to trust me now. I'm going to compel you to change. My will is going to rule yours."

She pushed. She knew Chris felt it, because his eyes grew worried. Very aware of Nate standing behind her, she upped the amperage. The air between her and Chris wavered with magic. Chris made a tiny noise like she was hurting him.

"Harder," Nate said before she could ease up. "You need to really slam your will into him."

"Just do it," Chris gasped at her.

She was trying. She remembered how mastering Nate had felt and knew this was different. Her authority didn't feel as decisive. Maybe she couldn't be as ruthless if the situation weren't life and death. Maybe she didn't want to be a stone cold alpha in front of Nate a second time. Shoving that fear aside, she closed her eyes to concentrate better. It wasn't working. Sweat broke out on her skin.

Then Nate dropped his hand to her shoulder.

All of them gasped in unison. Evina's eyes flew open. The contact was like a plug pushed into a socket. Nate's aura linked up to hers so neatly she was amazed it hadn't happened before. She felt twice as big, twice as strong, twice as unstoppable. She felt whole—without having realized she didn't feel that way before. Now she knew why this had been so easy at the lake. Nate made her more. Nate *supported* her alpha power.

"Change," she whispered, one hundred percent certain it would happen.

Heat surged from her heart chakra into Christophe's. His big hand tingled inside of hers, and then simply disappeared. He flashed from man to tiger in a split second, faster than she'd ever seen anyone change form. Light burst outward from where he'd been, radiant and gorgeous, like a soul she could actually see.

An instant later, a giant tiger shape was wriggling and huffing under

Christophe's plaid cotton sheet.

Evina started laughing and couldn't stop. His tiger looked completely silly trapped like that.

"Sorry," she said when he growled at her. Wiping her eyes, she got up and helped free him.

He lay down then, more than taking up the bed. Evina reached to rub him between the ears. He butted her hip, marking her with his scent glands. Then he looked up at Nate.

"*Can* I pet him?" Nate asked, slightly awed. Evina understood the reaction. Christophe was intimidating up close and in tiger form.

"Don't let him lick you," she warned. "Tiger tongues scrape like sandpaper."

Nate gave Chris an experimental scratch underneath the chin, which Chris encouraged by lifting it. Nate scratched harder. Chris's tiger's eyes drooped with enjoyment. If they kept this up, he was going to purr. He marked Nate too, then jerked his head toward the door with a sneezing noise.

"Okay," Evina said, "that's our cue to leave and let him change back again."

Since this only took a minute, she guessed her beta was over his hang up.

He came out again tying the drawstring on his sweatpants. The motions of his hands were easy, his skin once again flawless.

"That's more like it," Evina said, meeting his giant grin with her own. "Now all the hose bunnies can swoon after you again."

"Puh-lease," Chris said. "Women love a big guy with scars."

He reached for Nate's hand, giving it a manly slap and bump.

"*You*," he said meaningfully.

"Me?" Nate returned, his eyebrows quirking.

It was Chris's turn to burst out laughing. "You're a fricking alpha. And you're her damn bondmate. The other guys are going to have a collective cow. I hope you're prepared for it!"

"No," Evina said, even as the girly part of her nature fizzed like champagne. He was hers? Really, he truly was? "Christophe, maybe you're wrong."

"Nuh-uh," he said firmly. "My aunt and uncle are bondmates too. Their energy does the same stuff as yours."

Evina looked at Nate, whose jaw seemed to have fallen to the floor. "I'm alpha?" he asked.

"You're alpha to me, that's for sure. To all Evina's pride, I'll bet. I guess the wolves will have to speak for themselves."

"That's . . . not possible," he said. He looked like he wanted to be convinced, which Evina took as promising.

"I mistook you for an alpha when we met," she reminded him. "You certainly demonstrated a knack for making my crew back down. Heck, Nate, you inspired Rafi to change into boy form without a fight. He brushed his teeth for you!"

As proud as if he'd arranged this turn of events himself, Christophe clapped each of them on the shoulder.

"Look out, world. Resurrection has something new in it."

❦ CHAPTER FIFTEEN

NATE was lost in thought as they left Christophe's home. He stopped in front of his Goblinati, dropped his head, and rubbed the back of his neck.

Evina took his other hand. However their relationship turned out, she wanted him to know she was here for him. Strictly speaking, not reaching out would have been difficult. After what had just happened, the pull between them was strong. Her energy wanted his next to it.

"We can leave the car where it is," she told him. "We're close enough to walk to my place."

"Right." He must have felt what she did. He wove their fingers more firmly together.

Darkness had fallen while they were with Chris. Most of the development's residents were inside watching TV or fixing a late dinner. Evina led Nate the long way around to her unit, across the best grassy stretches toward the little woods her children liked to pretend was a deep jungle. Her family wasn't expecting her back just yet. She and Nate had time to talk. Much as she enjoyed the silence between them, she knew they needed that.

They walked close enough that their shoulders brushed. Without working too hard at it, they found a compromise between their stride lengths. Evina realized she wanted to do this every night.

"I always suspected that might be true," he said, cutting through the crickets and muffled cooking sounds.

"That you really are an alpha?"

"Yes." He rubbed his left eyebrow with a fingertip. "Of course, I also thought I might be kidding myself. Because I was resentful over not earning top spot in my pack."

"Is it going to be harder to work with them now that you know for sure?"

He thought. "No. I feel calmer. Maybe the validation helps. *I* know, so I don't have to keep pushing for them to see it too. Or maybe the calmness is your effect on me."

He squeezed her fingers, causing a thrill to run through her. They stopped walking and looked at each other. No electric lights were nearby but, behind Nate's head, the moon was three-quarters full, glowing like a spotlight with its power dialed to maximum. The moon was his people's symbol, their emblem of change and mystery. As well as she'd come to know him, his mysteries weren't all revealed. Evina's stomach was so jumpy she couldn't tell whether that excited or frightened her.

Nate stroked her braided hair around her head. "I believe what Christophe said. I believe you and I are mates."

Evina's nerves fluttered more forcefully. "You don't think that's crazy?"

"Only on the surface. Underneath it makes perfect sense. We bring out more in each other."

Evina bit her lip. Nate's expression was so serious she didn't know how to interpret it. "What do you want to do about it?"

He smiled gently. "I'm pretty sure that's your call."

She didn't want it to be hers, or—rather—she knew her preference already and needed to hear his. "I'm not the easiest woman to get along with."

He surprised her by laughing. "Did Paul put that idea into your head? You're easy, Evina. Any smart man you lived with would roll out of bed every day happy."

Any smart man you lived with . . . Was that what he hoped would happen? That they'd live together? She knew she shouldn't want more than that. More than that wasn't what most tigers did. "You called me bossy," she blurted.

"Do you think that scares me?"

"But now you know you're alpha!"

"Evina." He hugged her, quick and wonderful. "Paul wasn't secure enough in himself. You need a man who's stronger than him, not one who's more subordinate. I think, maybe, that's me."

There wasn't any *maybe* about him being stronger than Paul. Nate had confidence—and stubbornness—in spades. When Nate sank his teeth into a project, he never let it go.

"The question is," he said, his beautiful hands moving around her hair again, "do you want me in your life? Can you trust me after what I almost did?"

"You don't even have to ask!"

"I do. If you'd done what I had, you'd feel the same. Even if you're right about me letting you stop me."

When he put it that way . . .

Her arms were around his waist from his earlier hug, his rangy body warm in the loose embrace. "Nate," she said as soberly as she could, "if anyone were going to eat me, I'd want it to be you."

He stared at her, stupefied. Evina gave up the joke and broke into sniggers.

"Oh for crap's sake," he exclaimed. "That's not funny!"

"Apparently, it is," she replied, because he was laughing a bit himself. She wagged her brows at him. "You caught the double entendre, right?"

Nate shook his head in exasperation. To her delight, this was a prelude to kissing her. His lips settled over hers as if their mouths had been custom designed to fit. That was better. In fact, it was delicious. Nate's hands slid down her back to pull her as close as two bodies that still wore clothing could get. From what she could tell, he was very happy to be kissing her.

"Mm," she said, squirming against his various hard places. "Maybe I should eat *you*. You're so tasty."

"Jesus," he said, helpless to fight a smile. "Not. Funny."

"Well, then." Unable to resist, Evina ran her hands around the muscles of his tight butt. "Maybe I shouldn't eat you. Maybe I should just lick you here and there."

She rubbed her pelvis suggestively up his crotch, where the ridge of his erection seemed to have turned to stone. Since that drew a pleased gasp from him, she put more of her kitty slinkiness into the motion.

Sometimes it was nice to be flexible.

"Evina," he growled. Then he kissed her so deeply she couldn't speak for a few minutes.

It felt like he was pouring heat straight into her sex, like he'd tipped a bottle of steamy syrup, and she was filling up. Everything they'd been through hit her, everything she longed for, all the hurdles they still faced. She had to get him inside her, had to hold the two of them as tight as they would go. If she didn't, her heart *and* her lust might explode.

She broke free of his delectable tonguey kiss, both their eyes blazing fire. Because they were shifters, this sort of play cranked up their temperatures. She gripped Nate's hot hand in hers.

"Come with me," she said, tugging him after her.

They ran, laughing breathlessly, into the community's little stretch of woods. They didn't stumble. With the nimbleness of their beasts, they sought privacy among nature. The exertion was a pleasure, the anticipation it helped to build. Nate pushed her spine back into a tree trunk even as she yanked him closer by the collar. She loved that he was taller and stronger, loved too that he yielded to her pull. They were yin and yang jumbled up together, tinder and spark and a thousand other combustible metaphors.

Evina couldn't come up with them right then. She felt wilder and more wordless than she ever had before.

"I want you," he growled, low and sexy, ironing his crotch over hers. "I'm going to die if I have to wait."

172

She kissed him, clutched him. "Help me with my clothes."

He peeled off her upper garments in a single smooth motion. Cool air hit the tightened peaks of her breasts.

"Hey," she said. "Didn't I have a bra under there?"

Nate grinned and cupped her, thumbs reaching for her sensitized nipples. "I'm all about efficiency tonight."

He ducked his head and sucked. For a moment, all she could do was wallow in sensation. Each pull of his mouth licked nerves in her clit and pussy. Moaning, she drove her fingers so deeply into his hair that she undid his ponytail. This wasn't bad, of course. She loved combing through that warm black silk.

"Evina." He fell to his knees in front of her. His hands got busy opening her trousers, then shifted to unbuttoning his fitted business shirt. He must have kept extras at the precinct. The garment was as sharp as everything he owned. Dark oyster brown with pale cream stripes, the colors looked so yummy against his skin it honestly made her mouth water.

"Don't rip that," she pleaded as he wrenched his arms from the sleeves. "It looks really nice on you."

She felt him grinning as he kissed her navel.

"Lift your feet," he murmured against her stomach, his hands tugging at her sneakers.

A shiver of nervous excitement rolled up her spine. Did he intend to strip every scrap from her? Out in the open and everything?

She supposed he did. Once her shoes were pried off, he shucked her trousers and panties as handily as the rest. From his knees, he gazed up her body, the moon painting pale magic over her dips and curves. His expression was awestruck, like he hadn't imagined a woman could look like her.

"You're so beautiful," he breathed, his palms and fingers smoothing around her thighs, urging them to part for him. "You're exactly what a woman should be."

She couldn't laugh at his exaggeration. He sounded too earnest.

Plus, there was the distraction when he nuzzled between her labia and sucked her clitoris.

Her neck arched against the bark of the tree. Talk about being eaten. Nate was making a feast of her—licking, suckling, sliding two long fingers into her sheath to rub it coaxingly. Cream ran from her, coating those clever appendages. Christ, he knew exactly how she liked this. Evina clutched his head. Playing shy really was a waste with a man like him. With a grunt of pleasure, Nate worked his strong right shoulder under her spread left thigh.

Naked, forced to stand on one foot, Evina rolled her sex at him. Her inner thigh pressed his ear, the movement of his jaw intensely arousing. Sensing her urgency, he worked his fingers more strongly in and out. He held her too securely for her to fear losing her balance. This was good, because when his fangs lengthened with arousal, she totally lost it.

"Nate," she gasped, a sudden strong orgasm squeezing her pussy tight.

He panted in response, the ragged sound sharpening her pleasure. His fingers pumped faster, drawing out her climax. Knowing him, it wasn't an accident that one fang compressed a nerve so sweet the ecstasy almost hurt.

He seemed to know when she'd had enough. He eased his fingers from her, dropping one last kiss to her throbbing clit. He let her thigh slide off his broad shoulder, but didn't rise right away. Instead, he dragged his face from side to side on her belly. The gesture was indescribably vulnerable and sweet.

"I love you," she said, petting his lovely hair. "You're the best man I've ever known."

He tipped his face up, golden fires burning behind his irises. She didn't need the words back from him. Those soulful eyes were abundantly expressive.

With her hips to serve as his brace, he pulled himself to his feet. He didn't move. He looked down at her and breathed, the in and out of his ribs deep and exciting. Titillated by the thought of what they'd do next, Evina smoothed her hands over his bare chest.

"Open my trousers," he said.

The instruction rasped from his throat, inspiring a small shiver. Evina dragged her nails lightly down the arrow of hair on his muscular abdomen. His diaphragm moved faster, the large bulge behind his zipper drawing her scratches there.

"Fuck," he gasped, eyelids growing heavy as he widened his stance.

Evina knew an invitation when she saw one. Up and down his erection she drew her kitty nails—ten again, thank the Tiger Queen. She pushed them through his legs to where his balls were pulsing. Every inch of the route she took was worth repeating, a thoroughness he seemed grateful for. When she saw his canines sink into his lip, she undid the clasp at his waist and pulled down his zipper.

His swollen cock pushed out so heavily the teeth nearly parted without help. Slowly, teasingly, she dug down into his jockstrap.

"Ah," he sighed as she grasped his thickness and tugged upward. "Evina, that feels good."

"To me too," she whispered.

He was silk and steel, muscle and heat and oil where his tip leaked beads of arousal perfect for rubbing across his tip with her thumb. Sensualist that he was, he let her play for quite a few minutes. His body undulated, rolling in slow waves at the pleasure she stirred in him.

Then he caught her wrist with his hand.

"I need to show you something," he said throatily.

She rose on tiptoe to kiss him, their tongues tangling deep and wet. When both their hearts were thumping harder, she pulled away. His eyes glittered down at her as they opened.

"Show me what?" she asked.

"This."

He wrapped his hand over hers where she held his cock. She expected him to adjust her stroke, maybe show her how he liked to masturbate. That possibility increased the ache of want in her pussy. He surprised her by simply nudging her index finger onto a new spot.

The place was near the base of his erect penis, slightly hotter than the rest, and blatantly swollen. She fanned her finger across it, causing him to shiver.

"What is it?" she whispered.

"It's called a bulbus glandis. It activates in werewolves when partners who could be mates have sex."

"In werewolves."

"Yes." He pushed her finger across the gland again, shuddering at the feel this time. Evina's body creamed at his reaction. The spot must have had a lot of nerves. "It's been swelling up for you. It gets bigger when I come, and that tightens our fit when I ejaculate. Maybe you noticed I like to be really deep inside you then. The ring of muscles at your gate presses on me just right."

She had noticed that—and enjoyed it. "You didn't say."

"I wasn't sure what to make of it. It's only happened a couple times and never with someone I felt so drawn to. I didn't like it so much before, but with you it's incredibly pleasurable. I guess my body knew we were meant for each other before I was ready to admit it."

She smiled. Admitting this couldn't have been easy for a play-the-field guy like him. He smiled back. Possibly, she looked a little smug. She distracted him by rubbing the gland again.

As she did, an idea occurred to her: one her imagination found so compelling her inner muscles squirmed together. "I guess when this gland is swollen, being sucked feels especially good."

Nate inhaled. "It isn't the easiest spot to reach, since it's on the base."

"Is that a dare?" she teased.

He actually flushed when she ran her pointed tongue around her lips. Laughing, she shifted her hands to his hips.

"Stay where you are," she warned as she dropped down in front of him.

Beneath her knees, the long grass was cool and damp. Knowing he liked her assertiveness, she gripped the waists of his jock and trousers, and yanked them past his hips. Because his legs were straddled, neither garment fell. She had, however, succeeded in exposing his cock and balls.

She thought he looked nice in the moonlight too.

The ridges of his torso muscles were very clear, his erection monolithic from this angle. She saw the redder patch at the base of his cock. It was the size of a fifty-cent piece, two strong veins feeding it. With a hum of anticipation, she dragged the flat of her tongue up it.

Nate swallowed a moan and dug his hands in her hair.

This was fun, for sure. She pulled the head toward her mouth and slid her lips over it. That drew more heartfelt groans from him; especially when she stretched her tongue down to work his special spot. The sweetness of his pre-ejaculate washed over her taste buds.

"Evina," he said, hips rocking to her as her head rocked down him. "God. Don't make me go just yet. I want to be inside you."

She gentled her motions, but it was impossible to stop when he reacted this enchantingly. The power was so heady it sang in her blood like wine. No alpha could have refused it. She ran her hands up and down his trouser legs, knowing the instant his knees started to wobble.

She pulled back with a last lick up him. "Enough?"

He took her hands, helping her to her feet. The second she was on them, he bent his knees to align their heights. His body slapped hers back into the tree, his mouth claiming hers for a blistering kiss. That went on long enough to make her head spin.

"Whoo," she sighed when he let her go. She felt like she'd been plundered. Her heart pounded in her chest like a tribal drum. She was glad to hear his thumping at the same rate.

He dropped his sweaty forehead onto hers. "Can I let go for this?" he asked. "Will I scare you if I do that?"

Scared was the last thing she was feeling.

"Please," she said. "Don't hold back."

His hands glided to her bottom, fingers tightening around her ass cheeks. He hiked her into place, waiting for her to lock her legs and ankles into a helpful position. He let go with one hand, moving it between them. Evidently, he wanted to do the honors when it came to entering her. He adjusted his cock against her, setting the silken head where she was wettest. The way his penis trembled might have been the sexiest sensation she'd ever felt.

Before they left her, his thumbs and fingers caressed her labia, seeming to savor their soft cling on him.

"Ready?" he asked.

"Oh yeah," she promised him.

He reached above her, taking hold of a jutting branch. Evina slid her hands up his back to wrap around his shoulders.

His eyes caught fire as he pushed into her.

The thrust might have started slow but it ended emphatically. He let out a little grunt as he finished sinking. Loving that, Evina rubbed her face across his neck.

"That isn't all you've got," she whispered.

He drew his thickness back to her brink, the noise that accompanied this a barely audible whine. His gaze searched hers. *Yes,* she thought. *Give me everything.*

Perhaps he read the mental message. He let himself off his leash.

If a person could fuck like a dervish and make love at the same time, that's what Nate did to her. Evina met his fervor with her own, digging her heels into his butt and driving her sheath down him. Now that she knew it was there, she wondered how she'd missed the swell of his gland. It seemed to get bigger with every stroke, its entrance slicked by the excitement it pulled from her. The spot was hot in more ways than one. Nate cried out as she tightened deliberately on it.

"Shh," she warned, recalling they weren't in the actual wilderness. Nate couldn't seem to comply.

"Fuck," he groaned, jamming hard into her. "Jesus, Evina!"

The branch he was using to improve his leverage began to crack. "Fuck," he repeated, gripping it closer to the trunk.

Evina licked the sweat running down his corded neck, then nipped his lower lip. A tiny nick of blood hit her tongue.

Most shifters had a thing about blood and sex, the combination a cross between a fetish and an aphrodisiac. Werewolves weren't immune, apparently. She licked the drop from his lip, and his cock surged an inch longer. He'd reached the last millimeter of his control.

His cock jerked and went stonelike.

"Damn it," he cursed, abruptly yanking it out of her.

She didn't think he was angry; he wasn't panting the right way for that.

"Let go," he demanded, because her legs were still hooked on him. His voice was harsh. "Turn around and face the tree."

Understanding what he had in mind drove a spike of arousal through her pussy. She dropped her legs and turned, dug her cat nails into the bark, and arched her rear up for him. She loved when they were face to face but didn't hesitate to offer herself this way. She craved it too. Whether she was thinking like a woman or a tigress, he'd earned the right to ask. They'd been a team today, and he'd led them to victory. Now he would claim his prize. He growled, the sound pure admiration for the picture she was making.

Then he kicked her ankles another foot wider.

That made her cry out, the sound unmistakable for anything other than arousal. He surged up to her, his taller body hard behind hers. God, he was hot. Panting, urgent, he fit his cock against her and drove inward. Caught in her own heat wave, she moaned at all that steely maleness entering her from a new angle. Nate didn't have the patience to let her adjust to it. He started going at her the instant he was in. He felt so thick, so strong, his pumping motions even more frantic than before.

"Good?" he gasped, the word shaken by his thrusts.

"More," she pleaded, arching her hips to him.

She knew this was what he wanted, to be urged to take her without restraint. He slapped his hands on top of hers, wolf nails sinking into the bark with a solid thunk. That increased his leverage too.

"Unh," he said with a massive thrust that lifted her to her toes. "Evina . . . Evina . . ."

She came: tight, sharp, the sweetness running up her nerves in bursts. Her climax truly seemed to drive him crazy. Pistoning like this was a race he had to win or die, his clenched thighs wedged hers wider. He mouthed the back of her neck, canines taking hold of the delicate skin.

She knew he wanted to bite her like his beast would, wanted to hold her captive when his seed erupted.

"Yes," she cried, starting to crest again.

"It's coming," he said. "*God . . .*"

His cock and his gland pulsed inside her at the same time.

This was constriction. This was a pressure that drove her to the primal edge of being too taken. The first jets of his seed flooded into her, his hips jamming all the way in again. His ejaculation cast a spell on her responses. Suddenly, *too taken* was exactly right. Her pussy convulsed around him, tightening the fit even more. Snarling with pleasure, Nate yanked one clawed hand free of the tree and clapped it over her labia. The heel of his palm ground her clit back over her pubic bone, an increase in stimulation she wouldn't have guessed she needed. *Need* didn't matter much to Nate. He was all about making it better.

Thinking that was a good example to follow, Evina wrenched her hand free to wrap it over his. She made sure the joint pressure of their palms rubbed his now grossly swollen gland.

The orgasm detonated for both of them.

His teeth bit down, his tongue coming out to suck the mark. As it did, their auras merged like wildfires. His thrusts were only deep then, lightning-quick inch-long jerks that kept his prick way up in her core. His jaw was clamped on her neck, his groans of bliss singing down her vertebrae. He came until he couldn't come anymore, then continued to milk out her pleasure.

She was a little sorry when his canines released her. Her healing powers were back online. The sting faded in seconds.

"Evina," he gasped, the first intelligible speech he'd gotten out for a few minutes. "God, I love you."

A pang she hadn't known she was holding onto dissolved when he said the words.

Her knees were understandably shaky. Needing help staying upright, she rested her cheek against the tree trunk. Judging by the bark's texture, it was a birch.

Nice birch, she thought, laughing silently to herself. Nate had turned her into a literal tree hugger.

Nate wasn't much steadier. He was hugging her, his face ducked against her shoulder. They'd straightened some at the end, but his cock was still snug inside her, his quickened pulse vibrating strongly there. Evina twisted her neck to rub their cheeks together.

His slightly bristled skin was wet. His arms tightened on her waist. His breathing broke with a peculiar hitch.

"Nate!" She squirmed around before he could stop her. She touched his cheek, amazed by what she found. "What is it? Why are you crying?"

His face twisted sheepishly. "Sorry." He tried to drag the tracks away on his shoulder, but more fat drops appeared. "I guess every man fears the wolf inside him, that it will hurt the woman he cares about. I'm probably more wolf than most."

She dried his cheeks for him, knowing better than to make jokes. "You weren't too rough, Nate. You did exactly what I wanted."

"That's why it was so amazing. After what Iseult made me do, you trusted me completely." He shook his head. "That isn't all of it. I've been a seducer my whole adult life. I want to be worthy of how you feel about me. I don't want to hurt you in any way ever."

She ran her fingertips around the hollows beneath his eyes, searching for the right words to say. "I know you must have broken a heart or two. You're the kind of man a woman doesn't easily forget. All the same, I'm willing to bet that isn't how you get your jollies, and that you'd never deliberately break mine. That's all the worthiness I need, Nate. Everything else I know about you, I respect."

"I've never been in love before," he confessed.

She couldn't help it: her face split into a grin.

"Oh God," he sighed melodramatically. "You're going to hold that over me, aren't you?"

"Only secretly," she teased. "On the outside, I'll be perfectly mature."

"And on the inside?"

"Inside, I'll be crowing that I'm the Holy Foods Romeo's one true love."

He laughed and the moment magically turned flawless, a perfect diamond buffed by their shared humor. Evina didn't mind that the clothes he'd peeled off her were now so disreputable the Goodwill would have rejected them. They'd get her home without being arrested. Right then, that was all she needed.

Well, that and the honest-to-God ironed handkerchief Nate gave her to clean up with.

~

Evina's cubs let out enough of a caterwaul while running to her that there could have been ten of them.

"Mommy!" they squealed, flinging their arms around her. "You're home!

Nate watched her hug them back. She dropped to her knees on the kitchen floor, kissing them until they squirmed and giggled.

Abby was the first to push back. "Mommy, Nate's friend Tony invited us to a party!"

"Did he?" Evina asked, stroking her daughter's curly mop of hair.

"Yes, Mommy. Tomorrow night. He invited all the tigers you work with, plus Grandmom and Mr. Black."

Rita and the news producer had been playing a board game with the twins at the kitchen table—Portals and Ladders, Nate believed. Though Derrick Black wore a business suit, he looked surprisingly at ease. He seemed amused but not displeased to find himself where he was. His tie was tugged down and everything.

"Your friend called here," Rita said over the rim of her coffee mug. "Asked specifically to talk to the kids."

She seemed to consider this significant.

"You're supposed to stay home from work tomorrow," Rafi informed Nate. "He said you need a play day."

"He bought us tickets to the planetarium," Abby added. "He attached them to Rafi in an email."

"That was . . . nice of him," Evina said, shooting Nate a less sure look.

Nate didn't know what Tony was up to, precisely. He could guess, but the lowest ranking member of their pack had a talent for hiding his sneakiness under more of the same. Despite that, he didn't see the harm in this.

Only a monster could disappoint those two bright faces.

"I'd be happy to share a play day with you," he told the twins. "As long as it's okay with your mom."

"Yay!" both cubs yelled, which Nate found incredibly flattering.

His cheeks grew a little hot as he noticed Rita watching his reaction. Her tone when she spoke was dry. "Your pack member also mentioned the party would be at your loft."

"What?" Nate gasped before he could guard his tongue. Victory parties were never at his place. Adam always was the host. He'd have to clean. And shop. And cook, for all he knew!

As she watched these thoughts cross his face, Rita's smile was undeniably catlike. "Your friend is very persuasive. He also called my daughter's station. Two of her tigers have agreed to team up with two of your wolves to prepare the food."

"In my kitchen?" he burst out, so horrified the twins turned to gawk at him.

"That was my understanding," Rita said creamily. "Something about you having two dishwashers and every cooking utensil known to man."

Nate shut his mouth and swallowed. He could live with this. He was going to have to if he and Evina were serious. He hoped the wolves Tony roped into cooking were his parents. The Lupones were easygoing. They'd be unlikely to clash claws with Evina's crew.

"Is that okay?" Evina asked, coming over to touch his arm. "Whatever your friend arranged, you don't have to go along with it."

Her touch conveyed a charm he couldn't resist, settling his hackles in one warm wave. Nate grinned, which made her grin back. Probably, they looked sappy, but he really couldn't care.

"It'll be fun," he said, hoping this was true. "And so will the planetarium."

Rafi and Abby bounced up and down with childish roars.

"All right," Evina said, smiling indulgently at them. "Which of you mini-monsters has brushed your teeth tonight?"

Abby stopped bouncing to plant her fists on her little hips. "Mommy," she said as sternly as if she were thirty instead of six. "Tomorrow's Saturday. It's too early to get ready for bed."

Nate had to roll his lips together to contain his laughter.

~

Without actually discussing it, Evina and Nate mutually decided he'd sleep over. Evina was happy this was the case. Maybe it was too soon, and him staying would confuse the kids, but no way was she letting him leave her house tonight if she could help it.

She walked her mother and her friend to the door while Nate began the twins' elaborate pre-bed ritual.

It seemed Derrick Black and Rita intended to spend the night as a couple too. "I'll catch up," Rita said as he went to his car.

"Thanks so much for protecting the kids today," Evina said. "I owe you a million trips to the dry cleaner."

"You don't owe me anything. Those kids are my blood too. I'm glad you and I . . . I'm glad we get along now that you're grown up."

Evina hugged her. "I love you, Mom."

"I love you too, sweetie." Rita pushed back and tilted her head at her. "You're serious about this wolf, aren't you? This isn't fun and games."

Evina's cheeks grew hot, but she wouldn't deny it. "Nate is a good man."

"I agree," Rita said.

"You do?" She shouldn't have been amazed. Her mother's decided tone of approval simply took her aback.

Rita smiled. "He's certainly got better taste in women than Paul. And he doesn't have a nervous breakdown after a few fisticuffs."

Paul hadn't had a breakdown; he was just shaken up. Plus, Iseult being Liane's mother likely accounted for his wife's less-than-formidable character. Evina didn't waste breath explaining this. She had more important things to share. "Nate thinks I'm easy to get along with," she confided in an undertone.

"Well, then." Her mother framed her face in her hands. "All the more reason to treat him like a keeper."

❧ CHAPTER SIXTEEN

NATE enjoyed waking up with Evina and the hodgepodge breakfast she pulled together. It wasn't every morning he ate Faerie-O's with tuna salad on the side. To his relief, their trip to the planetarium with the twins didn't wear out his patience. Rafi and Abby were normal kids and not Elfmark Cards, but genuinely liking them smoothed any rough moments.

When Abby fell asleep and drooled on his sleeve during the tour of the Milky Way, he felt like he'd won a medal. Her brother might be shyer, but her fierce little heart was better defended.

Lunch at Bob's Kabob was the limit of how long he could go without checking in on his squad. He left Evina and the children pouring over the menu while he stepped out on the sidewalk to make his call.

"Everything is fine," Carmine assured him. "These suburban gangsters are a chatty bunch. They're so busy turning on each other I doubt anyone's gonna get a deal. Iseult thought she was being smart, setting up her crime ring in her daughter's neighborhood where nobody would suspect it. Instead, she wound up with a bunch of wannabe part-faerie amateurs. And of course she couldn't recruit anyone with as much mojo as she had. She wanted to be the one doling out the power with her rituals. That way, she'd assure their loyalty.

"Oh, and if I were inclined to gloat, no less than five of these yahoos told us they were convinced that she—as her Ellen Owen persona—actually preferred Ivan. She switched brothers when she couldn't push The Terrible around like she wanted. Set up the embezzlement scheme to drive them apart. Once Vasili killed his brother, she and her very well funded crew planned to step into the power vacuum, just like you theorized.

"The reason you set off alarms in that smoke shop was because Ellen Owen didn't exist before two years ago. She couldn't have gone to high school with your fake cousin. *Her* cousins—the dead drug dealers from the smoke shop—planned the whole thing with her. Helped her reinvent herself. Arranged for her to cross Ivan's path so he could be dazzled. The problem was, they were also the distributors for the baby parts, which meant you were too close to connecting her to something worse than being Galina arm candy. So you didn't screw up, really. You just got unlucky."

This was nice to hear Carmine say, but maybe not that important. "What about Beaumont? And the bank teller, Mrs. Norman?"

"Oh, *them.*" Carmine chuckled. "The bad doctor and Mrs. Norman are the DA's new favorite folks. I hear she's pushing for banishment to a demon realm, but she'll settle for the death penalty. This case is gonna be high profile. She's salivating to stick it to 'em good."

"Good," Nate said. He watched a gaggle of giggling teenagers dash across the street. They made it safely, despite the honking cars. "Did you guys catch the WQSN coverage?"

"We did," Carmine said. "They're calling the kids you guys saved Resurrection's little miracles. There's a big swell of support for the 'special needs' shifters. Child Services has been flooded with applications to adopt them." Carmine let out a snort. "One newscaster speculated spells must have been used to draw clients to that Wings of Love outfit, 'cause surely no decent parent would give up cute kids like that."

"It could be true," Nate said. "Iseult used magic for lots of things."

"Maybe." Carmine sounded cynical. "I did see one editorial that made sense. One of WQSN's producers—that Derrick Black—is calling for the fae to appoint godmothers to the rescued kids. Said if they didn't make a practice of neglecting their mixed blood by-blows, Iseult's peeps might not have turned to a life of crime. Those kids could use protection, that's for sure."

"That's smart," Nate agreed. "Somebody should call the Mayor as well. Really put a headlock on our founders."

"I'll drop that bug in Adam's ear," Carmine promised.

To their alpha's dismay, the city's benevolent yet terrifying head official liked chewing the occasional fat with him. Creature-wise, no one quite knew what the Mayor was—only that he out-juiced everyone.

Nate glanced at the restaurant's window, knowing he couldn't stand out here much longer. "Look," he said hastily, "about tonight's party . . ."

"Nope," Carmine said. "You are under strict orders to stay away from your loft. All you and your girlie friend are allowed to do is show up."

"But the tigers might—"

"Forget it," Carmine cut him off, proving authority didn't always depend on alpha genes. "Tony took care of everything. You show up at seven thirty and not a minute sooner. And in case you don't listen, we've put Grant on lookout to head you off."

They'd set the gargoyle to keep Nate away? While he was sure the squad didn't mean to, this situation made him feel shut out again. Besides wanting to ensure the interspecies cooks weren't breaking his place to bits, Nate had a specific reason he needed to get in.

"It's my *home*," he tried to say reasonably.

"Not until seven thirty," Carmine refused flatly. "Now go enjoy your play day."

He hung up, leaving Nate to stare at the phone.

Hell, he thought. He was startled from his glower by Rafi sticking his head out the restaurant door. "Come on, Nate," he urged. "Mommy said if you don't come back and order, she'll let Abby do it for you."

"Is that bad?" Nate asked, a smile rising to his lips.

"It's *awful*. Abby orders everything extra hot."

"Even ice cream?"

The boy looked up when Nate stroked his hair. "She would if she could," he warned ominously.

~

Considering the twins were felines, convincing them to nap so they wouldn't fall asleep at the party required more work than Nate expected. Once they'd succeeded, he and Evina took one themselves. The fact that he'd been banned from his home, where shifters he didn't know were doing who knew what, kept him from dropping off right away.

"You're worse than a cat," she teased, her head nestled cozily on his chest. "Someone closes a door and you immediately have to know what's happening behind it."

"So I'm territorial," he said. "I can bend if I have to. You know, if it comes to letting someone I care about feel at home in my space."

"Mm-hm," she hummed, patting him sleepily.

He could tell she didn't believe him, but it was true. Tony felt at home in his place, and Tony was a slob. He lay awake imagining what he'd do for her and the twins. The contents of his pantry would have to change, right off. Bottled olives and fancy imported crackers weren't exactly cub-friendly. He'd need a contractor to throw up some walls for bedrooms. Maybe an indoor ramp system like people built for housecats—assuming Evina wouldn't find that insulting. The kids would think it was fun, he bet, especially if he added tunnels and hidey-holes. Planning that entertained him until he remembered his weapons room.

Holy crap, he'd need better locks for that. Also, everyone might be happier if he had two bathrooms . . .

When he opened his eyes, it was late enough to dress.

He *thought* they'd started early, but it was seven forty-five before he parked the Goblinati in his loft's underground garage.

It was seven fifty before the freight elevator let them out at his floor.

185

Evina was suppressing laughter at his antsiness, but he ignored that.

"Huh," he said, looking around the landing. His door was shut and there didn't seem to be any noise.

"Where is everybody?" Rafi asked.

Nate hoped the answer didn't involve corpses. Before he could wonder if he needed to draw his gun, Tony opened the entrance to Nate's unit. "There you are," he said with a big bright smile. "The party's on the roof. We figured the weather's nice, so why not move the festivities outside?"

Nate's roof had nothing on it but air vents and pigeon poop.

Tony laughed at his expression. "We hosed it down. And strung up party lights. Go on." He made shooing motions. "Everyone is up there. Evina's friend Christophe is manning the bar."

He seemed a little too eager to get rid of them.

"What are you hiding in my apartment?" Nate asked suspiciously.

"Nothing," his packmate said.

Maybe he wasn't lying. Either way, Nate turned to Evina and kissed her cheek. "Take the kids up with Tony. I need to grab something from my place."

Evina laughed. "You want to make sure my tigers haven't destroyed it."

Unrepentant, he dropped a kiss to her mouth and smiled.

"Fine," she said. "Kids, let's join the party with Nate's friend Tony."

Nate could hardly get into his place fast enough. He walked into a wall of scents so rich his mouth watered: roasted meat and curry and fresh baked bread. Two tigers he hadn't met relaxed in his open kitchen with Rick and Tony's parents. The Brazilian black marble counters were piled high with dirty pans, but everything else seemed fine.

"Hey, Nate," said Mr. Lupone, looking tired but accomplished. His arm was around his wife, and they were sharing a glass of wine. The tigers saluted him with beer bottles, apparently not thinking introductions were required.

"Smells great," Nate complimented, falling in with the casual vibe. "Thanks for coming out to do this."

He slipped into his bedroom corner before anyone decided they ought to chat.

His safe was behind a painting of the local grocer Maria had done for him one Christmas. She'd included every detail: the grocer's dog, the prices on the fruit bins, even a poster for a play the local high school had put on. It was their neighborhood in a nutshell, worn and homey and colorful. Tony's sister probably didn't guess how much the gift meant to Nate—or the treasures he used it to protect.

His hand trembled as he turned the dial. He kept his mother's valuables in here: baby pictures of him, her two Extraordinary Bravery medals, a single love letter his father wrote to her. He'd left when Nate was four, but she'd always loved him, and had never tried to make Nate think he was a bad man.

He was a lone wolf, she'd liked to say. *He gave us as much settling-down as he had in him.* As an adult, Nate had sometimes felt he understood that. Tonight, he knew his father hadn't been as fortunate as he was. To meet someone you wanted to commit to was a blessing.

The item Nate sought was at the back of the cavity. The velvet box was so old it had faded from red to pink. This was his mother's wedding ring. His grandmother's too. Nana Rivera had passed it down to his wandering father. Both his parents' history was in it.

And now mine. Nate dropped to the edge of his bed to open it.

The antique ring was pretty, the diamond not huge but clear. His heart thumped faster when he touched it. Was it too soon to ask Evina to marry him? Should he wait until she knew him better? Until she was certain he'd do right by her and the kids?

He shut the lid and rose, shoving the box into his trouser pocket. He was certain, more than he'd ever been about anything. He wanted Evina to know his intentions now. If she wasn't ready, he'd keep asking until she was.

If you wanted a good territory, you had to stake a claim.

He smiled at that idea, nervous but happy. His course of action decided, he bounded up the building stairs to the roof. The noise of the party hit him the moment he pushed the door open.

And so did something else.

He blinked, completely flummoxed by what he was looking at. The roof, which he owned but had never gotten around to fixing up, was transformed. What used to be bare tarpaper was now a miniature park. Grass had been rolled over beds of earth, brimming with chrysanthemums and green things. Little trees and benches overlooked winding paths paved in cobblestone. On one side of the roof, a bar and a buffet table bustled. On another, an elaborate jungle gym had been erected. Nate's honorary nephew swung on it like a monkey, evidently demonstrating its finer points to Evina's admiring twins.

Nate had a jungle gym on his roof. Obviously, Nate didn't need one himself. Nate's pack was trying to help him please his tigress and her cubs.

His eyes welled up even before the partygoers spotted him and roared, "Surprise!"

When wolves and tigers roared at you, you heard it. Nate had to press his hand to his heart to keep it from jumping out. "Crap," he said once he could speak. "How the hell did you do all this in a day?"

From the front of the crowd, which had to be a hundred people, Carmine let out his belly laugh. "We snuck out between interviews. Plus, Adam had half the cops in the city pitching in. He'd have had more, but Tony was being picky when it came to construction skills."

Half the cops in the city had done this for him.

Nate looked at Tony and Rick and Adam, all of whom were grinning.

Evina stood next to Tony, his big hand resting on her slim shoulder. She was smiling too. She knew what this meant to him.

"Get that man a beer," Tony called. "He needs fluids if he's going to break down sobbing."

People laughed, but Adam brought him one.

"This is my apology," he said quietly. "For getting my back up and not trusting your instincts the way I should."

Nate accepted the bottle, though his throat was too tight to drink. His voice was rough when he spoke. "This is a hell of an apology, boss. And the jungle gym . . . That's a nice touch."

"Tony seemed to think it was good idea. Grant flew it up here in one piece."

The gargoyle lifted a wing and a paw at him. Touched, Nate's ribs constricted another notch. Not about to let him off the emotional hook, Adam waited until he looked back at him. His green gaze was so intense it had almost gone wolfy. "If this tigress is who makes you happy, she's who we want for you."

"Crap," Nate said as the water in his eyes spilled over.

Serious moment broken, Adam laughed and slapped his back. "Come grab a plate. We've got a mountain of food to eat. Those tigers don't mess around when they cook. Last I saw Rick and Tony's parents, they were actually speechless."

As they wound through the partiers, Nate saw a lot of cops he knew and a lot of firefighters he didn't. Evina's sultry friend Freda headed up a group of laughing male and female EMT's who were clustered around the bar sipping sunset orange drinks from martini glasses. Nate recognized some of the paramedics from crime scenes and acknowledged their friendly waves. His personal music collection was playing from hidden speakers, R&B people could dance to. Faerie lights had been strung around a small dance floor. In its center, Derrick Black the werepanther news producer was cutting an impressive rug with Rita Mohajit. Nate had been to and thrown parties in his life but hadn't had one thrown *for* him since he was a kid. Tonight felt a bit like wandering in a dream. Everything was too wonderful to be real.

"Everyone is getting along," he murmured, marveling.

"You can thank the good food for that," Adam said. "And Grant. Tony warned your guests he'd fly anyone who fought off the roof and drop them in the river."

"Don't tell the kids," Nate said. "That might sound like fun to them."

~

Nate seemed not to have informed his pack of his true status. Maybe he didn't need to. Maybe his underlying nature wasn't something a wolf could see. That Evina's tigers could perceive it was obvious. She watched her crew of sixteen meet Nate, take in his alpha energy, then glance speculatively at her. They knew her current lover was unlikely to leave the RPD. Police work was too linked to wolf nature and traditions. This being so, they didn't have to gird themselves for him becoming their co-boss. Working out his precise position in the pride would be interesting. Weretigers were as hierarchical as wolves. She wondered if Nate was aware of the paterfamilias role that was opening up for him.

She also wondered if he'd want it. Paul had, she suspected, but hadn't quite slid into the spot. Ironically, it was looking like it fit her wolf better. Christophe's story of how Nate had helped him change probably had something to do with that, but Nate's unique charisma accounted for it as well.

He was an alpha who hadn't spent his life as one, a natural leader who had experience following. He possessed both confidence and humility.

In addition to which, he was an unmistakable ladies man. His ability to charm didn't turn off just because he cared about Evina. Other males respected sexual success. It was possible she respected it herself. Males weren't the only ones at the mercy of anthropological tendencies.

"So, so fine," Freda purred at her elbow, her gaze on Nate as well. She handed Evina one of the Kashmir Mango Martinis Christophe was making it his mission to introduce Nate's wolves to. "I am genuinely regretful to be giving up fantasizing about that man."

Evina choked on a swallow of the strong vodka drink. "You were fantasizing about Nate? You only met him once!"

"Once was enough. I do hope that, as my friend, you appreciate my sacrifice."

"I imagine the fact that he has a number of hot wolf friends softens the blow."

"Just a tad," Freda said creamily. "You ask him to move in together yet?"

Evina choked on the drink again.

"Oh, come on," Freda said, patting her back to help her stop coughing. "You're alpha. You don't have to wait for him to ask."

"I have kids," she said.

"Who he obviously likes. Unless . . ." Grinning, Freda tapped her pretty cinnamon-colored lips. "Maybe you're holding out for something more old-fashioned."

"Well, I've done the living together thing," Evina admitted even as she flushed. "I'm just not sure Nate is that serious yet. Or if he'll ever be." She crossed her arms and frowned at herself. She couldn't help what she wanted: she simply wasn't certain wanting it was advisable.

"It's like that, is it?" Freda said softly. "You're, like, forever in love with him. That's nice, Evina. You don't have to be embarrassed. Anyway, wolves totally do commitment. It's not that long a shot."

"Maybe," Evina said and forced her arms to uncross again.

Nate chose then to turn and smile through the crowd at her. God, he was cute, his bad boy style on display tonight. Underneath that, he beamed happiness. She couldn't have been happier for him. He was back in the fold, surrounded by friends and family.

Evina wanted to be a part of that for him.

Someone turned the music louder, head-bobbing R&B pumping out of the speakers. Nate began dancing for her, his fingers crooking to call her out to him. Those hips of his were dangerous—and never mind his naughty smile. Ignoring the fact that her black leather skirt—the same she'd once worn to booty call him—was too short to move much in, Evina prowled through the bodies to join him.

She couldn't have him thinking tigresses weren't as good at swiveling their hips as wolves.

Nate bit his lip and shook his fingers to express how hot he thought that was.

She laughed and tossed her head. She'd worn her curls down for him, knowing he liked her hair that way. He took her hands and spun her to admire the full effect. She should have guessed he'd be fun to dance with, that he'd make her feel like a woman *and* a queen. His snazzy boots twisted and turned so neatly he could have been professionally trained.

When he went down without warning on one knee, Evina assumed he'd tripped on a cobblestone.

She offered to help him up, but then he dug a small hinged box out of his pocket. Evina's heart jumped into her throat.

"Evina," he said to her.

No one else was paying attention until the music suddenly cut off.

"Woot!" his friend Tony called, letting them know who the culprit was.

Nate called him a name she hoped her kids were too far away to hear.

"No, no," Tony teased. "We all want to hear this."

Nate called him the name again.

"Nate," she said, beginning to laugh softly.

"Fine," he huffed. Filling his lungs with a surprisingly shaky breath, he opened the box. On a silk-lined cushion a diamond ring twinkled—probably fortunate for her sanity.

"Evina Mohajit," he said almost steadily. "From the time I was a teenager, I knew how to be nice to women. Until I met you, I didn't understand what it meant to be good to one. You make me want to be good to you. Be my wife, Evina. Let me help your kids grow up."

"Give her the ring!" Carmine hooted, pretending to be Tony.

Nate stifled a snort and held it up. "Please," he said quietly. "Make my life finally feel whole."

Evina was shaking all over. This was ridiculous. She was the head of her pride, the head of a fire station. Too many times to count, she'd faced life and death dangers. Surely she could answer this one question—which wasn't in doubt anyway.

"Yes?" she managed to squeak out.

Nate rose and gave her a big hug. "Sorry," he laughed against her ear while their audience clapped. "I didn't mean for that to be such a scene. Here." He pushed back to slide the ring on her finger. The antique band was a little loose, but it was beautiful to her. "This was my mom's. I'm sorry you didn't get a chance to meet her. I know she'd have loved you."

His voice had gone husky. He'd truly given her a treasure. Evina looked from the twinkly diamond to him with sentiment-blurred vision.

"I love it," she said, squeezing him tightly. For some reason, him returning the embrace made her tears overrun. "Omigosh, I feel like a sap!"

He kissed her even as she cried, to the amusement of everyone. Thankfully, the music started up again. She and Nate grabbed their chance to step out of the spotlight. At the edge of the dance floor, Christophe had Rafi and Abby by the hands. Her cubs' eyes were saucer big.

"Big night," her beta said, smiling at her fondly.

"Mommy!" Abby burst out as if she couldn't contain herself. "Is Nate going to be our dad now?"

Nate went down on his knees to her. "I'll be one of them," he said. "If that's okay with you."

Evina watched her daughter struggle. Abby loved Paul dearly, but Evina knew he wasn't around as much as her little girl would have liked.

"I don't have to choose?" she asked.

"You don't," Nate assured her.

"And Malik will still be our brother?" This question came from Rafi.

"Absolutely," Nate said firmly.

Evina looked down to hide her smile. For a guy who was a neat freak, Nate was certainly jumping into her family messiness with both feet. She put her hand on his shoulder and squeezed the muscle there. She vowed she'd always remember how awesome he was being.

~

They made their goodbyes—or tried to—an hour later. Naps notwithstanding, the twins were flagging. Evina wanted to get them home to their own beds. Nate put Tony in charge of seeing the party wrapped up safely. After that, he found his alpha's wife, kissed baby Kelsey's wispy hair, and squeezed Ari in a hug. Ari seemed as happy as Nate that he and Adam had reconciled.

"Call me anytime you need a break from this one," she said to Evina while wagging her thumb at him. "You're pack now. We girls try to stick together when we can."

Evina seemed unsure what to make of the pint-sized, slightly punk alpha's wife, but she took the offer in stride. "Thank you," she said. "Whatever girl lunches and the like can do to improve detente, I'm in favor of."

The women's lips curved like they understood each other perfectly.

Nate told himself this was a good thing.

Ethan delayed their departure a little more by running over to chatter at Rafi and Abby. "Come back tomorrow!" he insisted. "We'll build a fort! And finger-paint! I *have* to see what you look like when you turn into tigers!"

"Ethan," his mom scolded, but the twins didn't seem put off, just more tired than he was.

"We'll set up a play date," Evina said to Maria. "I understand kids like to hang with other kids near their age. My friend Freda has a five-and-a-half year old. God help us, but maybe they'll all get on."

Nate was awed by the ease with which they settled this. Apparently, facilitating children's social lives was another skill he'd need to cultivate.

Evina's mom wandered over then, hugging her daughter and shedding a few tears. "A wedding," she sniffed. "You have no idea how much fun I'll have helping you pick a dress. You'd look absolutely gorgeous in an Edwardian gown! I can start searching online tomorrow for bargains."

With a slightly leery expression he had no trouble reading, Evina promised to call her later and got them all out of there. When they reached the freight elevator, he and Evina heaved relieved sighs.

The twins conked out in the back of his Goblinati five minutes after he'd begun driving.

All of this struck Nate as so normal it was surreal; as if in an instant they'd become a real family. How had he not known he wanted this so much? He took a moment to remember the babies for whom play dates and giggles and sleeping in back seats was over. Saving five out of two dozen had been a bittersweet victory, but Resurrection's citizens were correct: those five were miracles.

"We're lucky," Evina said, reaching to squeeze his knee.

He rubbed the hand she'd laid there. Words weren't sufficient to express how thoroughly he agreed.

"You know you probably won't have kids of your own with me," she said.

He touched her cheek, soft as velvet, warm as a summer's day. "I'll have two. And I already know they're turning out amazing."

Evina's eyes glimmered with quick emotion—and then twinkled with mischief. "I covet your dishwashers," she confessed.

Nate laughed softly. "That's convenient. I covet having you and the twins move in with me."

"So we'll work it out."

"Yes, we will," he promised.

When she laid her head on his shoulder, he knew they were both smiling.

# # #

ABOUT THE AUTHOR

EMMA Holly is the award winning, *USA Today* bestselling author of more than thirty romantic books, featuring vampires, demons, faeries and just plain extraordinary ordinary folks. She loves the hot stuff, both to read and to write!

If you'd like to find out what else she's written, please visit her website at http://www.emmaholly.com.

Emma runs monthly contests and sends out newsletters that often include coupons for new ebooks. To receive them, go to her contest page.

If sexy shapeshifters are your thing, you might try *Hidden Talents*, which stars Nate's boss, Adam. *Hidden Talents* is the start of the Hidden series.

Thanks so much for reading this book!

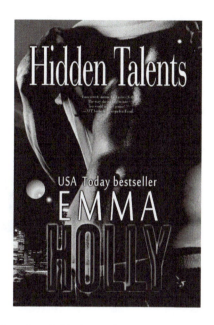

WEREWOLF cop Adam Santini is sworn to protect and serve all the supes in Resurrection, NY—including unsuspecting human Talents who wander in from Outside.

Telekinetic Ari is hot on the trail of a mysterious crime boss who wants to exploit her gift for his own evil ends, a mission that puts her on a collision course with the hottest cop in the RPD.

Adam wants Blackwater too, but mostly he wants Ari. She seems to be the mate he's been yearning for all his life, though getting a former street kid into bed with the Law could be his toughest case to date.

> "*Hidden Talents* is the perfect package of Supes,
> romance, mystery and HEA!"—Paperback Dolls

available in ebook and print

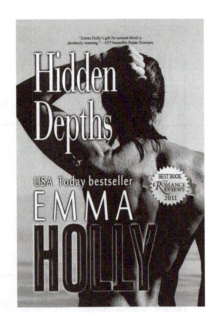

JAMES and Olivia Forster have been happily married for many years. A harmless kink here or there spices up their love life, but they can't imagine the kinks they'll encounter while sneaking off to their beach house for a long hot weekend.

Anso Vitul has ruled the wereseals for one short month. He hardly needs his authority questioned because he's going crazy from mating heat. Anso's best friend and male lover Ty offers to help him find the human mate his genes are seeking.

To Ty's amazement, Anso's quest leads him claim not one partner but a pair. Ty would object, except he too finds the Forsters hopelessly attractive.

"The most captivating and titillating story I have read in some time . . .
Flaming hot . . . even under water"—Tara's Blog

available in ebook and print

CPSIA information can be obtained at www.ICGtesting.com
Printed in the USA
LVOW01s0826100913

351743LV00008B/107/P